"Houston, do we have a problem?"

"Cute."

"Always."

"You can save the effort. That might have worked in high school, but it's not going to help you here. Especially since I already know the way you operate."

I did a pointed once-over, not exactly an easy task considering that I was squashed between Houston and some stranger who was snoring heavily and taking up more than his share of the armrest.

"I've known you for all of fifteen minutes. So I seriously doubt you know anything about the way I operate."

"I know that your dad asked me to find a program for you because he couldn't have you around right now."

I didn't flinch even though this latest parental betrayal stung like hell. Any sign of weakness is a fatal mistake when you're playing poker with a shark.

"*You?*" I said skeptically. "My *dad* confided in *you?* Again, I doubt it."

"He said you needed to get out of Portland so you wouldn't trash your life."

More by Marni Bates

AWKWARD

DECKED WITH HOLLY

INVISIBLE

Published by Kensington Publishing Corp.

NOTABLE

Marni Bates

KENSINGTON PUBLISHING CORP.
www.kensingtonbooks.com

K TEEN BOOKS are published by

Kensington Publishing Corp.
119 West 40th Street
New York, NY 10018

All Kensington titles, imprints, and distributed lines are available at special quantity discounts for bulk purchases for sales promotion, premiums, fund-raising, and educational or institutional use.

Special book excerpts or customized printings can also be created to fit specific needs. For details, write or phone the office of the Kensington Special Sales Manager: Kensington Publishing Corp., 119 West 40th Street, New York, NY 10018. Attn. Special Sales Department. Phone: 1-800-221-2647.

Kensington and K Teen Reg. U.S. Pat. & TM Off.

ISBN-13: 978-0-7582-6939-3
ISBN-10: 0-7582-6939-0
First Kensington Trade Paperback Printing: November 2013

eISBN-13: 978-0-7582-9152-3
eISBN-10: 0-7582-9152-3
First Kensington Electronic Edition: November 2013

10 9 8 7 6 5 4 3 2 1

Printed in the United States of America

This book is dedicated to everyone who feels judged based solely on their looks. Never forget that you have layers of awesome beneath the surface.
And that you're all beautiful to me.

Acknowledgments

Acknowledgment pages are hard.

Seriously. Everyone wants to have a particularly clever way of thanking people that goes beyond "I couldn't have done it without you."

But the truth is that I absolutely could not have written this book without . . .

Alicia Condon: my editor, aka the Patron Saint of Panic-stricken Author Emails. This book is immeasurably better because you worked with me on it. Thank you so much!

Laurie McLean: my rock star agent, who encourages me onward. I love being on this journey with you!

Marina Adair: my critique partner/best friend/savior of my sanity. I can't begin to express how much your friendship means to me. Your talent, persistence, kindness, and sparkling sense of humor inspires and humbles me. Thank you for insisting I remove the Navy SEALs.

Lisa Lin: Whether we are counting imaginary cows or plotting world domination, you never fail to brighten my day! Thank you for telling me to keep the Navy SEALs.

Suzanne Brockmann: Okay, maybe it's a little strange to thank someone I've never actually met. Regardless, your Navy SEAL romance novel *Prince Joe* began my love of the genre. Your staunch support of the LGBTQ community has inspired me for years. Thank you for all that you do!

Shoshana Werblow: I'm still giggling over your response to my plans for Chelsea. "You know what they say: 'Write what you know, Marni.'" I'll have to keep that in mind for next time.

Mom: Thank you for loving me no matter what.

Lewis & Clark College: I am honored to have you as my alma mater. Thank you for emphasizing more than test scores and for putting up with my personal brand of crazy for four years.

And the most Notable of them all: my *incredibly* awesome readers!

Thank you for making all of this possible!

Chapter 1

It never should have happened.

Oh sure, in the movies, the geeky girl gets the guy, but let's all get real for a second: High school doesn't actually work like that. No way. The absurdly sweet (yet popular) guy might continue being tutored by the geek, but he also keeps making out with his beautiful ex-girlfriend until they decide to give their relationship another shot.

That's how it *should* have worked, but apparently my good luck had run out a long time ago.

Because even as I gazed into the gray eyes of my perfect hockey-captain ex-boyfriend, Logan Beckett, and put it all on the line: told him point-blank that I missed him and wanted to get back together—I knew it was too little, too late. Instead of kissing me back when I leaned in and pressed my lips against his, he took a step away.

His eyes were full of pity. "I'm sorry, Chelsea. I just . . . don't feel the same way about you anymore."

Then he glanced over at his best friend Spencer's house and everything sort of clicked into place. He wasn't throwing away everything good that was still between us because he hadn't forgiven me for my middle-school mistake. Oh no, he was firmly rejecting me, Chelsea Halloway, because he was more interested in dating the most awkward girl at our high school. Actually, thanks to an embarrassing YouTube video, Mackenzie Wellesley had accidentally raised her profile beyond the hallways of Smith High School until she became best known as America's Most Awkward Girl.

Yet he was still choosing *her* over *me*.

It didn't make the slightest difference that I'd been in the midst of pouring out my freaking heart to him when he shot me down. That I was willing to grovel for ever breaking up with him and explain that, regardless of the rumors circulating in the wake of our breakup (mainly that I was ecstatic to have traded Logan in for a more popular high school boy), I'd been a wreck over our split.

But instead of hearing me out and then sweeping me off my feet in a passionate kiss . . . he just shook his head.

"Sorry, Chels. Take care of yourself, okay? I've got to—"

Go.

He had to scurry off to locate the girl who was so much smarter and sweeter and *better* than me in nearly every way. Leaving me, quite literally, out in the cold. No amount of pain from our first breakup had prepared me for *this* level of hurt. Nothing compared to smiling until my cheeks ached while I watched Logan leading a stumbling Mackenzie to his car with a transparent affection he never once showed me.

And I couldn't even cry without becoming fodder for another round of rumors.

"Hey, did you hear that Chelsea had a total meltdown at Spencer's party? Girl has some serious issues, if you ask me."

That was what I would have to pretend not to hear following me down hallways . . . into classrooms . . . even into the dressing room of Mrs. P's School of Ballet.

So I did exactly what everyone expected of me.

I tossed my long, shiny, blond hair over my shoulder, sauntered over to the nearest, hottest available guy, and began flirting like I didn't have a care in the world. As if my heart hadn't just been trampled over with a Logan-shaped footprint. But I forced myself to keep my voice even and my eyes dry because even the slightest crack in appearances could be enough to de-throne me as the Queen of the Notables. Which is why, instead of bawling my eyes out, I batted my baby blues at some guy whose name I didn't bother to learn before making my getaway.

My mom always instructed me that it was best to leave them wanting more.

Of course, she had said that in the context of my dance recitals, but it applied to flirting too. In both cases, it takes a lot of practice to hide sweat, nerves, and performance anxiety, but if you let any of it show, it kills the magic. And I had spent enough time faking happiness that I could flirt while replaying exactly how it felt to have Logan's lips against mine one last time—soaring hope and an overwhelming sense of rightness as my body recognized that this was exactly where I belonged.

But apparently Logan hadn't felt any of it.

I maintained that stupid fake smile even after a stranger splashed beer on my shoes as I headed toward the door. It was only when I was driving home that I began ranting to myself about the cosmic unfairness of realizing that I had never gotten over my first love only to find out that he had *definitely* gotten over me.

But it became pretty obvious when I pulled into my driveway that my night wasn't about to get any better. Because waiting for me by the door was my dad's suitcase. I had his teaching schedule memorized, and I knew for a fact that there were no upcoming academic conferences scribbled on the kitchen calendar for *months*. There was no logical reason for his luggage to be slumped against one of our enormous ceramic flowerpots.

Unless I was finally getting to see the closing night performance of the divorce walk of blame.

Not just a trial separation. Not a temporary experiment.

Not something that would blow over eventually, like it always did. Nope, this time he was really leaving.

And you would think that losing both Logan and my father in one night would forever earn it the terrible distinction of being the very worst evening of my life. My personal all-time low. Rock freaking bottom.

But it wasn't.

It's funny how being hunted down by a group of certifiable bad guys in a third-world country can change a girl's perspective on what constitutes a tragedy. Not *ha-ha* funny, *obviously*. It's more of a *laughing is my only alternative to disintegrating into a million pieces* type of funny. When your every decision is a matter of life or death, even truly ridiculous amounts of personal drama fade into insignificance.

Hunt or be hunted.

Hide or . . . wind up with a gun aimed at your head.

I found that out the hard way.

Chapter 2

My dad tried to break it to me gently.

"Now, Chelsea," he began in his dry professor voice, which I suspected made most of his students at Lewis & Clark College struggle to stay awake during his two-hour lectures. "You know your mother and I have been having some problems for a while now."

That was the understatement of the century, skating brilliantly over the fighting, the squabbling, the incessant bickering, the "trial separations," the therapy, the self-help books, and the return for even more therapy and positive visualization exercises. For as long as I could remember, they'd been unhappy together. Possibly because my mom's pregnancy wasn't exactly planned and she felt pressured into doing the "right" thing, according to her very Catholic upbringing. And then I was born and they were even more determined to hold their farce of a marriage together.

Probably because their therapists kept urging them to consider what was best for the child before making any hasty decisions.

If anyone had ever bothered to ask *me*, I would've set the record straight: One quick break would have been a lot easier to deal with than their constant on-again off-again emotional warfare.

That kind of stuff makes for good television but a really crappy home life.

"You don't have to treat her like a *child*, Paul!" my mom squawked indignantly. "It's not like she's too young to understand this!"

She was right about one thing: I could handle the truth. But my mom wasn't *actually* telling my dad to treat me like an adult; she only wanted to use this as yet another example of how he coddled me too much. Yet another one of my dad's habits that rubbed my mom the wrong way. Not that there had ever been a shortage of those. My mom was practically born with an ability to multitask, to set specific goals and not back down until she achieved each and every one of them (according to her exact specifications), which is probably what makes her such an incredible businesswoman. She has standards that she expects everyone to meet and preferably exceed, and a deep-rooted conviction that my dad's inability to employ her brand of "tough love" was what kept me from reaching my true potential.

"This is a very sensitive situation, Suzanne!" my dad countered. "You know what the books said about possible . . . reactions."

"It wouldn't be a problem if you didn't spoil her all the time. For god's sake, she's not made out of glass. If you spent a little less time with your nose in a book you'd know that!"

"And if you spent less time at your corporate retreats—"

I couldn't take any more.

"So about that divorce," I interrupted. "Good plan."

About freaking time.

I kept that part to myself. No need to give them anything else to squabble over. They already debated my upbringing enough. I was too wild. Too prone to hanging out with the "wrong crowd." Too many boyfriends, not enough IQ points. Too skinny. Too fat. Too much of *something*, they usually decided.

And that, *missy*, was usually only the beginning of an epic lecture.

"We want you to know that we considered all of this very carefully," my dad assured me, running a hand through his graying hair. Back when I was a little kid, I spent hours in my dad's office, drawing stick-figure ballerinas while he graded papers until his hair stood up in tufts just as it did now. At the time, I thought he resembled a very handsome duck with his feathers ruffled. I wanted to look just like him, but my coloring favored my mom: pale skin, thick blond hair, undeniably blue eyes, and a thin frame. My mom still loudly mourns the fact that I inherited her looks but not her ability to ace standardized tests.

I nodded and delivered the solemn response I knew he wanted to hear. "I understand. I know you guys examined all the possible alternatives."

It's about time for the two of you to finally come to your senses.

My mom somehow managed to snort elegantly in disdain. "There were no alternatives."

"Suzanne!"

My mom propped her hands on her hips and mimicked his outrage. "Paul!"

O-kay . . . time to get the hell out of there.

"Well, thanks for the update. I'm going to my room. I have dance rehearsal first thing tomorrow morning, so—"

My mom's eyes narrowed. "You're not going anywhere."

Great.

"Chelsea, your mother and I discussed this and . . . we really think it's for the best if . . . you should consider the benefits to—"

"Just spit it out, Paul!"

For once, I was in total agreement with my mom. I couldn't stand waiting for the other shoe to drop. And since I'd already been dumped, kicked aside, and informed of the dissolution of my family unit (such as it was) that night, I figured there was still plenty of time for it to get worse.

A lot worse, as it turned out.

"We think you should leave," he blurted out.

I stared at them blankly. "Leave where?"

"Here. Forest Grove. Oregon."

He still wasn't making any sense.

"Wait, do you mean leave my *home,* my school district, or my state? What's going on? You and Mom split and I have to join the witness protection program or something?"

"Don't be so dramatic, Chelsea." My mom buffed her shiny nails casually on the sleeve of her sweater.

"We just think some time out of town will be good for you, honey. Clear your head."

"My head is plenty clear, *thank you very much!*"

"It's so clear, it's empty," my mom added snidely, before she shrugged off our disbelieving stares. "What? You saw her SAT scores, Paul. Don't tell me you weren't thinking the same thing. Her grades are abysmal, her extracurriculars are a joke, she completely ignored her curfew, she reeks of alcohol, and her chances of getting into a good school are slim to none. Someone has to be the firm, responsible adult here—and it sure isn't going to be you!"

"Thanks, *Mom.* That's *exactly* what I needed to hear right now!"

"But she's right, princess. You need a totally fresh start if you're ever going to get your life together. You need accountability, intellectual stimulation, a whole new social environment, and right now . . . you mother and I aren't in a place where we can provide you with those things. Trust me, princess. We are just doing what's best for you."

"You picked one hell of a time to finally start caring," I snapped bitterly, as pain splintered across my father's face.

"We've always cared, Chelsea. You know we would do anything for—"

"You're only encouraging her to act out, Paul. She needs to accept that her actions have consequences and that this decision of ours is final."

There was a sickening silence that followed her pronouncement while I felt the last dregs of anger and outrage seep right out of me. It hurt too much to care. About Logan. About my parents. About leaving. About anything, really.

All of me ached and throbbed as if I'd just spent hours dancing in brand-new ballet shoes.

Except my heart was blistering instead of my toes.

"*My* decisions have consequences? What about *yours?* You guys want to split up, fine. That doesn't mean I should be forced to leave my friends and my school and my *life!*"

"It's only for a semester, Chelsea. You'll still be walking at graduation with your friends. And it's exactly what you need," my mom said staunchly. "Besides, international travel will spice up your transcript."

"So how long have I got?" Even to my own ears, it sounded like I was preparing to face an executioner. Not far off from the truth, actually, since this would effectively destroy my current life at Smith High School. It would rip away my every accomplishment, leaving nothing behind. A week had been long enough to turn Mackenzie Wellesley into the underdog story of the year; six months would leave me completely forgotten.

HERE LIES CHELSEA HALLOWAY: DANCE CAPTAIN, MOST POPULAR GIRL AT SCHOOL. FEARED BY ALL, MISSED BY FEW. TAKEN TOO SOON.

"It's going to take some time to make all the arrangements, passport, travel visas, shots, you know, all those sorts of things. But you'll be ready to leave with the program in just under two months."

"The program?" I repeated. I hoped they weren't trying to ship me off to some religious boarding school where I'd have to say the Lord's Prayer with every meal and watch out for angry nuns. The way I saw it, if there even was a god . . . then he was behaving like a total jerk by dumping all this on me.

And for stuff like allowing children to go hungry, be sold into slavery, and battle terminal illnesses.

But mainly because booting me out of Oregon *now* was just straight-up vindictive.

"We aren't throwing you out on the street, Chelsea," my mother scoffed. "There's no need to be so dramatic all the time!"

I gritted my teeth. "What program?"

My dad hastened to explain everything. "I asked around at work, and there's an opening on one of the study-abroad programs. At first it wasn't clear whether it would even happen because so few students signed up for it. But that's how I was able to convince them to take you along."

They both looked at me expectantly, as if I was supposed to be *grateful* for all the effort they had taken to ship me off.

Not so much.

"Let me get this straight: You convinced someone from your fancy liberal arts college to take me overseas?"

He didn't seem to like the way I phrased the question, but he nodded slowly.

"Okay, well, here's a problem: *I'm in high school!*"

"I called in a few favors, and they were willing to overlook that for me."

"I don't want to go."

"You should at least give it a chance before you write it off, Chelsea," my mom snapped. "This is going to be a great opportunity for you to spend some time figuring out what you want in life."

"I know what I *don't* want. And that's being stuck with a group of geeks in a foreign country."

"Aren't you the least bit curious about where you're going?" my dad wheedled.

Not really.

"It's a gorgeous country known for ancient relics."

Okay, well, when he put it that way, maybe their plan wasn't entirely without potential. I pictured myself zipping around Rome on the back of some hot guy's Vespa, eating gelato and pizza, and strolling along by the Trevi Fountain. Spending time sightseeing and shopping might be just the distraction I needed after Logan's rejection.

Still, I rolled my eyes before I capitulated. "Fine. Where am I going?"

"Cambodia."

Chapter 3

They were joking.

They were staring at me expectantly instead of laughing simply because they wanted to give me a little scare. Just to make Italy sound even better by comparison, because there was no way my parents were planning on sending their only child to *Cambodia*.

No. Freaking. Way.

I tossed my hair behind my shoulder and managed to paste a wry smile on my face.

"You're both hilarious. So where is the program *really* going?"

They traded looks while I felt the jagged bits of my heart ripping my intestines to shreds. Maybe if I got an ulcer they wouldn't make me go. I doubted that I could get the proper medical care for that in Cambodia.

Which was a nonissue, because I wasn't going.

"It's a beautiful country, Chelsea." My dad awkwardly broke the silence. "I've wanted to go there myself for years."

"Then why don't *you* go instead? Knock yourself out."

My parents both started squawking simultaneously at me.

"Don't get pissy with us, young lady!"

"This is difficult already, princess. There's no need to make it even harder!"

Right, because at the bottom of every problem there's always me.

"You do understand that I won't be able to do ballet, right? That successful dancers have to train every single day? What you're talking about could jeopardize my whole career!"

"It's not a *career*, Chelsea! It's a *hobby*. One you should've outgrown by now."

I couldn't stay in that room a second longer. Not without covering my ears and screaming.

"All right, well, if the two of you are done screwing up my life for one night, I'm going to bed. Unless, of course, you plan on kicking me out of that too. Oh *wait!* I forgot! You've already done that!"

A few years ago, I probably would've flounced right out of the house and conned someone into picking me up. A few well-placed calls and I could get a party started in minutes. I could make everyone think that I was simply too popular to call it a night, which sounded much better than admitting I didn't have much of a home in the first place.

But I couldn't go down that road again . . . not after what happened the last time. I shuddered as the nasty memory dragged its claws across my flesh. I refused to go back to being the girl at parties desperately seeking attention. The last time I had felt the sting of Logan's waning interest had been in middle school, and I hadn't exactly handled it well. In fact, I had accidentally conducted my own personal train wreck by latching onto the first guy to give me his undivided attention. And I had continued to cling to Jake Crane even when it became painfully obvious the relationship wasn't going anywhere good. Even though I knew he was more interested in maintaining the image of himself as a player around his friends than he was in *me*. That wasn't even the hardest part for my pride to swallow. Oh no, I was still flinching away from the memory two years later because if

Jake *hadn't* dumped me, he would still be treating me like a puppet whose strings he could yank, tug, or twist whenever it suited him . . . and I would be letting him get away with it.

I couldn't afford to let this new round of extreme parental crappiness pull me back into being that girl again. Which is why I also couldn't pretend it had never happened or could somehow be erased. Not even my dad could patch me up now that I was past the age where Scooby-Doo Band-Aids and ice cream cones were the solution for everything. Jake the Mistake couldn't be forgotten, Cambodia couldn't help me outrun Logan's rejection, and hiding out at Mrs. P's dance studio couldn't give me any lasting escape from my problems—just a wicked set of blisters from practicing in my toe shoes.

I discovered that the next day when I extended my ballet practice long after everyone else headed to the changing rooms to gossip. But at least the pain from my dancing gave me something tangible I could fight as I whipped around the floor.

Fouetté. Jeté. Fouetté.

Again. Again. Again.

My eyes stung, my back was soaked with sweat, and every single muscle in my body screamed for me to quit when I incorporated some *adagios* and waited to crumple under the stress of the slow movements. And when I inevitably sank to the floor, gasping for breath, it took a concerted effort to ensure I didn't hyperventilate my way into a trip to the hospital.

My parents might think of me as a drama queen, but that wasn't the kind of attention I wanted. The last thing I needed was to run into Logan's parents while they were on shift at Forest Grove General. Sure, both of them had been perfectly civil after the breakup, but their eyes always looked . . . pitying. As if they had known all along that I'd never be good

enough for their son and that the only one who hadn't figured it out was me.

They had probably done some dancing of their own when
Logan and Mackenzie made their relationship official.

I couldn't stand to be within twenty feet of the happy couple, but nobody at Smith High School seemed to share my
sentiment. Mackenzie's YouTube fame coupled with her Ellen
DeGeneres interview meant that even without Logan, she no
longer ranked among the losers. In fact, Mackenzie's new-
found celebrity status made her almost as popular as . . . me.

And she hadn't even *tried.*

Maybe it was a good thing I was leaving since everyone in
Forest Grove must have lost their freaking minds to even
fleetingly consider *Mackenzie Wellesley* cool. My best
friends, Steffani and Ashley, kept hastening to assure me that
the geek had nothing on me, but it wasn't like they could say
anything else. They both knew that even given the limited
time I had remaining at Smith High School, I could destroy
their social lives with one flick of my blond hair and a few
whispers in the right places.

Not that I would.

But the knowledge that I *could* kept them in line.

And just to maintain that illusion, I spent the next five
weeks pretending that my heart wasn't trapped in the ballet
studio, caught in an endless series of spins, going absolutely
nowhere while the minutes sprinted past. I kept up appearances. I auditioned for the school's musical production of
Romeo and Juliet—I even landed the part of Juliet—but I'd
be in Cambodia before it came time to rehearse . . . making it
a hollow victory at best.

That may have been the hardest part to accept: Nothing I
did mattered anymore because I wouldn't be around long
enough to reap the benefits.

Even befriending Jane Smith (known to the rest of the

school simply as Mackenzie Wellesley's fellow geek) didn't matter. Not when I was scheduled to leave so soon after we began to get to know each other. I couldn't even enjoy how uncomfortable it made Mackenzie to have her best friend turning to *me* for advice, because of my quickly approaching departure date.

A damn shame, if you ask me.

I spent most of my time pretending that I wasn't about to be banished to some backward country that might be completely unfamiliar with YouTube. Something I would know for sure if I had bothered to research the place the way my parents kept hounding me to do. Maybe denial wasn't exactly the smartest idea, given that my parents would shove me onto the plane kicking and screaming if necessary, but I couldn't help it. I couldn't even bring myself to Google it because that would make Cambodia a real place with real people where I was *really* going to hate my life.

Unfortunately, I also didn't want to be the only person on the trip who couldn't locate Cambodia on a map.

I procrastinated all the way up until two days before my flight, and then found myself casually scanning the shelves of the high school library for anything applicable. The entire time I moved along the shelves of books, I could feel myself being critiqued and judged. Usually, I can dismiss whispers and gossip as an unavoidable nuisance that comes packaged with popularity, but in the library I knew the geeks weren't discussing the clothes I wore, the parties I attended, or even speculating on the ex-boyfriend I was rumored to be pursuing.

They were wondering what Chelsea Halloway was doing in a *library*. Especially since it was considered common knowledge that this particular party girl was pretty—not smart. She didn't need to bother with books anyway. After all, she could easily bribe any geek at school to write a report for her. She wouldn't even have to pay them, since getting into her good graces provided plenty of incentive.

My mom put it even more bluntly when we first started checking out colleges together. "It's a good thing you're attractive. Maybe that'll get you into one of these big universities on a cheerleading scholarship. Let's just hope they don't have high academic standards!"

Real encouraging, Mom.

Still, I couldn't flee from the library without making people suspect that I was afraid of a few geeks. And while I might not have been staying at Smith High School, I wanted to leave my reputation perfectly intact, giving me no choice but to ignore all the staring faces. I sauntered casually over to a long row of books, acting for all the world like I came into the library on a regular basis.

Head up. Shoulders back. Hips cocked.

Until I spotted Logan in the arms of the one girl who somehow made me feel stupider than everybody else at our school combined.

They weren't just hugging either.

"You're in my way," I announced icily, desperate to say anything if it would snap the lovebirds out of their lip-lock.

My words effectively shocked Mackenzie into stumbling back against the bookshelf, but Logan caught her and pulled her against him before she could fall. He grinned as she clutched onto his shirt for balance, but the expression neutralized when he looked at me.

"Hey, Chelsea."

I forced myself to smile, even though I knew it wouldn't reach my eyes. "Hey, Logan . . . Mackenzie."

She scrambled to stand without Logan's support. "Hey, Chelsea! Are you here for something? Well, you must be, right? Because it's the library, and you wouldn't be here unless . . ."

Her voice petered out.

"I'm researching the history of Cambodia," I announced

coolly, as if I didn't have the time to spare from my intellectual pursuits for her blathering.

"Isn't it fascinating? I would love to spend some time wandering around the temples of Angkor Wat someday. Mainly because I can't resist ancient architecture when it is built on such a grand scale!" Mackenzie's face was practically glowing with enthusiasm. "I would probably geek out over every carving. Did you know—"

Of course she would geek out. That's the one thing she was good at doing.

"I'm guessing ancient temples aren't really Chelsea's thing, Mack." Logan's hand slipped into hers, and my heart lodged in my throat. "Working on a paper for World Civ?"

"Actually, I'm going to Cambodia."

His laughter resounded over the muted hum of voices in the library.

"Good one, Chelsea."

But I wasn't being sarcastic. Suddenly, listening to the same laughter I found so comforting back when I believed that we would beat the odds and stay in love forever now only pissed me off.

"I'm not kidding."

He instantly sobered. "You're going to Cambodia?"

"My parents have finally decided to pull the plug on their relationship." I shrugged as if it were no big deal while Mackenzie's eyes widened.

"I know how hard it can be to watch parents divorce, Chelsea." Her earnest tone of concern put my teeth on edge. "My parents split when I was younger, but—"

"Oh, you don't have to remind me what happened. It's hard to forget your first ballet solo—especially when some gravitationally challenged freak trips into the curtain and reveals that her own dad has been working on moves of his own with the instructor. Nobody was surprised when your parents split, Mackenzie. Nobody."

She blanched at the reminder, but my satisfaction at wiping the pity from her eyes was short-lived.

"Uh, yeah. Well, if you want to talk about it sometime—"

"Spare me." I tossed my hair before adding a deliberate eye roll. "It's a relief. I'd much rather be in Cambodia than stuck here watching the two of you act like lovesick puppies in heat."

Logan squeezed Mackenzie's hand comfortingly as she flinched back from me as if she'd been slapped. "Um, okay. Well, safe travels then."

I refused to acknowledge her with even a nod, choosing instead to head straight out of the library. But I didn't move quickly enough.

"What's wrong with looking like lovesick puppies?" I heard Mackenzie ask Logan. "Everyone loves puppies. And I think only grown dogs can be in heat—"

Logan laughed again, and I heard the distinctive sound of kissing.

For a genius, the girl wasn't very good at picking up on social cues.

But Logan still wanted her more than me.

Chapter 4

"We're going to miss you *sooo* much!"

Steffani wrapped her arms around me and squeezed, choking off all oxygen. Her cloying perfume was making me feel light-headed, and her death grip didn't help matters either. Still, it was nice of her to show up at the airport with Ashley in time to say good-bye.

It would have been even nicer if they had invited Jane to share a ride with them, but that thought probably never even occurred to them. Not that it really mattered, since Jane had successfully talked her boyfriend, Scott, into seeing me off at the airport with her, probably by luring him with the promise of a fun date in Portland afterward. Although it looked like she was having second thoughts as soon as she spotted the other two girls—at least judging by the way she began edging toward the exit. She only stopped moving when Scott pulled out his trusty Nikon camera and began snapping photos of her, probably because she was too distracted by her own muffled threats to make a run for it.

Right then, I envied my redheaded friend more than anyone else—except maybe Mackenzie—because every aspect of Jane's life was so . . . *stable*.

Pretty much the last word that could ever be used to describe mine.

Ashley glanced down at her watch and twirled her dyed blond hair around her finger. "We'd love to stay and chat, Chelsea, but I think it's time to go."

"Really? My flight doesn't leave for a while, so I was thinking—"

"Yeah, the thing is, there is, like, this *huge* sale at Urban Outfitters, and we don't want to miss it."

Ashley giggled. "It's not like there's anything to do here!"

Except wish me good-bye. But I kept that to myself.

"Of course," I said slowly. "Have fun shopping. I'll just talk to you both . . . later."

"Later!" Steffani paused only to blow me an air kiss before the two of them trotted toward the exit. Ashley didn't bother to say a word, as if I had already become irrelevant—especially since she was quickly approaching a dark-haired guy with a rumpled plaid shirt wheeling his bags to the checkout counter. Her lower lip jutted out when her sashay failed to capture his attention, while I took way too much pleasure in watching my so-called friend strike out.

"I hate those girls," Scott said without any real heat. Then again, he probably hated me too, but didn't want to say it with his girlfriend right there. "What do you call them again, Jane? Fake and Shake?"

Jane reddened, but she forced herself to meet my eyes. "Kenzie and I may have nicknamed them . . . Fake and Bake. Ashley, uh, might want to lay off the fake tanners?"

"Around Halloween she definitely fits in with the pumpkins."

It was a bitchy thing for me to say, but at least it was honest. Considering the way those particular friends had just blown me off for a sale, I felt barely a twinge of guilt for bad-mouthing them behind their backs.

"So how did you pick Steffani's nickname?" I asked Jane.

"Fake? The obvious hair dye, the fake nails, the questionable nose job . . . Give her thirty years, and I bet even her chin will be plastic."

I smiled as if none of it made the slightest difference to me, even as I braced myself for the inevitable. "So what am I? Cake? Lake?"

Jane shrugged. "Kenzie and I never came up with anything for you. You're not one of them. Not really. I mean, don't get me wrong, everyone fears the Notables. But somehow you've always been . . . separate."

A crazy-accurate social assessment, especially coming from two of Smith High School's biggest self-identified geeks.

"Calling her Lake makes sense to me. With a name like Chel*sea,* it's only fitting that her nickname continue in the same watery vein," Scott observed. "Plus isn't it a saying that still waters run deep? That fits too."

I eyed Scott speculatively, waiting to hear a catch. "I thought you didn't like me."

"I'm not sure I do. I said that still waters run deep, not that there is anything nice lurking in the depths."

Touché.

I poked Jane's arm to get her attention. "I think he might be a keeper. Any chance I can take him with me?"

She mock glared at me. "Nope. He's not up for grabs. Don't even try your hair tossing or flashing your megawatt smile. I *will* shut you down, Chelsea."

The steel underlining her tone had me fighting back a grin. Jane wasn't the same wallflower I had taken pity on during her *Romeo and Juliet* audition. And I liked to think that I'd played a small role in her recent transformation.

"Well, thanks for seeing me off," I interrupted before Jane could make any more ridiculous threats. "Both of you."

It was more than my parents had managed. They were too busy squabbling over furniture to give me a proper send-off. It should have come as a relief, since my dad would have spent the entire car ride asking if I had everything: toothbrush, deodorant, that sort of thing, while my mom accused him of babying me. Then I'd have been stuck listening to them tell me *again* how lucky I was to get this travel experience.

Classic guilt talk. They had to convince themselves that I was embarking on an incredible journey or they'd feel guilty for shipping me off to a third-world pit.

Jane's awkward attempt at hugging snapped me back to reality fast. "Are you going to be all right, Chelsea?"

There was no satisfactory answer for me to give. If I said yes, I would be lying. If I said no, I would sound like a drama queen.

No-win situation.

"I guess I'll have to be okay." And then, just to stop myself from doing something truly pathetic like crying, I fluttered my eyelashes at Scott. "Unless your big, strong man wants to rescue me from this nightmare. He could whisk me off and—"

"That's it, I'm out of here."

Scott headed straight for the doors, while Jane and I both laughed at his hasty departure. For just a second, I felt like the old version of myself. The Chelsea who existed before my parents ever considered shipping me off to *Cambodia*.

There were times when I missed that girl.

"I got you a going-away gift." Jane handed me a flash drive and grinned. "I don't know if it's your type of music, but I made a travel playlist for you anyway."

"Hipster music?" I guessed.

"Maybe."

I grinned. "I'll be sure to let you know what I think of it."

She rolled her eyes. "Of that, I have no doubt."

I wanted to say more, but I recognized Professor Hamilton's paunchy form approaching us. I knew that my trip leader's presence only meant one thing: My visiting hours were over.

"Take care, geek."

"You too, *Lake*. I expect to hear regular updates."

And before I could come up with any excuses about needing better Internet access than *Cambodia* probably supplied, she headed outside after Scott.

Leaving me officially alone.

Well, unless I counted the teacher who was barreling toward me with a foolish grin plastered all over his face. The guy was like an academic version of Tigger—bouncy, flouncy, pouncy, whatever—except his version of fun centered around economic trends in third-world countries.

If you weren't interested in analyzing that . . . then you were screwed.

"Welcome aboard, Chelsea! Are you ready for the trip of a lifetime?" His friendly punch to my arm instantly had me suppressing the urge to rub where he made contact.

I nodded, but didn't get the chance to say anything beyond, "Sure, Mr. Ham—"

"No need to start in with formalities! It's going to be a small group of us in Cambodia, so just call me Neal. First-name basis for everyone. No reason we can't all be friends, right?"

"Right. Friends," I repeated unenthusiastically, while Neal began craning his neck to look around the airport.

"So, where are your folks?"

"Not here."

He looked nervous, like he was waiting for me to start blubbering, *My parents don't love meee!*

Well, he wasn't going to get any of it.

The less speculation I received the easier it would be to sneak on board a flight to Italy. Although given that the other students were probably just as surprised to find a high school girl suddenly signed up for their trip, I could almost guarantee that I'd been the topic of at least a few conversations. I was willing to bet they were all wondering why my dad hadn't just shipped me off to military school or to one of those intervention programs where I would be forced to grow crops and live off the land.

And then they would want to know what *exactly* I had done to deserve total banishment.

I braced myself to be on the receiving end of sideways looks and furtive glances as a girl with messy dark brown hair, big brown doe eyes, and an enormous *I Heart New York* sweatshirt that dwarfed her curvy frame waved at Neal before approaching me.

"Um, hi! I'm Amy. It's nice to meet, uh . . ." Her voice began to peter out when I didn't return her smile. "You."

Sweet and easily controlled. Excellent.

I spared her only the briefest nod, since another girl in our group had captured my attention. At least, I was assuming it was a girl. The bright color clash between the hand-stitched turquoise pig on her shirt, her purple-rimmed glasses, her hot-pink-and-gold-painted nails, and her red-streaked hair . . . made her look like a parrot to me.

"Liz! Welcome, welcome, welcome!" Neal boomed enthusiastically, while I wondered how I would survive months of his nonstop cheerfulness. I had spent less than five minutes with the man and already I wanted to shank him with my nail clippers. Probably not a very good sign.

"Great to see you, Liz! And here come Houston and Ben. *Excellent!*"

Before I could get a good look at the guys, Neal delivered yet another hearty round of backslaps. I winced, Amy nearly toppled over, but it didn't seem to faze Liz in the slightest. She was definitely tougher than me.

So I'd have to work twice as hard to prove my invulnerability.

That's when I realized that standing right next to Amy was the plaid-wearing, dark-haired hottie who hadn't spared Ashley a second glance. Although I was quickly rethinking the "hottie" part of my analysis now that I was close enough to see that beneath the plaid he wore a black shirt with some crazy-looking scientist guy yelling, *"No edge!"* on it.

Geek alert.

Which explained why the guy had ignored Ashley. He probably went exclusively for girls like Mackenzie Wellesley who say stuff like "Math is an *integral* part of my life."

The reminder of my nemesis instantly twisted my gut. It didn't help matters that when his green eyes finally met mine, he merely raised one eyebrow skeptically before he continued his conversation with Amy.

Not that I cared about one dork's opinion, especially when I could be testing the potency of my most charming smile on his very attractive friend. This one was an appealing golden boy, whose hobbies probably included lounging shirtless on pristine white beaches . . . or maybe I was just reading way too much into his lifeguarding shirt. Still, I had no trouble imagining him sitting in a guard tower squinting out at the waves or flirting with bikini-clad girls. His fingers wrapped around mine in a firm handshake that lasted a breath too long for the physical contact to be a purely friendly gesture.

Now *this* was one game I knew how to play.

"So are you Ben or Houston?" I asked flirtatiously.

"That depends on whether you have a preference." His grin had probably inspired some exceedingly foolish girls to fake drowning, just so that they could receive his CPR.

"Of course I have a preference. I like hearing the truth."

That got a surprised laugh from him. "I'm Ben."

"Chelsea."

"It's nice to meet you."

I nodded and then leaned forward to adjust the tag on my suitcase, knowing perfectly well that the movement offered a slight glimpse down the neckline of my shirt. Not enough to be scandalous, merely a touch seductive. Ben's smile widened, but his friend Houston certainly didn't look impressed. If anything, Houston's expression twisted into outright derision before he refocused on his conversation with Amy. They kept right on chatting about their experiences with both Neal and the larger history department at Lewis & Clark while the professor under discussion happily discussed our travel plans with a ticket agent.

Not my favorite topics of conversation, but I wasn't about to let anyone render me irrelevant, especially since I suspected that Houston was doing it intentionally.

I just didn't know why . . . yet.

"Neal's pretty funny when you get some wine in him," I announced casually. "Although he makes a lot of puns about the Visigoths. Not really my scene, but tolerable."

"*You* have socialized with Neal?"

It wasn't exactly hard to read the subtext lurking behind Houston's words: *Yeah, right. Not even outgoing Neal Hamilton would waste his time talking to a pampered ditz like her. At least, not unless he was absolutely smashed.*

"He's only attended our annual Christmas party for, oh, the past five years." I matched Houston's disdainful tone to perfection. "He gave me a necklace with ballet slippers on it once. So, yeah, we've socialized plenty."

Houston tensed, as if he were waiting for me to go on the attack or something. Which was weird for a whole host of reasons, the primary one being that I had done nothing to alienate him. And I usually make a *very* good first impression.

"So was he fun?" Amy asked eagerly. "I've heard the professor who led the trip last year was super-strict. Do you think Neal will be more laid-back?"

The trip hadn't even begun and someone was already turning to me.

Score one for the high school girl.

Too bad the scoreboard didn't remain that way for long. In fact, it lasted only until airport security demanded to go through my bag and started disposing of the large bottles of lotion and hand sanitizer I had impulsively stuffed into it before heading to the airport. Houston scowled in annoyance, Ben's smile was one of wry amusement as he waited for his turn to go through security, Liz tapped her foot impatiently, and Amy kept glancing down at her watch as if she expected it to start berating her for being late. I struggled to keep my own face neutral as airport security confiscated the kitchen scissors I had completely forgotten about packing.

I knew exactly what everyone was thinking: *This* is what you get for taking a high-maintenance high school girl with more lip balm than brains to Cambodia.

Only Neal kept assuring me that little mistakes like this happen to everyone. He hefted my tote-bag and insisted on carrying it himself until we reached our boarding gate, even though I kept telling him I was perfectly capable of handling it myself. He merely chuckled and said that he wanted to personally ensure that my trip started off on the right foot.

I nodded politely, but I kept my mouth firmly shut. There was no need to tell Neal that the others were probably discussing ways to vote me off the trip. And telling him that I secretly wanted them to succeed in whatever plan they created to get me out of there wouldn't do me any good either.

Even before boarding the freaking plane, I knew I was only going to crash and burn.

I just had no way of stopping it.

Chapter 5

"I know all about you."

Not exactly a normal thing to say to the girl in an adjacent seat on a long flight to London, especially if you've only just met her and couldn't bring yourself to exchange more than two complete sentences back on solid ground. But it appeared the geek had been biding his time, waiting for the right moment to go on the offensive. I couldn't help being slightly impressed with the way he timed it. The minuscule airplane seats definitely added a level of difficulty to any escape I might have otherwise attempted.

I turned to Houston and wished that I had trusted my gut instinct to trade places with Amy. Even sitting next to our overly enthusiastic teacher had to be better than chatting with the one person who appeared to have it in for me. If my parents hadn't signed me up to spend *months* with him in Cam-freaking-bodia, I already would have told him exactly where he could go shove his condescending glances.

I batted my lashes instead. "Houston, do we have a problem?"

"Cute."

"Always."

"You can save the effort. That might have worked in high

school, but it's not going to help you here. Especially since I already know the way you operate."

I did a pointed once-over, not exactly an easy task considering that I was squashed between Houston and some stranger who was snoring heavily and taking up more than his share of the armrest.

"I've known you for all of fifteen minutes. So I seriously doubt you know anything about the way I operate." I reached down to grab my tote, which was resting where my leg space would've been if the guy in front of me hadn't pushed his seat all the way back. It was probably going to take over an hour of ballet before my cramped body would loosen up again.

"I know that your dad asked me to find a program for you because he couldn't have you around right now."

I didn't flinch even though this latest parental betrayal stung like hell. Any sign of weakness is a fatal mistake when you're playing poker with a shark.

"*You?*" I said skeptically. "My *dad* confided in *you? Again, I doubt it."

"Paul said you needed to get out of Portland so you wouldn't trash your life. You know, when most kids tank their grades they get *summer school,* not a free trip to Cambodia. I bet you have no idea how freaking lucky you are either."

The geek probably thought that being on a first-name basis with my dad would impress me.

Not so much.

"Yeah? Well, I guess that means you're just as clueless as my dad. Congratulations. That's quite an accomplishment."

Houston shot me a piercing look. "Given what I've heard in his office, I'd say he knows plenty."

"Spend a lot of time pressing your ear to the door, do you?"

"I'm his TA."

"That stands for 'Terrible Ass-kisser,' right?"

He smiled grimly. "Let's get one thing straight, *princess:* Your dad's a good guy who doesn't deserve to be saddled with a stuck-up snob for a daughter. So you can keep trying to play your pathetic little games with airport security or you can accept that I'm going to be keeping an eye on you for him. Either way, your troublemaking days are over."

I brushed back a few strands of hair that had escaped from my ballet bun and leaned in close so that he could look right into my eyes.

"Well, Houston, it looks like you really do have a problem. Because I'm not going to waste my time listening to some geek who owns more plaid than common sense."

Then I popped in my headphones and blasted the Ben Fold's song "You Don't Know Me" loudly enough to drown out both Houston and the armrest thief on my other side.

Damn straight, Houston didn't know me.

Although, apparently, that hadn't stopped him from helping my parents ship me off to *Cambodia* before ordering me to behave. And then he had the audacity to call me a stuck-up snob . . . based on what, exactly? Even if my dad had mentioned I was the most popular girl at school, that was still one hell of an assumption. I almost snarled at Houston that well-developed social skills aren't synonymous with snobbery, although I could easily understand why he wouldn't see the difference. The guy was definitely plagued by residual nerd envy from his own days in high school and was now trying to overcompensate by pretending that being an International Affairs major made him cool.

Well, I refused to feel guilty about my talent for getting my own way. Maybe, if given the choice, I might be tempted to pick Jane's skill with standardized test taking over my ability to manipulate and maneuver. Then again . . . maybe not. Either way, it's not like I ever actually had the option of exchanging my skill set for another. The only practical thing for me to do was to work with what I was given—and I wasn't going to tolerate *anyone* shaming me for it.

So if some brown-nosing twit planned on ordering me around, he was going to have to get used to receiving the middle finger for his efforts. Hopefully, that would be enough to make him rethink his bizarre loyalty to my dad, or at the very least prevent him from stalking me for the next four months in Southeast Asia. I briefly considered emailing my dad—demanding that he call off his watchdog—but I doubted it would make a difference.

My dad didn't *actually* care about how I was feeling. Oh sure, he talked a good game, but if he had really been as worried about my reaction to the divorce as Houston claimed, he would've assured me that I'd always have a home with him.

But he hadn't.

So I had no trouble believing that my dad would probably just assure me I had nothing to worry about with a serious, academically oriented college boy like Houston . . . with a stick up his butt.

Okay, so maybe that last part was more my opinion than my dad's.

It was still true.

And if I was really going to escape from the program, I had a feeling Houston posed a more significant threat to my freedom than our perpetually upbeat teacher. Although I had absolutely nothing to lose by trying to irritate him into keeping his distance. I started out by stealing his armrest and squealing my way through three relatively unfunny chick flicks before I bumped up the plan into high gear. All it took was one quick tug and my long blond hair tumbled around my face. That's when I began tossing my head every few minutes as if I were auditioning for a shampoo commercial. And if I *happened* to whip his face in the process . . . well, accidents happen.

By the time the flight attendant asked everyone to return their tray tables to their full, upright position in preparation for landing, Houston sat contorted as far away from me as humanly possible given his six-foot-tall frame. If he were anybody else, I might have enjoyed the way our relative height discrepancy made me feel delicate and feminine. Instead, I was too distracted by his stupid disdainful glances to feel anything more than annoyance. That's when I decided I might as well embrace the role of pain-in-the-ass teacher's kid and show Houston just how well I could play the part.

Our three-hour layover at Heathrow Airport gave me the perfect opportunity to stage a little demonstration. I lied easily about picking up some new hand lotion and strolled right into the duty-free where it took only a few minutes of flirting with the guy handing out liquor samples to down three of them like a champ.

If I was going to be labeled the party girl, I wanted to deserve the reputation.

"I'm not even twenty-one, which means there is no way in hell you're old enough to drink," Houston growled as he dragged me away from the store and herded me toward the Starbucks where everyone else had gathered. I smirked up at him.

"The drinking age is eighteen here."

"Yeah? Well, you're not that either."

"What are you going to do, Texas? Rat me out to my dad?"

Before he could respond, I shoved his hand off my arm and headed straight for the bathroom so that he couldn't follow me. The last thing I needed was yet another lecture about my behavior. Unfortunately, from my hiding place in the handicapped stall, I couldn't help overhearing Amy and Liz as they began talking freely about me.

"Chelsea seems . . . decent," Amy said in what could only

be described as a halfhearted endorsement. "I bet she just needs some time to warm up to people."

"She certainly didn't waste any time warming up to Ben."

"Well, Ben's a friendly guy. Maybe—"

Liz cut her off. "Did you see her drinking in the duty-free? I thought Houston would have a coronary when he dragged her out of there. I mean, does she *want* to be plastered this entire trip?"

That idea actually held a certain amount of appeal for me. At least that way I would be able to temporarily forget that this trip was already turning out even worse than I'd imagined.

"Maybe she's a nervous flier?"

"Yeah, she sure looked nervous when she boarded the plane in Portland," Liz scoffed. "Oh, wait. No, she didn't."

"Well, maybe she's just sad. Houston mentioned something about her parents splitting. Just because she's acting like a spoiled party girl doesn't mean she can't be hurt."

My body stiffened as I soaked in that bit of new information. Apparently, the geek wasn't content just narcing me out to my dad and making snap judgments about my life; oh no, he had probably told everyone that I was nothing more than an airhead party girl with terrible grades and an even worse personality.

Well, I had already heard enough.

The Chelsea Halloway who ruled Smith High School would *never* stoop to cowering in bathroom stalls. It was time for me to end this bullshit once and for all by going on the offensive.

I swung open the door and sauntered to the sink, ignoring the way Amy's eyes bugged out and her dark bob swayed as she glanced over at a speechless Liz for support.

"You know, everyone says high school is completely different from college, but I just don't buy it."

The two older girls continued staring at me in silence.

"The classes might be harder and the parties might be better, but honestly, it sounds like high school two point oh."

"Uh—" Amy began, but I cut her off.

"Now if we were all back in high school and I overheard someone spouting off shit about me in the bathroom, I would threaten to make their lives a living hell. But since you're both in *college*, I guess I'll have to take a slightly different approach."

I glanced at the reflections of both girls in the mirror, as if I couldn't be bothered to turn around to face them directly.

"You mess with me and I *will* take you down. And nobody will notice two extra bodies in Cambodia. We clear on that?"

They nodded.

"Excellent." I flashed one of my blinding smiles. "Enjoy the bathroom, ladies. You might want to close your mouths. It's not a good look."

Maybe not the best way to bond with my fellow group members.

Then again, friendship is overrated.

Chapter 6

It was too quiet.

All the usual airport noises were present and accounted for: the announcements about various gates and flight delays, snippets of strangers' conversations, and the ever-present wail of an unhappy baby; but among the Lewis & Clark group I was practically in solitary confinement. Apparently, word had already spread about my little bathroom speech, and everyone thought it was in their best interests to give me a wide berth. Everyone except professor "Just Call Me Neal" Hamilton, who kept trying to distract me from the fact that I was about as popular as avian flu by asking me all about my ballet dancing. I guess it never occurred to him that it might be a sensitive subject since this stupid program was responsible for interrupting my training with Mrs. P.

I couldn't even appreciate how hard he was trying to make me feel at home with the group, because that would involve actually caring about something, and the helplessness of my situation was effectively placing a damper on my emotions. I couldn't seem to feel much of anything anymore. Even when Neal awkwardly mentioned that my drinking violated school policy and asked if there was anything I needed to discuss, I did little more than shrug. There was nothing left for me to say.

Certainly nothing that Neal would want to hear.

The initial buzz from the alcohol at the duty-free hadn't lasted, probably because I'd been careful to remain hydrated on the plane—not that anyone in the group would believe that I was cautious when it comes to stuff like drinking. My reputation had already been sealed the second I lifted that first vodka sample. Still, I held my head high while I waited along with everybody else for my passport to be stamped. The only physical giveaway of discomfort I couldn't control was the restless way my feet shifted from first position into third.

My mom always hated it when I practiced ballet in supermarket lines, but I ignored her voice in my head telling me to *Stand still, for god's sake!* Instead I focused on relieving my cramped muscles by making small movements to match the beat of my music. And then I visualized each move I would make if I were back in Mrs. P's dance studio and I had the place to myself.

I could see it all in such detail. The dull shine of the wooden floors, the dents and scratches in the barre, even the blurry patches on the mirror that no amount of Windex managed to clear. I could see myself too. Hair bundled in a tight bun, black leotard, tan tights, and my favorite pair of toe shoes in place. I nodded my head to the beat of my music while I calculated just how long I would hold each movement that I mentally choreographed.

Fast. Slow. One and two, three, four.

"Hey, *princess,* you're slowing down the line."

Houston let irritation and condescension drip from his every word. So much for all that crap my parents said about "making a fresh start." Yeah, right. I looked over at the Cambodian man grumbling something that probably translated to *stupid American tourists,* while he signaled for me to approach his desk.

Somehow I had managed to piss off the Americans *and* the

Cambodians in under fifteen minutes. That required some skills.

"Shut up, Dallas," I said easily before sauntering over to the desk.

In a matter of minutes the rest of the group had passed with us through security, but I didn't expect Amy to sidle up to me and whisper, "It's Houston. You know . . . his name? Not Dallas."

"Really?" I feigned ignorance while I made sure that everyone could hear my words. "Are you *sure* it's not Austin?"

Amy nodded earnestly. "It's Houston."

"Not San Antonio?"

Ben laughed, releasing a rich chuckle as he draped an arm across my shoulder. "You're a hellcat, aren't you?"

I batted my lashes up at him. "I have no idea what you mean. Unlike Texas over there, I'm perfectly nice to everybody."

"That's a state, not a city," Houston pointed out crisply.

"And Houston is a city, not a name."

"Uh, let's huddle up, everyone!" Neal called out enthusiastically. "We're going to take a taxi to the hotel and break into rooms of two or three."

"Um, Neal?" Amy raised her hand as if she were sitting in a classroom. "When are Jeffrey and Micah going to get here?"

Neal cleared his throat uncomfortably. "Uh, well, they're not coming."

Everyone else stared at Neal as if he had casually announced that water wouldn't be available for the rest of the trip.

Houston was the first to speak. "What happened?"

"Well, they decided to travel independently before meeting up with us, and Micah got into a motorcycle accident in Thailand yesterday. He's going to be fine," Neal rushed to assure us. "But given the circumstances, the two of them are going to fly back to make sure that Micah gets the proper medical help he needs."

"So this is the whole group." Houston didn't look happy about it. His green eyes darkened as he ran a frustrated hand through his hair, mussing it up in the process.

Which, of course, looked downright sexy on him.

Talk about unfair. After the number of hours spent cramped in airplanes, he should at least have had bloodshot eyes and a waxy glaze of exhaustion.

"Yep, this is it!" Neal was trying way too hard to make it sound like that was a good thing. "We're going to be a tight-knit pack by the time we return."

Simply scanning my eyes over Houston's dark good looks, Ben's golden boy sheen, Liz's chaotic explosion of color, and Amy's pale, worried face confirmed my suspicion that *hell no,* we weren't going to become sitcom-family close. Lewis & Clark might be a college of misfit toys, but that didn't mean they would accept a packaged Barbie in their midst. Excluding Neal, the only one in our group to make even the slightest effort to be nice to me was Ben. And it didn't take a genius to figure out that he was primarily interested in getting into my pants, especially when his eyes lingered on the front of my V-neck shirt.

I was the odd girl out. And I was so fed up with being unwanted, I was tempted to try sprinting back toward the terminals. It wasn't as if my heart was so exclusively set on Italy that I wouldn't consider other destinations. London definitely held appeal. I could easily picture myself walking the cobblestone streets in my favorite heels alongside a charming British boy who was distantly related to Lord Something-or-other. The two of us could throw some darts together in seedy pubs before checking out the coolest underground clubs.

My daydream dissolved as my suitcase was loaded into a taxi and Houston gave me a not-so-gentle shove into the car.

I glared, but, if anything, his smirk only widened in response. I could practically hear him thinking, *Daddy's little girl isn't the center of the universe anymore. Bet she doesn't like* that!

I pointedly ignored him and stared out at the streets of Siem Reap, Cambodia. Actually, calling them *streets* was overly generous, in my opinion. The paved road leading away from the airport soon became dirt-packed and bumpy. Small dilapidated houses broke up the landscape, but they didn't look like they had ever seen better days. Instead it was as if the glorified shacks had come into existence looking ramshackle and were fighting just to stay that way. There was no mistaking the poverty around us. All the locals wore ripped jeans that were not distressed by design, yet along the main road were advertisements for Gucci and Prada. Photos of skinny white women clutching purses were everywhere—their big blue eyes staring sightlessly down at the people struggling to carve out a life for their families.

Portland definitely had its share of people living in poverty, but it was never like *this*. Not for me. It was something that I'd been able to ignore. Then again, in Portland I also didn't see men holding signs asking for donations because *land mines* had blown off part of their legs. That wasn't something I could easily dismiss.

I felt so uncomfortable.

"Pretty crazy, isn't it," Houston murmured, and I knew he was talking to me. "Shows just how safely you were tucked away, right, *princess?*"

There was that disdainful edge in his voice I had come to expect.

"Yeah, it's *my* fault that I was born into a middle-class family," I scoffed. "I should donate my entire college fund to charity. Move to Cambodia and . . . what? Play nursemaid to the orphans? Would that be pious enough for you?"

I hissed the last part, wanting to lash out with my fists as well as my words. I was so sick of not being enough. Not smart enough. Not sweet enough. And now, apparently, not generous enough.

Houston shook his head. "Never mind. I shouldn't have bothered. You just stay in that tower of yours, princess. It looks like you're pretty comfortable there."

"Thanks, *cowboy*."

A weak retort, but I hoped it grated on Houston's nerves the same way that being called *princess* annoyed me. Hearing it from a snarky college kid just made me wish I had told my dad to knock it off years ago. The endearment sounded so forced and . . . fake. I was nobody's princess. But telling Houston the truth would be a damn big tip-off that my home life wasn't the way he thought.

The way my dad had represented it to him.

That part still stung. I wondered what *exactly* my father had let slip. Did Houston know about the month I spent in middle school looking glassy-eyed and lost while I tried to find a way to keep Jake the Mistake from leaving me? Had Houston heard a rumor about the way I had convinced myself that Jake's cutting little remarks about my looks and my intelligence were his way of helping me grow?

No way.

It just wasn't possible since I'd never told anyone—not even my dad—about the true extent of my self-destructive mistakes.

Then again, my dad still could've speculated aloud . . . with Houston.

I pressed my body even more fully against the door of the cab and farther away from the plaid-wearing jerk.

All I had to do was make it out of Cambodia in one piece.

Chapter 7

The sun was shining. The birds were chirping. And the monkeys were . . . humping.

Why yes, that was exactly the way I had imagined Cambodia.

Our group hadn't even managed to make it through a whole week of tramping around temples and listening to lectures before witnessing the primates' more *amorous* activities up close.

And that didn't include watching Ben flirt with almost anything that moved.

"Um, well," Neal said awkwardly while he readjusted the collar on his shirt. "Let's all pay attention to our guide, Mr. Hournj. I'm sure he has a lot to tell us about the history behind this temple complex."

And I was sure that I didn't give a crap.

My body couldn't seem to adjust to the heat leaching away my energy. Probably because Oregon wasn't exactly known for being all sunshine and light—especially near Portland. If my parents had shipped me to England, I wouldn't have had a problem adjusting. It would have been easy trading in my version of cloudy and overcast for the grayness that lingers over London. But no. They had to pick *Cambodia,* where my skin perpetually felt hot and sticky. Roasting in the sun while touring a temple complex that looked remarkably similar to *all the other freaking temples we had already seen* effectively reduced me to a tired, mindless state.

Luckily, all I had to do was nod every time Neal and Mr. Hournj looked at me, and then wait to board the bus, where I'd be able to nod off to sleep.

I was beginning to feel like a freaking bobblehead.

At least I wasn't the only one who hated having Neal cheerfully pounding on our doors at six each morning with his "Up and at 'em!" greetings. Liz woke up with a pissed-off look on her face and always claimed the farthest seat away from Neal on the tour bus until mid-afternoon. I might have made a play for that spot myself, if she hadn't looked so ready to rip somebody's face off.

And my parents complained that *I* wasn't a morning person.

So I just sort of stared at the humping monkeys while Mr. Hournj yapped at us in what I could only assume was English since his accent was too thick for me to decipher most of it. I also hadn't managed to say his name right. Although if you've got a name like Hournj, I don't think it's fair to get all bent out of shape if someone calls you "Mr. Horny."

It wasn't like I called him that on *purpose*.

The first nine times.

Sadly, his name was the only thing I found even remotely interesting about our guide. So I tuned him out. If we were going to be tested on anything that came out of his mouth, I fully accepted the fact that I was going to fail. I expected it. Especially since I couldn't ask any of my classmates for help. I wasn't clear on who had initiated the silent treatment, but I wasn't going to be the one to break it.

Not that it really mattered. My parents didn't expect me to return to Oregon with B's. Or C's. Hell, they probably would be psyched if I maintained straight D's.

The whole thing was pointless for me to speculate on,

since I had no intention of sticking around in Cambodia long enough to be graded. My dad had asked me to keep an open mind and give it a chance . . . well, I had done that. And after spending almost a whole week sweating on the stones of temples, I was officially ready to leave. Ben slung an arm across my shoulder. "Penny for your thoughts?"

Okay, so I was on speaking terms with Ben and Neal. That didn't do much to relieve my sense of isolation. I mean, one of them only spoke to me because he thought he had a shot at getting in my pants and the other was my professor.

Oh yeah. My social life here was *great*.

I glanced from Ben, to the monkeys, and then back to him. "Sure. I was just thinking that between the two of you . . . the monkey probably has better technique."

"Ouch!" Ben leaned in closer. "You know, there's really only one way to test that theory. . . ."

I laughed. "So not going to happen."

"You sound pretty sure about that. Don't you want to see the size of my"—he paused suggestively—"*banana* first?"

"That's the lamest line I've ever heard."

It was exactly what I was thinking, but the words hadn't come from my mouth. Houston was looking at us both irritably, probably because it put his nose out of joint whenever anyone dared to have fun without his express permission.

I cranked up the megawattage on my smile. "Sounds to me like Detroit wants to see your banana in action way more than I do."

"Nah, he's already seen it."

That made my jaw drop.

"Roommates," Houston explained, although judging by his gritted teeth, he felt more like punching somebody than talking. "It comes with the territory."

"Um, what?" Now I really couldn't stop laughing. "Is that some secret housing requirement? Must be comfortable with—"

"No, it's not a *requirement!*" Houston's eyes were flashing fire, and I thought I saw faint traces of a blush moving up his cheeks. "It's what happens when you get sexiled and your roommate forgets to lock the door!"

"Dude, that happened *twice!*"

Houston shot Ben a *get real* glare.

"Okay, so it happened four times. Who's counting?"

"Me. I was counting. And it was six times, you moron."

Ben crossed his arms over yet another one of his lifeguard shirts. And while the guy had a killer smile, I wasn't interested in hooking up with anyone except Logan Beckett. Especially with someone who was making it pretty freaking obvious that the extent of his interest was purely skin deep.

I rested my hand on Ben's shoulder and ignored the way Houston seemed to become increasingly tense. "I appreciate the offer, but it just doesn't hold my interest. Sorry, Ben . . . better luck with someone else!"

Then, with an easy hair toss, I put on headphones to make it look like I couldn't hear the boys while I walked toward yet another temple. Eavesdropping shamelessly the whole way.

"I think she's still interested in me and just wants to play games first."

"Drop it."

"But—"

"Drop. It. Now."

"Have you looked at that girl, Houston? I mean *really* looked? Her ass is—"

"Off-limits," Houston finished for him, although I doubted that was how Ben wanted to describe it. Maybe it was stupid, but it felt good knowing that a college boy wanted me, even if that particular college boy didn't strike me as being very selective.

"Like hell it is!" Ben retorted. "We're in Cambodia. You

know what they say: What happens in Cambodia stays in Cambodia."

"Nobody says that, Ben. *Nobody*."

"Well, they should. There's no reason the two of us shouldn't have a good time and . . . get to know each other."

"Form a book club then. But you can't mess with Paul Halloway's daughter."

"Why? Does she have scales?"

That was all I heard, and frankly, it was a good thing Mr. Horny distracted me, because I was about to laugh and give myself away.

Ben had no clue that there were actually two Chelsea Halloways. One of them was comfortable dancing and flirting in high heels and a tight dress . . . but the other was still figuring out how to be alone. And neither version could handle having a one-night stand. I wasn't even sure I was ready for another relationship, considering that my last serious boyfriend . . .

My mind skidded away from old wounds. I may have been forced to look at super-old temples every day in the sweltering heat, but there was no need for me to dwell on *my* past.

"Did you know that the name Angkor Wat means 'City Temple' and refers to this whole area?"

I turned to Liz and crossed my arms defensively. "Nope. Then again, I also don't know why you think I care."

"Because we're going to be tested on it, and you clearly can't understand Mr. Horny."

That startled me. After our little bathroom conversation, I hadn't really spoken to Liz or Amy beyond, "Hey! Could you hurry up, already? I want to shower!" So I wasn't prepared for her to be . . . nice. Let alone for her to use my stupid nickname for Mr. Hournj.

"And you care if I fail the test?" I raised an eyebrow but kept my tone light. If this was a legitimate gesture of goodwill, I didn't want to screw it up.

Liz shrugged. "Not really. Unless you start crying afterward, because I *really* don't want you using up all the Kleenex or hogging the bathroom."

Then she nudged me with her shoulder and I found myself grinning back. As if we were actually friends and her quasi-insult was an inside joke.

"I think I can handle the test," I lied.

"So then you already knew that the temple is both the symbol for Cambodia and depicted on the national flag? Oh, and that the design and construction of this one began in the first half of the twelfth century under the rule of—"

"Okay, okay, I get your point!"

She smirked. "I'll be leading group study sessions when we get closer to the exam. And you'll be buying a round of drinks."

"Why are you being nice?" I demanded. "Studying with me . . . drinks . . . What gives?"

Liz cleared her throat. "Amy *may* have pointed out that we didn't exactly give you much of a chance. She's feeling guilty about it."

I glanced over at Amy, who was scribbling down Mr. Hournj's every word.

"Really?" I couldn't keep the skepticism out of my voice. "Amy doesn't strike me as the type to worry about much beyond her books."

Liz laughed. "Yeah, well, she does. And since we're stuck sharing a room with you . . . I thought we could blow off the group and get pedicures or something. Y'know, girl bonding time. And stuff like that."

There were so many ways I could have declined.

I could have made excuses:

Sorry, Liz, I can't make it tonight. Neal's been hounding me to have a private chat. He keeps wanting to talk about my feelings. Maybe we'll connect some other night?

I could have created a conflict:

I promised my parents that I would try to get an Internet connection in this godforsaken country. Sorry!

Or I could have unleashed my inner bitch:

Pedicures? With you? Um . . . pass.

But I accepted the invitation. In fact, I used it as an excuse to duck out of the heart-to-heart session Neal kept trying to schedule to make sure I was "adjusting" to the program. He had straight up told me that if I ever needed to talk about *anything*—translation: the divorce—that he was always available to listen. Ordinarily, I'd be pissed off to have someone acting like my surrogate dad. My parents might not be the best, but that didn't mean I wanted someone else to try to fill their roles.

Except . . . I hadn't been able to get mad at Neal. I found myself at a complete loss for words, including snarky comments. I couldn't even zap him with one of my best patronizing looks because Neal had already expressed more interest in my dancing than my dad had ever managed.

So I bailed on him in favor of exploring Siem Reap with the girls.

Mistake number . . . five thousand.

Chapter 8

It's not exactly a girls' night out if guys insist on coming along.

Unfortunately, Neal got all freaked out at the idea of the girls wandering the streets of Cambodia on their own and insisted that we let the guys go with us. I thought Liz made a particularly good point that his attitude was paternalistic and overprotective. Still, in the interest of *not* wasting time while Liz duked it out with him, Amy and I dragged her out of the hotel . . . while Houston and Ben watched in amusement. Still, it wasn't all that bad. Most of the time Ben's gaze was focused on checking out all the women in the marketplace.

Which meant that he definitely wasn't going to be hung up on me.

At one point he gave an attractive girl his patented once-over and then announced, "I'm happy to let her work out her daddy issues with me."

Just . . . gross.

I didn't catch Houston's response because Amy's face grew flushed with anger.

"That's *wrong*. It's disrespectful and it's just *rude*."

"Um, well, you're right. But I think Ben intended it to be fun—"

"Who said anything about Ben?" Amy demanded. "Wait, did he buy one of those shirts too? Because I *will* burn it."

Liz must have picked up on my confusion because she pointed at the stall in front of us. "Amy hates those shirts."

I glanced over at them. "Elephants are now offensive?"

"No!" Amy growled. "The one that says: *Danger! Cambodia land mines!*"

I waited patiently for the lecture I knew was coming.

"It's awful! I mean, people are *dying* from land mines here, and these *tourists*"—Amy spat it out like a dirty word—"are making light of the situation." She deepened her voice. "It's all, *Dude, cool shirt. Land mines.* But it's not cool!"

"You sure you're not blowing this whole thing out of proportion? It's a shirt, not an actual bomb."

Amy started flapping her arms at me. I should have known that her quiet exterior covered up a passionate nutcase underneath.

"It's a very big deal," Amy insisted. "There are *thousands* of land mines here just waiting to *blow up!* So turning it into a joke is just—"

"Unspeakably awful?" I suggested. It certainly felt to me like there were no real words that could encompass the pain of the country every time I passed amputees with donation bowls resting where their legs used to be. It was overwhelming.

"O-kay, it's terrible. Awful. Now that we have that settled—" Liz pointed to the rows of comfy-looking chairs where women of all ages were waiting to give massages. "I vote we stimulate their economy by getting pampered."

My kind of thinking.

Until Ben and his best buddy, Houston, intercepted us as we began moving toward the masseuses. Apparently, they were finished looking for shot glasses and patches or whatever type of souvenirs guys collected.

Ben winked at me. "You know, if you wanted a rubdown, Chelsea—"

"Cambodia is the place to get it," Houston finished for him. "I think I'll join you guys myself." He flopped into one of the big overstuffed chairs next to me, ignoring both Ben's scowl and my raised eyebrow.

"You playing bodyguard now too?" I exaggeratedly batted my lashes while Ben shuffled off, muttering something about getting a beer. "Protecting my honor?"

Houston shrugged. "Your dad just wants you to return home with the same dubious amount of honor you possessed when you left."

I stared at him in disbelief. "I can't believe you just said that."

"Total douche-bag behavior," Liz agreed.

Amy nodded. "Out of order, Houston."

Wow. It was kind of nice having people jump to my defense. Sure, if we were all back at Smith High School, Fake and Bake—um, *Steffani* and *Ashley*—would've backed me up. Except they would have been doing it because I potentially posed a threat to their social lives . . . not quite the same thing.

Houston nodded curtly. "Okay. That may have come across a bit harsh."

Rather weak as far as apologies go, but he didn't seem like the type to give them lightly.

I narrowed my eyes. "*A bit* harsh? No freaking kidding, you jerk!"

"But," he continued as if I had never spoken, "since I promised your dad that I'd look out for you, consider yourself on a hookup hiatus."

For the first time since I came to Cambodia I found myself laughing hard.

"You think that you can stop me from *flirting?* Trust me, Tallahassee, I could have any guy I wanted wrapped around my little finger back in *middle school*. If I turned on the charm, not even you would stand a chance."

Liz moaned from her chair as her masseuse began rubbing her legs with oil. "God, this feels good. Wait . . . *middle school?*"

That's when I realized just how close I'd come to sharing far more than I was willing to tell anyone.

So I merely shrugged while a middle-aged Cambodian woman rubbed my legs systematically. Liz was right: It felt amazing. It was too bad that our conversation had me so tense I had to force my hands to unclench.

"Yeah. Middle school."

"So what happened?" Amy looked like she was about to fall asleep in her chair, but apparently she was still paying attention. "Did things work out with the guy?"

Deep, even breaths. No need to panic over a perfectly innocent question. Especially since I had told the truth . . . mostly . . . about having guys wrapped around my little finger.

I had just left out a whole bunch of details—like the fact that I had also completely lost myself in the relationship. That what I had with Jake had spiraled into something twisted that sickened me more every day. I could still remember feeling my heart swell when he murmured, "Nobody will ever love you as much as I do, Chelsea" into my ear. It had been so thrillingly romantic. It made me feel sexy. Desired. Wanted.

I didn't realize it was a threat.

Nobody will ever love you as much as I do, Chelsea.

Because they don't really love you at all.

If you *really* loved me back, you would stop wasting all your time teaching kids at the dance studio. You would let me take naked pictures of you. You would stop flirting with other guys. Stop saying that you were just trying to be friendly, Chelsea. We both know differently.

Nobody will ever love you as much as I do.

So you'd better not screw this up too.

I didn't think anyone in the group would understand.

If someone tried to manipulate Liz's emotions, I was willing to bet they'd find themselves kicked to the curb, holding a handcrafted sign: RELATIONSHIP TERMINATED DUE TO SUDDEN OUTBREAK OF UNACCEPTABLE BEHAVIOR. As for Amy . . . I doubted that she had ever been in a relationship, which meant the closest she had probably come to heartbreak was waiting for her crush to *finally* notice her.

It sure sounded like Ben got laid and moved on with no hard feelings on his side. It wouldn't even surprise me to hear that he rolled off a girl after sex and high-fived her before searching for his pants. I didn't really understand how he could dive into casual flings and one-night stands without feeling, well . . . used. But it didn't seem to bother him in the slightest. I seriously doubted he would have any trouble disentangling himself from a hookup that was approaching its expiration date.

That left only Houston. I eyed him speculatively, but I couldn't get a read on him. Part of me wanted there to be a female Jake the Mistake lurking in his past that would conveniently explain why he was so suspicious of me.

But I seriously doubted it.

"Yeah, Chelsea. What happened?" Houston smirked as if he already knew whatever I was going to say wouldn't be the truth. Not the full truth, anyway.

He was right.

I rolled my eyes. "I dated a high school senior back in middle school. We broke up. He left for college. Satisfied?"

Amy's eyes snapped open. "*Seriously?* You can't stop *there.*"

But that's exactly where I wished the story had ended. I wanted it to be nothing more than a temporary footnote in my romantic history—one that glossed right over a year of warped mind games followed by an inevitable breakup and a two-year tailspin. I definitely wanted to forget how desperately I had needed someone to reassure me that Jake had it all wrong.

That I wasn't broken and unlovable.

But I didn't know how I would recover if Jake's words were only confirmed, so I didn't risk it. Instead, I pretended that I was perfectly fine and focused on maintaining my popularity. Nobody could hurt me if they thought I had the power to make them regret it. All they could do was whisper about me behind my back as I smiled, tossed back my hair, and put on the performance of a lifetime. By the time I figured out that all the guys I was surrounding myself with weren't going to ease my gnawing self-doubt—that only Logan had ever been interested in hearing what I had to say—he had already moved on to geekier pastures.

Not that I would admit any of that out loud.

Houston laughed, but I couldn't tell if he actually found any part of the conversation funny. "I take it back. I'm calling you jail bait now instead of princess. That's just—" He shook his head for a moment before the laughter died and he suddenly went very still. "Your dad doesn't know you were in middle school when it started, does he?"

Crap.

I had completely forgotten that Houston was a total narc, which was incredibly stupid because he kept reminding me of that fact every freaking chance he got. So I said the first thing that came to my mind.

"What happens in Cambodia stays in Cambodia."

"I told you, Houston!" Ben announced proudly as he sipped his newly purchased beer and lowered himself into another one of the massage chairs.

"Still not a real thing, Ben."

"Yeah, well, you're going to keep your mouth shut about this, Michigan," I snapped out so angrily that the woman massaging my calves looked up at me in concern. "Whatever happened *years* ago with Jake is none of your business. And if you say anything about him to my parents—"

"He won't," Liz assured me. "He's just messing with you. And for the first time . . . I agree with Ben. I don't care if it sounds stupid: What happens in Cambodia stays in Cambodia."

Ben pumped his fist into the air. *"Yes!"*

"Shut up, Ben," Houston said without any real heat.

I laughed and for a second I thought that we might all go back to hanging out and relaxing. Maybe do some more shopping in the stalls of the marketplace.

"Your secrets are safe with us, Chelsea. So what happened with Jake?" Liz waggled her eyebrows suggestively.

The one question I had no intention of answering.

Ever.

Chapter 9

I forced myself to laugh.

"You're going to have to get me plastered if you want to hear *that* story. And since a certain *someone*"—I glanced pointedly at Houston—"will never let me do that, you're just out of luck."

Liz rolled her eyes. "Fine."

Ben turned the power of his dark chocolate eyes on her. "What about you, Liz?" he asked smoothly. "Any secrets you want to share with the class?"

"My love life isn't all that interesting right now. My girlfriend is studying abroad in Australia, and since we've been together since freshman year, there's not much to tell."

"Wait, *girlfriend?*"

She burst out laughing at Ben's surprise. "You didn't know? *Really?* It's not like I'm in the closet, guys. I've been leading LGBTQ events for *years.*"

Amy's eyes softened as she tapped her finger against the leather of her chair. "Wait a sec. I think I know her. Sara, right? She was in my Shakespeare class."

Liz smiled, and for the first time it hit me that she was disgustingly pretty. She might not look conventional, but one mention of Sara and she practically glowed.

"She's amazing." Liz laughed self-consciously. "And if you get me started, I won't shut up. So . . . your turn, Amy."

"My turn for what?"

Classic stalling tactic. I would have called her on it, except I didn't want to draw any more attention to my love life either. Especially since I had already let Jake's name slip. Damn but that had been clumsy of me.

"The details on *your* love life, Ms. English Major. Spill."

Liz was even nosier than I originally thought. Amy turned bright pink and began fiddling with her purse. "Um, nothing to tell."

I doubted that was an exaggeration, so I interrupted to distract Liz before she could embarrass Amy further.

"I think it's time for Texas to have a turn. After all, he claims he knows *so* much about me."

Houston merely smirked. "Listen, jail bait—"

"Keep it up with that nickname and I *will* feed you to those flesh-eating fish." I pointed behind us to a huge fish tank that I had made the mistake of checking out earlier. Apparently, the pool was fully stocked with little fish that ate the calluses off people's feet.

Gross.

"He just broke up with a girl named Carolyn because he didn't want to do the whole long-distance-relationship thing," Ben volunteered. "That's what he told me, anyway. I think he just wanted an excuse to stop seeing her."

Liz perked up at that. "Why would he want an excuse?"

"I wouldn't and I didn't."

"Because she's about as bland as oatmeal."

"Hey, what's wrong with oatmeal?" Amy protested. "It tastes good to me."

"Yeah, but would you want to *date* it?"

"No. Then again, I don't form romantic attachments with any breakfast items."

"Well, take my word for it, Carolyn was nothing special."

I waited for Houston to defend his ex-girlfriend's honor, but he didn't say a word. "Are you really not going to stick up for her?"

He shrugged. "Ben's entitled to his own opinion. And no offense, but I'm not sharing the details of my love life with a kid."

A kid.

I saw red. Admittedly, I was younger than all of them—kind of obvious, considering that I was a high school junior and they were a mix of *college* sophomores and juniors—but that didn't make me a *kid*. Not the way he meant it at least. Then again, it was probably all part of his stupid "protecting her as a favor to her dad" plan.

All things considered, I thought I had done a damned good job of looking out for myself. The last thing I needed was someone else deciding that they would be better at it. Not to mention that if my dad had really wanted to make sure I was safe, he should've done something himself instead of sending me off with his freaking *teacher's assistant*. What exactly did he think Houston would do if I got into trouble, anyway? Write it down in a grading booklet for further evaluation?

"Fine, Houston," I snapped, handing my masseuse a five-dollar bill, effectively giving her a 300 percent tip. "Keep your secrets. I really don't care. I'll see the rest of you back at the hotel."

Then I quickly started moving so he wouldn't be able to follow me through the crowded streets, where vendors urged tourists to check out their wares and guys on temperamental-looking motorcycles with carriages attached weaved around on the dirt road, hustling to pick up new customers.

In my haste to hail one of them, I held up some of the cash from my wallet. Nothing like a twenty-dollar bill to get people's attention. Although that might not have been the smartest idea, since I effectively created a traffic jam as four different drivers

attempted to pick me up. Still, I dropped my wallet back into
my enormous tote bag, slid into the contraption closest to
me, told the driver the name of our hotel, and gripped the
railing tightly . . . just as the entire thing wobbled from the
additional weight of someone lurching in right behind me.

For the first time I found myself relieved to see that particular plaid shirt and the scowl that went with it. As much as I
disliked Houston, the alternatives for companionship in
Cambodia could have been a whole lot worse.

"Do you have a death wish or are you just an idiot?" he
demanded. "Here's a little tip for you, *princess:* Don't wave
wads of cash around before hopping into a freaking tuk-tuk
alone!"

"Into a what?"

Houston raked a hand through his hair, making it stick up
comically. Except I didn't think he was going to be laughing
about it, or anything else, anytime soon.

"This!" He gestured at the glorified open-air carriage.
"*This* is a tuk-tuk. God, do you listen to *anything* or are you
too busy flipping your hair to pay attention!"

Ouch.

I lifted my chin and glared right back at him. "Can you
even pretend to be a halfway decent human being, or is that
asking too much of you?"

The tuk-tuk began moving with a lurch that steadied out
once the driver really started darting and dodging his way
down the street.

"You're right," Houston said finally. "You are absolutely
right, princess. I've been stressing out over my babysitting
obligations this entire time, and that's not the experience I
signed up for. It's not my job to hold your freaking hand
every step of the way. So . . . you're on your own."

I sat in silence that was broken only by tuk-tuk horns and
intermittent road rage–inspired swearing, while I stewed over
his words.

"I never asked you to hold my hand. In fact, I never asked you for anything. If you treated me like everyone else, we wouldn't be having this problem."

"Chelsea, you are *three* years younger than most of us. You might not want to hear it, but you are most definitely a kid."

I laughed even though his expression made it clear that he wasn't kidding. But it was way too funny for me to squelch my grin.

Because I hadn't been a kid in years.

Definitely not after *Jake the Mistake*.

"Keep telling yourself that if it makes you feel better. We both know that a measly three-year age gap doesn't make the slightest difference here. But maybe if you just keep repeating it, you'll actually believe it, Walker Texas Ranger."

The tuk-tuk stopped at our hotel, and I handed the driver some cash before Houston could intercept and pay the bill. Normally, I don't care if a guy wants to foot the bill for me, mainly because I never *rely* on it. My after-school job working as an assistant dance instructor for Mrs. P's studio was more than enough to support my Starbucks addiction. In fact, I had even started a small Get Out of Oregon fund that my parents didn't know about. Just in case their fighting ever got bad enough that I needed to bail for a while. It wasn't much—maybe enough for a week at a cheap Oregon motel— but I've always been good at budgeting.

But with Houston it was different.

I had something to prove.

Which was why I pretended to ignore him completely as we walked through the hotel's fancy lobby, complete with marble floors, a gleaming concierge desk, and plush leather couches that reminded me of the one in my dad's study. A sudden rush of homesickness threatened to overwhelm me. It was such an insignificant thing to make me miss home that I straightened my shoulders and decided not to even mention it in my email to Jane. But before I could ask the front desk about paying for Internet access, Neal approached us from the elevators with a big, goofy smile on his face.

"Chelsea! Houston! How was your evening?"

"Um, fine, Neal," I said, glancing at the desk in the hope that he would take the hint and let me leave. "I think the others will be coming back pretty soon."

"That's great!"

I really wished someone could find his enthusiasm off switch—or at the very least dial it down.

"What are your plans for tonight?" I couldn't tell if Houston was asking to be polite or if he was actually interested, but either way he screwed up my plan for a quick getaway.

"Well," Neal began, "I wanted to take a shower earlier, but the plumbing in my room didn't work!" He chuckled as if he were sharing an absolutely *hilarious* anecdote. "So I came down here to ask for a different room. And when I got to it, you'll never guess what I found there!"

Houston and I both kept our mouths shut and simply waited for him to tell us.

"Two Buddha statues!"

Okay . . . I was officially bored with this conversation.

"Well, that's great, Neal. I'm, uh, glad you got the plumbing issue fixed. I'll just be go—"

But Neal wasn't finished. "I was just coming down here to thank them for the gift. Isn't it the most thoughtful thing you've ever heard of happening in a hotel?"

Um, no.

"It sure is," I agreed. "Well, I'll just let you do that while I—"

"The two of you should look at them! They will give you a whole new appreciation for the culture, Chelsea." Neal practically swelled with excitement, and I knew Houston and I were stuck.

Not that Houston seemed to mind. If anything, he actually

looked interested in checking out the stupid statues, as if he hadn't just seen thousands of cheap wood carvings meant to capture the hearts and wallets of tourists while exploring the marketplace stalls of Siem Reap. Neal's statues were going to be more of the same. Maybe if our dork of a professor was lucky, he had been gifted a whole five bucks' worth of wood in the shape of a fat man.

Not exactly exhibit-worthy material.

"Why don't you show Houston while I—"

My last-ditch attempt for freedom failed miserably when Houston tossed a casual arm over my shoulder and announced, "We'd love to see them, Neal."

Well, wasn't that just fan-freaking-tastic.

The three of us rode the elevator up to the third floor while Neal chattered on about how we were in for a real treat since we'd be visiting a working Buddhist monastery the next day. Then again, since Mr. Horny would still be the one explaining everything to the group, I had a hard time working up even fake enthusiasm.

Yippee.

Still, I couldn't help being a little impressed when Neal swiped us into his room and I actually saw the statues. These weren't the dirt-cheap market creations I had expected but legitimate works of art I could picture my mom buying for her office to make her seem more worldly. Purchased online, of course. Less hassle that way.

Then again, beautifully carved or not, Buddha was still a beaming fat man. My mom would probably put him in her exercise room in order to steer herself away from the path of carbohydrates.

"Wow, Neal. They're really pretty." I gently stroked the smooth wood that formed the head of one statue. "Nice gift."

He beamed while Houston examined the other statue. "Chelsea, I think you should keep one of them."

"Uh, that's okay!" I instantly tried to backpedal as Neal held out the Buddha as if it were Simba about to be introduced to all the beasts in *The Lion King*.

"I insist," he said grandly. "They're supposed to bring good luck. Or happiness. Not sure which, actually."

Great. I could've used some help turning down a gigantic wooden fat man, but Houston only smiled.

"He's . . . awfully heavy," I lied, knowing that it couldn't weigh more than five or six pounds when I had the stupid thing clutched in my arms. "You sure you don't want to keep him, Neal?"

"No, I really want you to have him, Chelsea, only . . ." He paused uncomfortably. "Maybe you shouldn't show it to the others? I don't want anyone getting jealous."

Right. Because *everyone* wants to haul a wooden statue around a third-world country.

But I could tell from Neal's expression that he was really worried about hurt feelings. And *that* was undeniably sweet. I mean, the guy was still plenty annoying, but at least his heart was in the right place. Which was how I became the not-so-proud owner of five pounds' worth of his "good intentions." I opened the dance tote bag that I was in the habit of carrying everywhere and shoved most of the Buddha inside. Half of his head and part of his enormous belly jutted out, but all things considered, it fit pretty well.

"How's that?" I asked Neal. "Discreet enough for you?"

"Marvelous!"

Of course, because everything in Neal's world was daisies, butterflies, and happy fat men. The guy was growing on me, but he still put out a little too much good cheer for me to stomach.

"Well, we're going to see if the others are back yet," Houston said as the two of us edged our way out the door and into the hallway. "See you tomorrow, Neal."

"Get a good night's sleep, you two! Don't forget, we have a busy day tomorrow."

On that note, he waved good-bye to us and shut his door with a soft click.

Finally. Now I can relax in private.

That's what I was thinking when several men whose classy suits couldn't hide the fact that they were built like tanks passed us in the hallway. Taking a nice hot bath before my roommates showed up was my top priority—right before the men used a swipe card of their own to enter Neal's room.

Which was when all hell broke loose.

Chapter 10

I'm used to arguments.

Call them whatever you want: squabbles, disputes, moments of heightened dialogue; none of it fazes me. So when I heard indignant voices emerging from Neal's room, I remained rooted in the middle of the hallway, but it wasn't from fear. It actually reminded me of home. Only this time I couldn't try to drown it out with my music, and most of the voices spoke with thick Cambodian accents.

"Who are you?"

"What are you doing in this room?"

I had no trouble imagining Neal's good-natured smile as we heard him say, "Oh, this must be some hotel mix-up. See, I had this problem with my plumbing—"

Except the Cambodian businessmen didn't calm down, or chuckle, or say anything along the lines of, "Let's just ask the concierge about this little mistake, shall we?"

Oh no.

There was the unmistakable sound of shattering glass and a startled cry of pain before I distinctly heard Neal gasp, "Wait! I can explain!"

That's when I began screaming.

Loudly.

I've always had the ability to project my voice really well, which was why Smith High School cast me to play the female lead in their musical production of *Romeo and Juliet*. It's always better when the leads don't have to wear mics in order to be heard at the very back of the theater. And to think that I had been disappointed to have the opportunity ripped away from me because of my stupid program in Cambodia.

Nobody could miss the performance I was putting on now.

Especially since I wasn't just flat-out shrieking like girls always do in horror movies. Oh no, I was also bellowing for the police—until a large hand covered my mouth from behind. I tried my best to evade the tightening grip because there was no way I could let some insane business guys beat the life out of Neal.

No freaking way.

Someone was speaking rapidly in my ear while I writhed and squirmed, and it took me a second to realize it was Houston who'd grabbed me.

"*Run, Chelsea,*" he ordered me firmly. "Go back to your room. Lock the door. And call downstairs for help. *Now.*"

Except his string of orders came too late.

The door to Neal's room flew open, and one of the men came lurching out to shut me up. He needn't have bothered. One glimpse of Neal, sprawled out on the floor like a discarded stuffed animal after too many rounds of tug-of-war, cut off all sound to my throat. Not to mention that I still had Houston's hand clamped over my mouth.

There was so much blood.

That was new for me. It always looks so dramatic on television when the cops go to investigate a brutal murder and there are pools of blood surrounding the victim. The camera inevitably pans to their wide, sightless eyes and . . . roll opening credits.

Except this was different.

The blood wasn't created out of cornstarch and food coloring or whatever.

This was Neal.

"You—you . . ." I stuttered at the stranger, unable to complete my sentence because it was so unthinkable. For the first time words were well and truly beyond me because I couldn't bring myself to say, *"You killed him!"*

I couldn't even admit the possibility that it could be true.

The stranger seemed temporarily unsure what to do about two young witnesses, but the largest of the three men—Mr. Enormous, as I automatically began thinking of him—decisively shut the door in our face. Although not before I caught a glimpse of Mr. Boss Man (who I assumed was in charge because his suit was the nicest) kicking Neal right in the stomach.

I dimly heard one of the strangers snarl, "You think to double-cross Mr.—" before Neal's retching drowned out the rest of his words.

That should have been my cue to get the hell out of there. In fact, the smart thing would've been to bolt at the first sign of trouble. Maybe that meant everyone at Smith High School was right about my intelligence after all, because I couldn't move. I stood frozen in place while the small part of me that desperately tried to remain objective pointed out that if Neal was puking he couldn't be dead . . . yet. He just needed to stay in that condition long enough for help to arrive.

"Answer me, thief! Where is it?"

The man standing far too close for comfort appeared to make up his mind as he headed right in our direction. Houston didn't exactly let me linger around there any longer. Snatching hold of my hand, he pulled me down the hall toward the elevator while a handful of nosy guests stuck their heads out of their rooms.

"Call the police!" Houston shouted. "Room three fourteen! *Now!*"

The same tiny, logical voice that was somehow managing to remain calm wanted to point out that I'd been about to yell the exact same thing before he'd shut me up. And that for someone who had recently proclaimed that he was anti-hand-holding, he had a pretty tight grip on me now. I decided those particular comments could probably keep until we didn't have a three-hundred-pound crazy man chasing us down. Most people tend to be more receptive to feedback when their lives aren't in mortal danger.

So I kept my mouth shut and ran.

My tote banged into me with every step I took, doubtlessly mottling my side black and blue in the process, as Houston and I barreled down three flights of stairs. I never got the chance to reposition it, because Houston's pace didn't slacken even when we burst into the lobby. His breathing became choppier with every step until he was wheezing like a shrill teapot trying to signal that the water had reached boiling.

My feet could easily match Houston's strides, but my head was struggling to catch up. I knew we had to keep moving, that sprinting far away from the group of thugs currently beating the stuffing out of our professor was our top priority . . . I just didn't understand the *why* of it all.

None of it made sense.

All Neal had done was complain about a shower. Even with some leeway for cultural differences this was one major overreaction over a faulty appliance. And *I* couldn't be fleeing for my life with the one person in Cambodia who hated my guts, all because of a random plumbing miscommunication.

If my death was that freaking meaningless, I fully intended to haunt my parents forever for sending me on this stupid trip in the first place.

Houston pulled me through the lobby without missing a step, simultaneously yelling at the overwhelmed help desk lady to call the cops as we sprinted toward the door. I took her panic-stricken face as a good sign that she was taking the danger seriously. Then again, the alternative was to see her expression as a bad sign and, frankly, I didn't need anything else to freak out over because the big guy behind us didn't appear to be calling it quits.

He simply decided that nonlethal force was no longer his method of choice—not when it came to stopping the two of us. That became pretty darn clear when the handful of tourists sitting in the lobby started screaming, "He's got a gun!"

Although I thought the real giveaway was probably the blast of heat as the bullet tore into a framed wall painting next to me. Not to mention the fact that his buddies were probably still upstairs kicking the living daylights out of my professor. That was a big clue that these guys weren't exactly future Nobel Peace Prize material.

More like excellent candidates for *Cambodia's Most Deadly,* if such a thing even existed.

But I didn't have time to say anything sarcastic like, "*Really? He has a gun?* Gee, I never would have guessed!" because I had to conserve my oxygen for more important things, like charging toward the lobby door. There was another loud blast as our pursuer fired off another round, this one slamming through my tote. I probably should have just let the bag go flying across the room, but I clung to it even as my arm wrenched from the effort. I just concentrated on putting one foot in front of the other, and I didn't slacken the pace when we made it outside.

A tuk-tuk was waiting right by the curb, probably because the driver was hoping to receive some late-night business from barhopping tourists. Not that I cared why it was sitting there. I had barely climbed inside before Houston shoved me down to the floor.

"Go!"

Our driver didn't need to be told twice.

Probably because he wasn't interested in getting riddled

with one of the bullets intended for us. He swore fluently in both English and Cambodian as he peeled away from the hotel. I couldn't help panting as if I'd just gone through Mrs. P's hardest routines . . . . twenty times. More than Houston's arm was draped across me now; his whole body was pressed against mine. Even as I struggled to push past the adrenaline flooding my system, I shut my eyes and pretended that when I opened them again, I'd be safely tucked under the covers in bed. In Oregon.

Instead of underneath an incredibly hot college guy who appeared equally shaken.

"Chelsea," he rasped finally, and I shifted to meet his eyes. For the first time I noticed that they were green with dark gray flecks. And they definitely didn't look coldly cynical or distant anymore.

"Chelsea," he repeated. "What the hell have you gotten mixed up in?"

Chapter 11

I glowered up at Houston.

"You don't really think . . ." But it was obvious that he did. "I had nothing to do with this, *thank you very much!*"

"Then why . . ." Houston appeared at a loss to know what he should say next.

"How do I know?" It felt good to channel some of the adrenaline pumping through my system into yelling at him. Houston deserved it too. He *should* have said something significantly more swoon-worthy like, "Are you all right? Sit tight, princess. Let me check for injuries." Now *that* was an acceptable reaction after someone randomly opened fire in a hotel and tried to use two American students for target practice.

Other guys would've said it without any hesitation. Plenty of other guys also would have used our horizontal positions in a getaway tuk-tuk as an opportunity to make a play for second base. Houston's hands were bracketed on either side of my face, but they didn't so much as brush against my cheek. It looked like he was trying his hardest not to unnerve me with our close physical contact . . . even as he accused me of being behind the epic debacle of awfulness. The moment would have been so sweet if he hadn't gone and ruined it by tossing out ridiculous accusations at me. I slugged his shoulder. Hard.

"This isn't my fault!"

"I didn't say that you *intended* it to happen, but let's face it: You're a walking disaster. We both know that's why your parents decided to send you on this trip in the first place. And since disasters don't usually come from out of nowhere, I'm betting you're involved somehow." Using his body weight to keep me pinned to the floor, Houston clearly had no intention of moving.

"You're insane! Certifiably insane!" I tried to whack him again, but he kept my arms immobilized. "What's my mastermind plan here, Houston? I flipped through the Yellow Pages and hired some Cambodian Rent-a-Thugs to beat the crap out of Neal, *shoot* at us, and all for . . . what? A direct flight back to the U.S.?" I snorted in contempt. "If I wanted out that badly, there are a billion better ways I could have arranged it. None of which would include hurting Neal!"

Houston levered himself off me, and breathing suddenly became a lot easier.

"So you had nothing to do with this?"

"That's what I just said, genius!"

We glared at each other, and for a moment I could almost pretend we were still arguing over his snarky comments that had pissed me off not even an hour ago. Except then he had to go and take the fight out of me by raking a hand through his hair and muttering, "I'm glad you're safe, Chelsea. Let's focus on keeping it that way."

I nodded, but instead of leaving the conversation there, I locked onto his piercing green eyes and blurted out the one thing that really mattered to me.

"Do you think Neal is going to be okay?"

Even as the words escaped my lips, I knew it was a dumb question. Neal was probably still being beaten up by a group of men who had looked awfully comfortable kicking him in the stomach. *Of course* he wasn't okay. Not by a long shot. I simply couldn't bring myself to ask point-blank if Houston thought he was dead.

"Let's concentrate on finding the others," Houston replied evasively, before he shifted upright so that he could holler out directions to the tuk-tuk driver. I didn't move from the flooring. I didn't even try to pull myself up onto one of the seats. Instead, I closed my eyes and felt the vibrations of the motor rumble through me.

It should have been soothing, but I couldn't catch my breath until we pulled up at the same open-air massage place I had stormed away from an hour earlier, but which already felt like a lifetime ago, and found Liz and Amy happily getting pedicures. Ben sat nearby flirting with two random girls as he worked on what was probably his third or fourth drink of the night.

Ben spotted us first and grinned. "Aw, have the two of you kissed and made up already?"

Not so much.

My expression must have given away that everything was far from okay because Liz stared at me hard. "What happened?"

"It's Neal," I managed to say numbly. "He's . . . in trouble."

Amy's big Disney eyes widened. "What kind of trouble?"

"The kind that comes with guns. Lots of guns."

Ben started laughing. "Good one, Chelsea. You almost had me with that one. You're not a half-bad actress. Maybe you should consider it professionally. Or you could always look into modeling."

"She's not joking." Houston's voice was low and calm, but I could sense his body vibrating with adrenaline just like mine. "We were leaving Neal's room when these guys showed up."

"Boss Man, Mr. Enormous, and Backup," I interrupted. Then shut up when Houston shot me his patented *you're not helping* glare.

"They confronted Neal about being in their room and then one of them got really pissed—"

"Boss Man."

Houston rubbed his forehead, probably to resist the temptation to throttle me.

"Okay, *Boss Man* started beating up Neal, Chelsea started screaming, and . . ."

"*And?*" Liz demanded.

"We ran."

There it was. The reason I felt like the crappiest human being on the planet. My teacher, the one adult who actually cared enough to try to discuss my feelings, was *pummeled* right in front of me, and all I'd managed to do was scream and run away.

Oh yeah, I was real brave.

Mackenzie Wellesley probably would've figured out a way to help Neal. She would've whipped out her phone and snapped a picture of the thugs to show the police. Or maybe she would have simply bored them to tears with a discussion on the history of Cambodia. Either way, she wouldn't have bailed for the nearest exit with an enormous wooden Buddha weighing down her tote bag. Mackenzie never would've taken all that extra poundage with her.

Then again, I wasn't as smart as Mackenzie Wellesley, geek extraordinaire.

"You ran?" Liz repeated.

"Yeah." Houston shoved his hands into his jeans pockets as if that would help him regain his famous control. "One of the guys chased—"

"Backup."

I really had to stop interrupting.

"Backup started shooting at us and . . . what else could I have done?" He looked disgusted with himself. "Chelsea was a sitting duck, and I couldn't—"

"*Hey!* Don't you dare blame this on me!"

Houston shook his head. "That's not what I'm trying to do here, Chelsea. You already told me you had nothing to do with it. So . . . that's it."

Liz, Amy, and Ben looked at me expectantly. As if now that we had *that* all cleared up, I would start barking orders for everyone to follow. There was a thickness to the air, a nervous energy, a heightened tension that was only building around me.

It paralyzed all of us.

High school popularity might have prepared me for a lot, but nothing like *this*.

"So. . . ." Amy's voice shook as she finally cut through the helpless silence. "Uh, what . . . what should we do now?"

Ben draped an arm across her shoulder as he obviously did his best not to panic. "I vote we go back to the hotel. We can do some amateur sleuthing while Houston and Chelsea hide out here. Sounds like they could use a few more massages while we make sure the coast is clear."

Right. Because as soon as the massage oil came out I would totally forget that, minutes ago, someone was trying to lodge speeding hunks of metal in my body. Then again, I couldn't go back to the hotel. If I ever had to walk through the main lobby, with or without bullet holes, the hotel would have another mess on its hands. I couldn't even *think* about it without wanting to retch.

Still, if Ben wanted to be the voice of reason while I had my own private meltdown, he wouldn't hear any complaints from me.

"Okay," I muttered, sinking into the chair that Amy had vacated. "That's great, because I'm not going back there. Ever." I fought back a wave of hysterical laughter as I added, "Could someone grab my suitcase? My tote isn't exactly going to cut it for long."

I lifted my bag to show them just how unprepared I was for life on the run, but it only made the Buddha inside stare at all of us with that big, foolish grin carved on his face.

"Why exactly are you lugging around a *statue* with you?" Liz demanded. "Please tell me you didn't steal it from the lobby on your way out."

"Yeah, that's exactly how it happened." Maybe it was the fear-based adrenaline pumping through my system that had me desperate to cling to this distraction. Anything to postpone the inevitable moment when the events of the past twenty minutes became sickeningly real. I couldn't resist rolling my eyes. "I asked Backup to stop *shooting* at us long enough for me to grab a Buddha. Pudgy men always make me sentimental."

Maybe it wasn't fair of me to dis on the closest thing I had to a spiritual adviser. I hadn't actually been shot, so he had sort of upheld his whole "lucky" end of the bargain. Then again, good luck shouldn't have included fleeing for my life from professor-beating thugs.

Houston's lips quirked upward into a reluctant smile, and it struck me just how absurdly attractive he was when he chose to make himself agreeable. If the guy ever loosened up enough to turn on the charm, he could probably be every bit as persuasive as Ben . . . or me.

I wanted to attribute that observation of mine to shell-shock. That was the only thing that made even the slightest bit of sense to me. It was also the one semi-logical explanation I could come up with to excuse the goofy smile spreading across my face.

I was one more hysterical burst of laughter away from being committed to a psych ward.

"Next time, don't drag the bag with you, princess."

So apparently I wasn't the only one who had an inappropriate response to catastrophe. "Funny, I'd rather make sure there isn't a next time, Texas."

For a second I thought we might legitimately have a nice moment together, one that didn't involve frustrated hair raking or eye rolling or general snarkiness, even though the timing couldn't have been worse. Something that Ben didn't hesitate to point out.

"*Seriously?* The two of you are going to be all cutesy together *now?*"

"Don't be jealous, Ben," Liz told him, dragging Amy with her toward the nearest available tuk-tuk. "We'll help you find someone. *After* we find Neal."

Ben's scowl only deepened as he strode towards the bustling street full of tuk-tuks. "I'm going to hold you to that promise."

Even in the midst of a full-blown crisis, it was hard to take Ben seriously. The guy acted like a little boy who had just been promised a bowl of ice cream if he ate all of his broccoli. Houston might care about the three-year age gap, but I wasn't particularly impressed with the way the others were handling Neal's situation. Amy looked terrified by the idea of scouting the hotel, Ben paused briefly to check out a stranger even as he hailed the nearest tuk-tuk, and Liz . . . okay, she looked like she had everything under control.

But *some* of that had to be an act.

Although for the very first time I found myself hoping that someone else could continue delivering the star performance. Our group needed someone to keep it together because this particular mess was already way out of my league.

I didn't even need Mackenzie Wellesley to point it out.

Chapter 12

"We've got good news and bad news."
Those were Ben's first words when the three of them finally returned to the massage parlor where Houston and I had been waiting with growing levels of impatience.

"Just tell us what you know," Houston said tightly, which was a good thing because I wasn't sure I could speak beyond a croak. The image of Neal lying facedown in his hotel room kept flashing through my mind in a slow-motion slide show.

Flash.

Boss Man screaming at Neal.

Flash.

Boss Man drawing back his foot like a professional soccer player.

Flash.

Boss Man's foot plowing right into Neal's gut.

Flash.

"Neal's not dead," Ben said reassuringly, and I went boneless with relief. "According to the woman we talked to in the lobby, he was still breathing when he left."

"Left?" Houston looked skeptical. "The thugs just let him go?"

"Only one of them was able to make it out of there before

the police showed up. Apparently, uh, drug dealers prefer to keep a low profile even when someone messes up a deal."

Ben paused while Houston and I soaked in that bit of news. *Drug dealers?* It kind of made sense . . . until Neal entered the picture. Because no way would he ever get mixed up with anything illegal.

"You suck at this, Ben," Liz said disgustedly. "Okay, here's what we heard: The cops showed up to find two big guys using Neal as their own personal punching bag and booked the three of them for drug trafficking."

"Neal was *arrested?*" I couldn't hold back my incredulity. "No way."

Amy burst into tears. She wasn't pretty crying either; big messy tears rolled down her face and mingled with snot, and yet I still thought she looked like an anime character. Just a very sad one.

"Hey," I said soothingly. "It's going to be okay, Amy. We'll get him out of there."

"Oh yeah? How are we going to do *that,* Chelsea? They found *cocaine* in his room and hauled him off to jail so that they can kill him!" That last part emerged as a gasp/sob combo. *"They're going to kill him!"*

Yeah, well, since it sounds like Backup may be recruiting more backup right now, your scene could leave us equally dead!

I didn't think she could handle hearing that, even if it was the truth. Taking my suitcase from the pile they'd grabbed from the hotel, I pasted a confident smile on my face.

"Why don't we walk?" I suggested, even though moving through the crowds and vendors would be slow going. "Neal's safe now, Amy. We'll just explain to the authorities that there has been a misunderstanding and get him out. This is good news."

Amy's red-rimmed eyes became pitying. "You don't get it, Chelsea. This is *Cambodia*. The government takes its cues from the drug dealers, okay? Just like American politicians are owned by big business. So if these thugs want to shank Neal in jail, he's a dead man. And even if some people in power *don't* listen to the cartel, they're going to give him a death sentence to prove that Cambodia is tough on drugs now."

I was speechless.

"He's a dead man. He was caught in the room with drugs so . . . game over."

"She's right," Liz said. "I hate to admit it, but she's absolutely right."

I stared at them in disbelief. "So you want us to just wipe our hands of him and say, 'Oh well, not *our* fault!' "

Houston raked a hand through his hair in exasperation. "What do you think we should do, Chelsea? March over to the nearest police station and tell them they've got the wrong man? Yeah, that'll go over well."

"We can't do *nothing*," I insisted, clutching my tote in one hand and my suitcase in the other. "Wow. And you guys thought *I* was the shallow one!"

The weirdest part was knowing that this was the perfect opportunity for escape. I couldn't have invented a better excuse to flee the country. My professor was in jail, and not even my parents could blame me for buying the first ticket home. They might not be happy to see me, but they still couldn't twist this into becoming *my* fault.

But they didn't want me around. The only person who genuinely did was Neal.

And sure, his whole bubbly *aren't we all one big, happy family* routine was annoying. The guy was probably chatting with the guards or trying to *visualize* his way out of trouble. His geekiness was off the freaking charts . . . but he was also the nicest person I had ever met. Any other professor at

Lewis & Clark would have balked at the idea of taking an outraged high school girl halfway around the world, but I doubted Neal had even hesitated. Instead, he had welcomed me at the airport the same way he did everything else—with boundless enthusiasm. And despite my general attitude, not to mention the whole drinking-in-the-airport incident, he had refused to think the worst of me. If anything it had just made him more determined for us to bond.

And somehow his plan had worked because I couldn't turn my back on him now. Even though a large part of me *really* wanted to bail.

"It's not that simple," Liz protested.

"Yes it is! It's exactly that simple. We either help him or we let him die. Those are the options. So let's come up with a way to save him. You guys are all shelling out thousands of dollars for a fancy liberal arts degree. So think!"

Ben nodded. "We should call Lewis & Clark. Get them to start calling the embassy on his behalf and pay for us to catch the first flight out of here."

"That doesn't guarantee Neal's release, but it's probably our best shot," Houston agreed.

"Not good enough. What about bribery?"

Houston, Ben, Amy, and Liz all stared at me as if I had just lost my mind.

"What? It works, doesn't it? Usually."

Liz shook her head. "The drug cartel's pockets are way deeper than ours."

"Okay, then let's keep brainstorming on our way to the embassy. Here's a tuk-tuk, let's—"

"Stick our noses where they don't belong?" Houston interrupted.

"I'm going to get *all* of us out of this stupid country alive, Houston. And I'm done running away just because you're scared. If you want to take off again, that's up to you."

He gritted his teeth. "I'm not running away."

I smiled sweetly. "Then you won't have a problem with the plan."

"Um, I do." Amy waved her hand as if she wanted me to call on her in class. "How do we know one of those guys isn't still looking for us?"

Ben shrugged. "It was just an interrupted drug deal, right? There's no reason to start chasing us."

Amy's nose crinkled. "It just . . . doesn't make any sense. The thugs enter the room, see Neal, and freak out because they've got some new guy crashing their transaction. All of that stuff fits. I even get why they would beat him up. But that doesn't explain why one of them ran through the lobby shooting at Houston and Chelsea."

"Oh, I can come up with plenty of reasons to want to shoot Chelsea," Houston muttered.

I glared at him. "Nice."

But Houston was back to being all business. "Amy's got a point. The guy kicking Neal—"

"Boss Man."

"He said something about being double-crossed. Maybe somebody showed up while Neal was in the lobby with us and screwed Boss Man over?"

Amy's face was so scrunched she looked like a frustrated hedgehog. "That's a pretty small window of opportunity, but I guess something must have happened."

"This is important; I want everyone to read my lips: *I had nothing to do with this. Nada.* Nothing. Zip. Zilch."

"Still not blaming you, princess."

For the first time Houston didn't sound like he was gagging on my dad's term of endearment. Then again, he might have been slightly too preoccupied with the whole *Cambodian drug dealer fiasco* to layer the word with the proper amount of scorn.

"You say that now, but whenever you need a handy scapegoat, everybody starts looking sideways at me!"

"That's just because you're pretty." Liz elbowed me lightly in the stomach to diffuse the tension. "We can't take our eyes off you."

I snorted. "Save it for your girlfriend, Liz."

Her eyes instantly went all soft and dreamy. "I wish she were here right now."

And for half a second everything almost seemed normal. We were back to being a group of college kids (okay, and me) discussing our love lives in a Cambodian marketplace, as if the past few hours had never happened.

Except there was an imprisoned teacher and a hotel riddled with bullet holes to prove that it had.

"If Sara was in this mess with us, you'd be way more freaked out." Amy pointed out.

"Nah, Sara can hold her own. She'd probably start up a massive campaign to free Neal. Email all the human rights organizations that she supports. And if *that* failed, she would probably try to deal with the cartel directly." Liz grinned. "Never mind. I take it back. She's better off in Australia."

"You know some of those ideas aren't half bad. Maybe we could—"

Houston didn't give Amy a chance to finish. "Right now we need to focus on our immediate concerns. You know, like finding a place to sleep without tipping off any guys with guns."

I had to agree with him. It wasn't cold yet, but the temperature was definitely dropping, and I didn't relish the idea of sleeping on the streets. Especially since that was an excellent way to have all our possessions jacked. Sure, the locals in Cambodia had been warm and friendly, but that's because we were tourists willing to spend money on Buddha statues and shot glasses and cheesy shirts. That didn't make the poverty level any less striking . . . or potentially dangerous.

Liz nodded and began shepherding us into a pair of tuk-tuks, squeezing inside mine after directing the drivers to take us all to the cheapest place around, which apparently meant we would be staying at the Happy Wonder Hostel. It looked like the preferred destination for broke college-age travelers and enormous Cambodian spiders alike. I can tolerate being around people with questionable hygiene for limited stretches of time, but disgusting, hairy creatures with too many spindly legs are a different story. I'd rather have another showdown with a gun-toting maniac than wake up to find a spider skittering across my leg. I shivered in revulsion, as my mind involuntarily replayed the moment I had spotted an outdoor vendor selling spiders that were fried before being *eaten.*

That's right: My parents had banished me to a country where people enjoyed snacking on spiders. Maybe that should have seemed insignificant in the wake of Neal's drug-related problems, but it's not easy dismissing something so disgusting. The least my dad could have done was warn me about the culinary surprises in store for me. Had I known about the spider thing, I probably would have tried to convince airport security to detain me in London. And then I wouldn't be stuck wondering if there was a very scary man with a gun searching the streets of Cambodia for me.

At the very least, I wouldn't have been forced to stay in a crappy hostel while I tried to figure out a way to get all of us home alive.

Oh yeah, my parents had a whole lot to answer for already.

Chapter 13

We booked one room for the five of us.

Correction: *Houston* booked one room for the five of us, and when I pointed out that some people appreciate a little thing called *privacy,* he ignored me.

Actually, that's not quite true.

He not-so-politely asked me to shut my enormous yap. Then he ignored me.

Jerk.

I should've called him out for it. I should've told him that Neal's absence didn't make him the adult in charge. There was no transfer of power that had taken place. No wills had been signed—not even a deathbed promise had been given. All of us were in the exact same position: lacking one overly enthusiastic leader. As far as I was concerned, that didn't give Houston any right to make decisions for the rest of us.

But I was too tired to put up a fight . . . and this time it wasn't just because my body hadn't adjusted to the heat. The exhaustion went bone deep, leaving me with barely enough energy to express anything more than mild annoyance. I silently tagged behind Liz all the way up to the room, clamping down on my bottom lip every time my tote banged painfully against my side. The others probably wouldn't have noticed a muffled yelp, especially since I was willing to bet they were all thinking the same thing: *A few more steps and I can collapse.*

I clenched my teeth and tried my best to fight the urge to spend some quality time facedown on a mattress.

Neal desperately needed help.

We didn't have a plan. We didn't know who those guys were or what they wanted or how Neal had been dragged into this mess. We didn't even know if the three not-so-funny Stooges had friends already combing Siem Reap for the blond high school screamer and her male companion.

And I didn't think sleep would magically produce those answers.

But it was like part of my brain had walked into an area with crappy reception, leaving the remaining half muttering, *Hello? Can anybody hear me? Hello!* Meanwhile, the rest of my body was repeating: *The person you have dialed is currently unavailable. If you would like to leave a message, please leave your name and number after the beep.*

Yet even in my exhausted, zombie-like state I still balked at the idea of sharing a space with the boys.

Stupid.

Completely childish.

It's not like I thought their cooties could get me while I was asleep or that one of them would become overwhelmed by lust. At most, I might have to listen to one more of Ben's ridiculous come-ons.

Hey, babe. Guess you really dodged a bullet tonight. Still . . . want to see my guns?

Eye roll.

But when I saw the room and imagined sleeping with one of the guys right next to me . . . I panicked. Five students, two double beds. It didn't take a genius to figure out *that* was going to get awkward.

"I'll take the floor!" I volunteered. "Toss me a pillow and let's call it a night."

Houston eyed me suspiciously. "Is this a pity play for one of the beds, *princess?*"

"Nope. Actually, if I can just have a pillow, I'll sleep in the bathtub. That's probably spider-free, right?"

"There's room for all of us in the beds," Amy pointed out. "Although you should probably share with Houston and Liz."

Ben raised his eyebrows, and I couldn't help wondering if our resident good girl was trying to make a move on him. Weirder things had happened. Probably.

Amy blushed. "I didn't mean it like *that*. Chelsea and Liz are smaller than I am, and since you're bigger than Houston it seemed like a good way to . . . reach equilibrium?"

"Uh, yeah. That's not going to work for me." Taking matters into my own hands, I leaned over one mattress and snatched a pillow. "Problem solved. If any of you need to use the bathroom, I suggest you do it now."

"Is it because I'm gay?" Liz demanded, folding her arms under her chest. "I'm in a relationship, Chelsea. Although even if I wasn't with Sara you still wouldn't be my type. So if that's why you're freaking out, you can relax."

I shook my head and wished there was a way to skirt the issue entirely. "I won't share a bed with anyone. I don't even like sharing a *room,* but since Cowboy over here insisted, I'm trying to adjust."

I didn't want to say the words because I knew they might make me sound . . . damaged. But since the only alternative was to let Liz believe my personal space issues centered around homophobia, I didn't really feel like I had a choice. Not unless I was willing to tank a growing friendship in the process.

And surprisingly, that was no longer a sacrifice I was willing to make.

Houston studied me as if I were a tricky multiple-choice question on a final exam. "Why the trouble sharing, Chelsea?"

"That's none of your business."

"Okay, well, thanks for clearing that up." Houston's voice sounded low and sleep-heavy, and for some reason the combination struck me as oddly intimate. I couldn't remember ever hearing Logan slip into that low register.

Maybe it was a college-boy thing.

Still I had more important things to focus on than the way his wry tone tugged on my impulse to smile, such as transforming one Spartan bathtub into a makeshift bed composed entirely of towels. As far as I was concerned, passing out in an uncomfortable white cocoon was still infinitely better than sleeping with my body pressed against someone else.

I hated that Jake still affected such a basic decision. Our relationship was supposed to stay in the past, not rear its ugly head in Cambodia. But that didn't change anything. Knowing intellectually that I had no reason to distrust Houston and Ben didn't alter my knee-jerk reaction to flee.

Maybe because the person I didn't trust was myself.

All it had once taken were a few nice words to leave me desperate for more attention. I'd been caught in a downward spiral long before I even recognized the danger.

You've got moves, girl! Dance with me.

Sure, it had started out that simply. Some grinding on a makeshift dance floor and a bit of hair swishing later and I'd be drinking in the compliments. And when reality pressed a little too closely, I would toss back another shot so I could pretend that I actually wanted to be there.

I played the part everyone expected of me.

And by the time it sank in that the role only left me feeling empty, it had become an automatic response.

The only way to kick the habit was for me to be the one in control, and as luck would have it . . . I became pretty skilled at getting my way. Which, contrary to common opinion, isn't necessarily a *bad* thing. I tried to explain that to my dad once, but he didn't get it. He insisted that using my social skills to score free English tutoring sessions was morally wrong. And okay, maybe I should have paid Mackenzie Wellesley something for her time.

But she was using me too.

I benefited from her brain, but whenever Alex Thompson or his football-playing cronies wanted to start a rumble, she could use my name to gain social protection for her merry band of dweebs. Something that wouldn't have been possible if I hadn't stood in the way.

It was a trade, but one where I ultimately had the control.

And was my father impressed with the way I had out-maneuvered the smartest girl at my school?

No, he was not.

My mom might have gotten a kick out of it . . . before she used it as another opportunity to rant about my low SAT scores. So I decided to keep my mouth shut and give her as little information as possible.

After all, knowledge is power.

Maybe that's why I was wary about falling into line behind Houston . . . or any of the others, for that matter. Sure, they could probably write very long, boring essays on the development of agrarian-based societies, or whatever, but that didn't necessarily make them smarter than me.

Okay, so they were *textbook* smarter.

But that still didn't mean they were equipped to make decisions in everyone's best interest. Case in point: None of them had noticed the inherent awkwardness in the sleeping situation.

Although judging from the snoring that filtered into the bathroom, maybe I was the only one who would've been losing sleep over it. I yanked the shower curtain in place before I began digging in my tote for a better sound barrier. My fingers made contact with my wallet, cell phone, and a smooth Buddha belly, but nothing of any practical use. Reluctantly, I gave up. I climbed inside the tub, while I tried to ignore a rising sense of claustrophobia as the room began to feel too dark and too cold and . . . too lonely.

I was tempted to thwack my head against the hard ceramic, since it would either knock some sense into me or knock me out. Except if I was going to come up with a way to break Neal out of jail, I needed to be concussion-free.

So curling up in the cramped space, I instinctively did what I've always done when I overheard my parents arguing at night.

I lied to myself.

It's going to be okay, Chelsea.

It's all going to be okay.

Four long, deep breaths and I could picture Smith Middle School in excruciating detail, right down to the scuffed tile floors and the fluorescent overhead lights and the lingering scent of sweaty social desperation.

And then I saw him struggling with his locker combination, swearing indistinctly, and looking about ready to kick it with one black Converse-clad foot.

Logan.

His features became clearer as I approached, until he looked just the way I had seen him with Mackenzie in the library. Gray eyes shining, dark hair mussed, crooked grin in place.

It was a high school boy in a middle school dream, but this time that warm smile was all for me. That's when I sort of separated from my body and watched the middle school Chelsea rise up on tiptoe, grab Logan, and kiss him. No cartoon birds or double rainbows made a surprise appearance, but it still looked magical to me. Maybe because when it had *actually* happened for the first time, in his kitchen while his parents were at work, I'd foolishly believed it could last. That there just might be something to the whole love-at-first-sight concept, because that's sure how it felt to me.

I had found my other half.

And suddenly, I wasn't hovering above the scene like a creepy voyeuristic ghost, I was looking into Logan's eyes as he told me . . .

"Answer your freaking *phone!"*

Okay, I was pretty sure that wasn't what Logan had been about to say. I opened my eyes blearily and was momentarily blinded by white. It took me a minute to put all the pieces back together.

Bathtub.

Cambodia.

Misery.

If I had to choose between dreaming about how great things used to be with my ex and worrying about big guys with guns . . . yeah, I wanted to fall back to sleep.

The shower curtain was jerked aside, and I found myself looking at one seriously annoyed college student with a bad case of bed head.

"Huh?"

Oh yeah. I'm eloquent in the mornings.

Although to be fair, it's not like I'm greeted on a regular basis with a truly excellent view of a half-dressed guy. Okay, maybe that was a slight exaggeration. He was wearing a shirt with *DFTBA* written on it, whatever that meant, and boxers. Plaid ones.

How very Portland of him.

"Turn off your phone!"

My phone. Right. Yesterday I had planned for an early-morning wake-up so that I could shower before Neal yelled, "Wakey wakey! Chicken bakey!" I had set the alarm back when my biggest annoyance was the college student currently raking a frustrated hand through his hair, which he only succeeded in rumpling further.

It felt surreal knowing that this was the first morning after . . . I still didn't know how to refer to it. *The Event?* Too casual. *The Debacle?* Too vague.

The Night We Ditched Neal and Ran Away from Armed Thugs?

Accurate, but a little long.

But today there would be no temples or lectures or tours. And my phone was wailing away as if last night had never happened.

"Turn that damn thing off already!"

I jolted into action, dragging my tote into the bathtub with me as I fumbled inside for my phone. I struggled to get my hand in past the Buddha's enormous belly as I pawed at the bottom of the bag.

Almost . . . almost . . . score.

Except when I finally succeeded in pulling it out, I found my fingers coated in a fine white powder.

My first thought was, *Oh crap! My makeup must have spilled. This won't be fun to clean.*

Except that's when the other half of my brain, the part that wasn't still fantasizing about kissing Logan Beckett, decided to click on. And I realized it wasn't makeup.

"Uh, Houston? We've got another problem."

He glared at me. "That is seriously getting old."

"Yeah, well, this should freshen it up for you: I think I found the drugs."

Chapter 14

There's no easy way to break the news that you accidentally stole a Buddha full of drugs.

But maybe blurting it out wasn't the best approach.

Houston skewered me with an arch look that said I'd better not be joking. So I waggled my fingers, letting some of the powder disappear against the ceramic whiteness of the bathtub.

"The drugs aren't missing anymore."

"Holy shit."

Yeah, that nicely summed up what I was thinking too.

He grabbed my arm and dragged me out of the bathroom, which I might have considered, you know, kind of caveman-ish and sexy if it hadn't *hurt*.

"Hey!" I protested. "I'm not the drug lord here!"

But Houston ignored me, switched on the hotel room light, and used his significantly more muscular arms to force me to sit on the edge of a bed.

"Turn off the light!" Liz muttered. "I can make you wish you were never born."

Well, that was comforting.

"Wake up," Houston ordered. "Now. It's important."

"And in a few hours you can tell me all about it." She nestled her face farther into her pillow. "Until then, keep it to yourself."

"Chelsea ran off with cocaine from a Cambodian drug cartel."

And I thought *I* had been too blunt.

"I didn't do it intentionally! And it might not be cocaine!" Houston shot me a withering *get real* look and I raised my chin defiantly. "It could be heroin."

"Well, in *that* case we have nothing to worry about! Everyone knows that drug cartels only notice when their *cocaine* goes missing."

Okay, he had a point. "I'm just saying that we don't have all the facts yet. All we know is that my Buddha is leaking white powder."

"Who is leaking white powder?" Ben sat up in bed, making the blanket slip down and exhibiting a nicely chiseled set of muscles. Okay, so he had a bad habit of hitting on every girl within a ten-block radius, but that didn't make him any less ridiculously hot.

"The statue in her bag," Houston explained as he began pacing the small room. "It should've been so *obvious!* I can't believe it took us this long to figure it out."

"Right," I quipped, rolling my eyes. "Because when guys with guns are chasing after me the very first thing I think is *Hm, I bet they're after the fat man in my purse.*"

Amy shook her head. "You know that's religiously disrespectful, Chelsea."

"You're right. I'll try to be more politically correct. The full-figured gentleman? I'd call him big-boned, but I don't think that explains his waistline."

Amy kept shaking her head but failed to repress her smile. "So wrong."

"So sue me. Or shoot me. Oh wait, we've already got people trying to do that!"

Houston didn't stop pacing, which might explain how he

stayed in such good shape. If he strode around every time he got stressed, then an uptight guy like him had to be clocking in serious mileage every day.

"Everything makes sense now." Houston still looked disgusted with himself. "They came for the statues, only saw one, and started pummeling Neal. At least until Big Mouth over here started screaming and they spotted it sticking out of her goddamn bag."

Just like that I was the screwup again. If I hadn't taken the statue, none of us would have been in this mess. All I'd had to do was drop my freaking bag and let the thugs reclaim the white powder. Then they would've had no reason to keep pummeling Neal.

It was all my fault.

Nobody said it, but I knew they were thinking it. Just like I knew they expected me to flip back my long blond hair while they tried to clean up my latest mess.

"Okay, so I think it's safe for us to assume that they want it back."

"Nah, they only care if it's cocaine, and we might have heroin."

Okay, even by regular Houston standards, that was way too heavy on the snark.

Liz pounded a fist against her mattress. "Will both of you please shut up! *I want to sleep!*"

"Dude." Ben shook his head while Amy cleared her throat.

"Maybe this isn't a bad thing."

"Oh yeah?" Houston forced himself to sit down. "How do you figure that, exactly?"

"Well, now we know what they're after and exactly where it is."

"Yeah, on us, and guess who they'll be coming after!"

None of it felt real. Because Houston was right; the full extent of our crisis sounded like a joke straight off the pages of a worst-case scenario handbook. Freeing our professor while avoiding one seriously pissed-off drug cartel in a country known primarily for its history of death, destruction, and land mines? Yeah, if it hadn't been my life at stake, I might've enjoyed waiting for the punch line.

"Correction: They're coming after *me*," I said coolly, as if the thought didn't have me breaking into a cold sweat. "They saw *me*, they saw *my* bag. *I'm* the target."

"Maybe we could hand it over to the government while we explain about Neal."

"And you called me naïve, Amy? How do you propose we explain that one? *Yes, sir, I brought this Buddha full of cocaine for you. I want to trade it for the American you've got on drug trafficking charges. He didn't do it. How many pounds of coke am I carrying? Gee, I dunno!*"

Ben broke the resulting silence by whistling. "Okay, it's official. Chelsea definitely has to make her mark in Hollywood." He grinned. "You deliver one hell of a monologue."

"I also have a point. You guys aren't involved. If any of you want out, leave now."

"If they leave, can I *sleep*?" Liz snarled. "At the very least someone should have the decency to make me some coffee."

Houston released a tense breath. "None of us are ditching, Chelsea. We just have to figure out a plan that doesn't include death or incarceration."

"We could always contact the Cambodian embassy once we're safely in Thailand," Amy suggested.

"No way. We can't risk getting caught with the drugs."

Somehow her eyes managed to widen. "We'd leave those here, of course!"

"We can't just abandon our only source of leverage." I lifted the Buddha dramatically, only to lower it quickly when my aching shoulder muscles complained. "This is all the protection we've got if things go south."

"You know you can always come to me if you're worried about *protection*, Chelsea. . . ."

I stared at Ben in disbelief. "*Really?* You think *now* is a good time for your stupid pickup lines?"

He shrugged. "I thought you might need a distraction."

A pillow smacked his face with impressive force considering that Liz's head had been buried under it only seconds earlier. She forced herself into a sitting position, glaring at all of us equally.

"Here's what we're going to do." Her voice still sounded rusty with sleep. "We're going to find an Internet café and let our families know we're okay. Then we're going to contact Lewis & Clark so that they can handle the Neal stuff."

That actually sounded like a pretty good plan except—

"How are they going to free Neal?" I demanded. "It's not like the dean of a liberal arts college has much pull in *Cambodia*."

"Yeah? Well, neither do *we!*" Liz snapped. "And since I'm rather fond of my body parts, forgive me for not wanting to go on a suicide mission. Time to move on."

"So you want to ditch him." I couldn't believe it.

"No. I want you to get it through your very thick skull that we're not bulletproof!"

It wasn't fair for me to expect them to risk their lives for Neal. Especially since I still wasn't sure I could handle standing in the line of fire. That kind of stuff might look cool in action movies, but I still remembered the heat radiating off the bullets Backup had sent in my direction. The smartest move was to dump the drugs and flee the country.

Which meant that all the whispers about Chelsea Halloway were right. Pretty girl but not very bright. Doesn't have two spare IQ points to rub together. No wonder Logan chose Mackenzie Wellesley over her; he probably wanted to have an intelligent conversation for a change.

Screw it.

I didn't care.

Not when it came to helping the one person who'd ever treated me like I was more than my looks.

So yeah, maybe the brilliant Mackenzie would have cut her losses and played it safe. But instead Neal had Smith High School's most reckless idiot determined to free him— alone, if necessary.

Lucky him.

Chapter 15

It was surprisingly easy to ditch the group.

I waited for them to leave for the Internet café before I packed in the bathroom, making sure I took all the essentials: a few shirts, my shortest skirt, and my sexy black heels, along with some smaller items like my iPod, passport, wallet, laptop, cosmetics, oh, and a Buddha full of drugs. No way was I letting that out of my sight. At least not until Neal was back where he belonged.

Then, before I could chicken out, I faced myself in the mirror and pulled out a pair of very sharp-looking scissors I'd swiped from Amy's needlepoint bag.

It's amazing what a few strategic snips can do to alter someone's appearance. Instead of flowing down my back, my hair now barely dipped below my shoulders. Okay, so maybe my own personal transformation required more hacking than snipping. Whatever. It still looked good and I wasn't finished yet. I rummaged through Liz's bag until I came up with her hair dye.

I'd never pictured myself as a redhead. Then again, I'd also never imagined I would have to alter my appearance to evade a drug lord. And given the option of going red, blue, purple, or *dead,* ginger was definitely the winner. I might be on the run, but I still didn't want to look like a Smurf.

Still, it was weird checking myself out in the mirror post-transformation, because the girl who gazed back looked . . . badass. I imagined everyone's reaction to the change: Ben would probably make some stupid crack about redheads burning up the sheets; Liz would yell at me for pawing through her suitcase; and Amy would carefully choose her words to sound vaguely complimentary, like, "Well, it's certainly a change."

As for Houston . . . at most he'd raise an eyebrow before refocusing on the task at hand: getting everyone safely back to Oregon.

Everyone except for Neal.

Which was why I'd decided to make a plan of my own—one that didn't involve sticking around an empty room waiting for everyone to return from the Internet expedition that they had decided was too dangerous for me. Houston had practically ordered me to sit and stay in the room like a disobedient puppy, while he updated *my* dad on the situation. He claimed it was because between the two of us, I was more likely to catch the eye of a criminal. I thought it was far more likely that he wanted to control the narrative and make sure that my parents received the truth, the whole truth, and nothing but the truth.

But this time his overbearing impulses worked to my advantage.

Their excursion gave me enough time to work my makeover magic and write a note before I began strolling down the streets of Siem Reap.

Nobody looked at me twice.

Okay, that's not exactly true. Plenty of eyes lingered on the way my distressed jeans emphasized my legs and my tight, clingy shirt highlighted my other, um . . . assets. I'm used to getting *those* looks, though.

That's the nature of high school. At least for me.

Still, I had to keep fighting the urge to double-check that

no one behind me was loading their gun for round two. It took all my years of ballet training to create a deceptive air of nonchalance as I sauntered through the bustling crowds until I found an Internet café far enough away that I knew I wouldn't be running into any familiar faces. I handed over a few dollars to a guy behind the desk, sat down at an abused-looking computer, and logged on to my email account. Then I quickly deleted all the stupid Facebook notifications cluttering up my inbox so that I could concentrate on the handful of important messages waiting for me. My dad's email was painfully abrupt; the subject line (*I hope you made it safely to Cambodia!*) said it all. My mom's was significantly longer, but only because it was packed with suggestions for possible college essay topics she wanted me to consider.

Ignoring both of them, I focused on the emails from my friends.

> *Hey Chelsea!*
> *School is soo not the same without you! It's like you're gone for 5 minutes and the geeks totally start freaking out. And you wouldn't believe the number of fashion casualties wandering the hallways now! Yesterday I saw a freshman wearing a plaid jacket over a striped shirt and I had to be all, "Um, visually challenged much?" Anyhow, Steffani has been flirting with Spencer! I told her that your ex-boyfriend's best friend is totally off-limits, but she wouldn't listen to me. She probably thinks he's going to help her cinch up a Junior Prom Queen nomination or something. Crazy, right?! I was wondering if you still have those photos from her birthday party last year. Do you think I could get a copy? Just in case she needs help remembering her roots.*
> *Kisses!*
> *~Ashley*

I knew exactly which photos Ashley wanted me to send—the ones that ensured that Steffani would never speak to me again if they leaked. The ones I had no business taking in the first place . . . or using as insurance in case she ever considered trying to overthrow me as the most popular girl at school. The whole thing twisted my stomach, partly because it was a crappy thing to do . . . but mostly because the pursuit of scandal was the only reason Ashley had bothered writing to me.

I had no qualms about leaving her message unanswered and moving on.

> *Hey Chelsea,*
> *I thought you might be feeling homesick so . . .*
> *here is a very special update from reporter Jane*
> *Smith with all the latest news. Our top story*
> *tonight: The Fake and Bake Battles. Two girls*
> *have turned the fight for the number-one spot on*
> *the Smith High School social ladder into an all-*
> *out war. Clashes in the cafeteria have put the*
> *whole school on edge as the showdown continues.*
> *In related news, geek hazing appears to be at an*
> *all-time high. This reporter credits some of the*
> *tension to the absence of yours truly.*
> *You might want to use your Jedi mind tricks to*
> *fix this disturbance in the Force. If you get the*
> *chance, I'm sure it would be greatly appreciated.*
> *Seriously.*
> *So how are you liking Cambodia? I keep*
> *Googling it to make sure you haven't overthrown*
> *the government yet. If any teenager could success-*
> *fully create a revolution in less than two weeks,*
> *it's you.*
> *~Jane*
> *P.S. Scott does not send his love. He wants to*

know if you've plumbed new depths yet. His
words, not mine.

I clicked reply and got down to work.

> *Hey Jane,*
> *Thanks for the update. Sorry, I can't help with*
> *Fake and Bake right now. I'm dealing with a huge*
> *problem of my own. It's life or death, Jane. Which*
> *is why I need you to call in every favor you've got*
> *for me. Every connection of Mackenzie's too. If*
> *there is a string you can pull, you've got to start*
> *tugging.*
> *Here's the situation: I accidentally stole drugs*
> *from a Cambodian cartel. No, I'm not kidding.*
> *Just trust me when I say that my professor, Neal*
> *Hamilton, is innocent of his possession charges.*
> *And it's his life at stake. That's on the off chance*
> *that the really scary guys with guns haven't killed*
> *him already.*
> *I know that right now you're probably shaking*
> *your head and thinking that normal people don't*
> *accidentally create international incidents. And*
> *maybe you're right, but since I've also ditched my*
> *group, you're all the help I've got.*
> *So I need you to start making some noise while*
> *I try to negotiate with drug dealers. How is that*
> *for a crazy breaking news report?*
> *~Chelsea*
> *P.S. You can tell Scott I'm definitely not feeling*
> *shallow right now.*

I sent the email and felt a jolt of satisfaction as it disappeared into cyberspace. Maybe help wouldn't arrive soon
enough to save Neal . . . but at least now I had the smartest

person I knew working on it. That had to count for something.

Although I had a feeling the rest of the group wouldn't see it that way. In fact, I half expected to see Houston barge into the Internet café and drag me outside so he could yell at me. Sure, I had left a note in the hostel, but I doubted that would diminish anyone's anger over my disappearing act. Obsessing over their reaction wasn't doing me—or Neal—any good. If Houston caught up with me, I was fairly certain he'd try handcuffing me to a bedpost . . . and not in a sexy way either.

Still, I could worry about that later.

I had researching to do.

Chapter 16

It was *probably* heroin.

Unfortunately, the un-cited Wikipedia article I found wasn't exactly overflowing with hard evidence. Apparently, Cambodia had a bit of a reputation for supplying tourists with heroin instead of cocaine. Interesting, but far from a reliable answer. Then again, the article also mentioned how easily drugs could be acquired in Cambodia.

That matched my firsthand experience.

I quickly scanned the article. Drug abuse among street kids was on the rise . . . as were the number of HIV/AIDS cases from shared needles. It twisted my stomach, but I had to stay focused on the problem at hand. Saving thousands of street kids from drugs, diseases, and freaking land mines was much-needed work for an entire organization, not one high school girl who already had a Buddha-shaped target on her back. So I skimmed over the drug transportation part and then . . . I totally hit pay dirt.

Rithisak Sovann.

His brief bio read like Hollywood's idea of the perfect übervillain. Rumored to be the biggest drug lord in the area, Mr. Sovann was a card-carrying member of Cambodia's wealthiest elite. He dined with military officials, vacationed with leading politicians at his luxury hotel in the capital city of Phnom Penh, and just so happened to own the country's largest daily newspaper.

Oh, and the guy was certifiably insane.

If the rumors were to be believed, Rithisak Sovann had once pulled out a gun on a cruise ship and demanded to be treated with more respect . . . and then a year later he shot the tire of a taxi cab because the driver didn't want to wait for his friends to show up. His trigger-happy reputation probably would have made me laugh if I had no connection with him whatsoever. But there was nothing funny about a psychopath with the funds to send an army of thugs to hunt me down.

He certainly didn't seem like the kind of man who would react calmly to the news that half of his shipment had been stolen. Nope, he would make it his mission to destroy the guilty party, if only to send a warning message to his rivals.

If this guy was involved—which admittedly was something of a stretch—I was in a world of trouble.

I peered at the screen, trying to memorize the drug lord's features so that I would be able to recognize him anywhere. There was nothing particularly remarkable about him. Dark black hair combed back with enough product to look professionally slick. Eyes that were on the border between brown and black, a wide-set nose, and a pair of full lips that were spread in a welcoming smile. I scrolled down and stopped abruptly at a candid photo of him. Rithisak Sovann wasn't smiling in this one, but he also didn't look overly concerned about the swarm of journalists around him. Probably because he had a security detail of his own keeping them at bay.

One of whom bore a striking similarity to Boss Man.

I couldn't be positive since the image was grainy and I hadn't exactly conversed with the thug during a stress-free afternoon tea. Maybe beating the crap out of someone was business as usual for Boss Man, but it had definitely rattled me. Which meant that it was entirely possible I had confused him with another imposing Cambodian man . . . but I couldn't shake the feeling that Mr. Sovann's bodyguard and the Boss Man I had encountered last night were one and the same.

This was my guy.

As if Houston could read my thoughts, a new message popped up in my email inbox with a subject line that left virtually nothing to interpretation: *WHERE THE HELL ARE YOU?*

The contents of the actual email were equally direct.

> *You need to get back here, Chelsea. Right now.*

I hesitated only momentarily before responding.

> *Sorry, Houston, I can't do that. You guys can leave anytime, but I'm staying to help Neal. Deal with it. Hey, at least this way you can tell my dad you tried to talk me out of it!*
> *xoxo!*
> *~Chelsea*

All things considered, I thought it was a pretty nice response. Polite. Concise. The *x*'s and *o*'s were downright affectionate. My parents would be so proud of the way I was taking the moral high ground.

Actually, they would probably be spitting mad.

Since they were the ones who had insisted I make a new start for myself in Cambodia, I didn't think they had the right to whine about the way I went about it.

Houston's quick response took me by surprise though.

> *We aren't leaving without you.*

I stared at the screen in disbelief. All of their worst thoughts of me should have been confirmed. Neal was in prison because I had stolen a Buddha full of heroin! They should have been *thrilled* to distance themselves from any association with me. Frankly, an *hasta la vista, princess* was all that I deserved.

> *I'm not leaving without Neal. So where does that leave us?*

At an impasse, probably. Houston wanted to play it safe in a high-risk/high-reward situation, and I was determined to play the hand we'd been dealt. Maybe I was behaving like the spoiled princess he accused me of being, but this time I wasn't going to be the first to fold.

> *Fine.*

I blinked in confusion as I searched Houston's one-word answer for some kind of hidden meaning. *Fine, you're on your own. Try not to get yourself killed, princess.* That seemed like something he would write.

I braced myself for the worst as more words appeared on my screen.

> *Come back and we'll talk it over.*

The authoritative tone made me roll my eyes at the sheer *Houston-ness*, but it also made a foolish grin spread across my face. He really meant it. They were actually willing to stick around for Neal . . . and oddly enough, for me. Even though they would all be safer leaving me behind to fight a war of my own making.

We just needed to get one thing straight first. . . .

> *My rescue. My rules.*

I leaned back and braced myself for the first round of battle. It wasn't long in coming.

> *It's called teamwork, princess. I realize that might be a foreign concept to you, but the rest of us find it quite effective.*

Right. Because *I* was the only one who didn't always play well with others.

> *It's called leadership, cowboy. And this time I'm in charge.*

I drummed my fingers on the scarred table while I waited him out.

> *Fine. Where are you?*

I didn't need to see my reflection to know that my smile had transformed into an *I've got you exactly where I want you* smirk. An expression that has been known to terrify freshman girls at Smith High School into speechlessness. Sure, I probably had one seriously angry drug trafficker gunning for me, but for the first time since leaving Oregon I finally felt like I was back in control.

I had the drugs, a semi-feasible plan, and now a group of teammates backing me up. My smile only widened as I typed my final email and logged off.

> *I'll see you guys at the Siem Reap bus station in an hour. Please bring my suitcase.*
> *The rest is for me to know and you to find out.*

Oh yeah. My luck was definitely about to change.

Chapter 17

I hadn't expected them to greet me with open arms. Considering that I'd rummaged through their suitcases for makeover supplies before ditching them—and that I'd do it all over again, if forced, without hesitation or apology— yeah, I could understand their anger. Still, I had hoped for a tight-lipped smile or a halfhearted wave or two when I met them at the bus station.

Instead, I found myself on the receiving end of four furious death glares.

"So I take it the thugs caught up with you," Ben said easily. "That explains the hair, right? It's some new kind of torture technique."

I fingered one of the strands defensively. "It's not *that* bad!"

"Liar, liar, head on fire." His mouth tilted upward, and I knew at least one member of the group wasn't going to stay mad at me forever.

"Okay, maybe not my best look. I can accept that. But it's still got a high score on the disguise-o-meter, right?"

Even before the words were out of my mouth, I knew it was quite possibly the geekiest thing I had ever said. I mean, *disguise-o-meter?* Not even Mackenzie Wellesley would go that far.

I tensed as I waited for them to mock me.

Nothing happened.

It probably shouldn't have surprised me. They might be furious with me for sneaking out of the hostel, but that didn't mean it was open season on all things Chelsea Halloway. They weren't going to leap at the chance to ridicule me the way Ashley or Steffani would if I were still back at Smith High School.

Now I just needed Amy to stop acting like I'd personally killed Bambi's mother. Liz rolled her eyes. "You know the red looks good, Chelsea. Stop fishing for compliments."

I shrugged and pointedly studied the chalkboard bus schedule. The first bus for Phnom Penh would be departing in fifteen minutes, and I had every intention of being on board.

Whether or not anyone else still wanted to join me.

"So where do you think we're going?" Houston's tone was mild but there was an undertone of anger. He may have agreed that it was my mission, my rules, but that didn't mean he would back down without a fight. His eyes looked extra green as he struggled to keep himself tightly under control.

I held up my twelve-dollar bus ticket. "I'm going to Phnom Penh to see a guy about a Buddha. Feel free to join me . . . or not. Totally up to you."

Liz eyed me warily. "Who is the guy, Chelsea?"

"Right now? He's my first solid lead."

"You seem to have thought this out." Houston's words came out clipped and measured, as if he was forcing himself to spit out only those specific words.

"That's right."

Amy nodded stiffly before marching right over to the counter. "One ticket for Phnom Penh, please."

The others followed behind her, and I felt a surge of relief that we were finally doing *something* instead of just complaining about the situation. The terrifying sense of paralysis eased even further as I climbed aboard the bus and took my first breath of recycled air-conditioned freedom.

Amy wordlessly claimed the seat next to mine, and after trading shrugs and nervous glances, everyone else settled two or three rows behind us. Probably because they knew what was coming when she finally spoke in an unnaturally low voice.

"I thought you were dead."

And just like that, the biggest dork at Lewis & Clark College stunned me into absolute silence.

"You want to know what happened, Chelsea?" Amy didn't wait for a response. "At first we thought you weren't coming out of the bathroom because you wanted some privacy to cry. But then we started getting worried and—" Her voice faltered as tears welled up in her eyes. "Strands of your hair were all over the place. All that red dye looks a lot like blood, so . . . I thought you were dead. I actually thought that if you'd gone with us to find the Internet café you might still be okay. But you hadn't. We left you and you were *dead* and there was nothing I could do to fix it."

Amy began full-on weeping, and I had no idea how to comfort her. Apologies didn't come in a large enough size for what I had accidentally done.

"I, uh . . . left a note," I pointed out. "I never thought that—c'mon, Amy. Don't do this. I'm sorry, okay?"

"Yeah, well, now I want to kill you myself."

"That seems . . . counterproductive," I said wryly. "Any chance we could focus on saving Neal instead?"

"You scare me like that again and I won't forgive you."

I grimaced. "I promise I will never intentionally scare you again, Amy. Does that work?"

Amy shook her head in disbelief. "How can you be so calm about all of this? You're just—" She pitched her voice an octave higher. "Let's go rescue Neal from almost certain death! *Ready? O-kay!*" The last part came out sounding like a bad cheerleading routine.

"I've just had plenty of practice faking confidence under pressure. It sort of comes with the territory when everyone thinks you're stupid."

The truth slipped out so easily, it wasn't until Amy rolled her eyes that I realized just how much I had revealed. I tensed instinctively as I waited for her to go right for the jugular.

Maybe if you studied harder you wouldn't have to fake anything, princess. Did that ever occur to you?

"Nobody thinks you're stupid, Chelsea."

I nearly laughed out loud. "Do you really think I don't know what people say about me? I'm a pretty girl—not a smart one." I shoved back a strand of red hair just so I would have something to do with my hands. "That's a direct quote from my mom, by the way. They sort of have a point. I mean, I totally choked during my SAT test. And then my ex-boyfriend, Logan, dumped me for the smartest girl at school. So he traded up. And every time I see them together it's like—" I broke off. "I wasn't good enough. No matter what I do or how hard I try, I never seem to be good enough. So I really am sorry that I hurt you, Amy. And you should know that it's entirely possible Neal's rescue will be just one more disaster to add to the list. But at least this time—even if I screw up—the attempt will mean something. *That* is why I can act so calm."

Amy's arms were suddenly wrapped around my neck, and I couldn't protest her stranglehold because it felt like . . . friendship. The close kind that forms at a summer camp and disintegrates because the promises to call each other are soon forgotten. And yet, with Amy I thought it could last beyond our crisis with a Cambodian drug cartel.

I still wasn't entirely comfortable with her very public display of affection, so I glanced over the back of my seat, fully expecting to see Ben chatting up some female traveler while Houston and Liz planned our next move. Instead, I found all of them staring straight ahead with their attention caught on . . . me.

The pit of my stomach dropped as I soaked in the mixture of guilt and defiance in their expressions. Houston's unwavering gaze told me what I needed to know: They had overheard everything. All that stuff about my SAT test and *Logan* was now common knowledge.

If there was a gunman on the bus, I found myself hoping he would just take his shot, already. At least that way the situation couldn't become any more awkward.

No such luck.

I coolly held Houston's gaze, not even bothering to raise my voice. "You say a word about any of this to my dad and—"

"I already promised that I wouldn't." He rolled his eyes before he muttered, "What happens in Cambodia stays in Cambodia."

"I knew that was going to catch on!" Ben crowed victoriously. "That was all *me*."

"Yeah, you're a regular Shakespeare."

All four of us gawked at Amy, who looked surprised to find that she had spoken.

Liz beamed proudly at her. "Nicely delivered, Amy! We'll have you trash-talking in no time."

Houston grinned too—a genuinely amused expression that I'd only glimpsed once or twice before, but which fit his face to perfection. Not that it mattered. What we needed to be figuring out was how to help Neal, not wasting time *smiling* at one another.

That's why I changed the subject. Not because I found myself wondering what it would take to see that expression on his face more often. And definitely not because I felt a surge of something that felt dangerously like attraction when his eyes met mine.

Nope.

I was too aware of all of Houston's flaws to ever be taken in that easily.

And just to prove it to myself, I started passing out prepaid cell phones from the batch I'd bought right after I logged off with Houston. The ones I'd charged to my dad's emergency credit card.

Then I leaned forward confidentially.

"Okay, so here's the plan."

Chapter 18

I waited until I had their full attention.

"If any part of this plan goes wrong, you bail. You take the nearest tuk-tuk to the American consulate and you stay there. Are we all clear on that?"

They nodded, but I couldn't let it go.

"No stupid risks either. If you even *think* you're in danger, go to the consulate."

Houston laughed. "Seriously, Chelsea? I hate to break it to you, princess, but you are the only person here who needs to hear that warning. I bet you have no intention of following your own advice."

I put on my best look of disbelief. "Are you kidding? I'll be in the first tuk-tuk headed for the embassy."

Just as long as Neal is right there with me.

I knew better than to say that last part out loud.

Liz nodded. "Okay, so we flee to the embassy if the plan goes horribly wrong. What's the plan again?"

"It's sort of a work in progress, so let's withhold some of the judgment, okay?"

Ben and Houston traded looks that made it pretty freaking obvious that they had no intention of withholding anything.

"Okay, so we *don't* know where the police are holding

Neal. And we *don't* have the political power to make the authorities release him."

Everyone looked thoroughly unimpressed with that bit of information, so I quickly moved on.

"But we do have a Buddha full of heroin."

Houston raised an eyebrow. "I thought you said it was cocaine."

"I Googled it. And now we just have to use the heroin to our advantage."

Ben grinned. "You want to try using it to bargain with a dirty cop?"

Not the *worst* idea but definitely more complicated than what I had in mind.

"Let's try to avoid any run-ins with the law. In fact, I vote we leave *that* part to the experts."

"The experts in what, exactly?" Liz asked. "Bribing politicians?"

"Exactly."

That momentarily stunned everyone into silence.

"You're kidding." Amy looked as if she expected me to laugh at their gullibility. "Please tell me you're kidding."

"Look, it's a very simple trade. We return the Buddha to a drug cartel and in exchange they give us Neal. Everybody leaves happy."

No response.

"It's simple!"

"Sure. Perfect. As long as you don't factor in *this* scenario: The cartel shoots you. The cartel takes the drugs. The cartel leaves happy. You leave in a body bag."

Well, when Houston put it that way, my plan sounded significantly less brilliant.

"I admit it's a possibility. But what exactly would they have to gain by shooting me?"

"It would send a message to all their competitors." Houston

nodded. "But I see your point. Bloodshed isn't a requirement."

"*See!*"

"They'll profit far more by selling you into the sex trade. Young. Blonde. Pretty. They might make more off your body than they would from the drugs."

That thought made my blood chill. "You're being overly dramatic."

"*Right.* Drug kingpins are known for their high moral standards. And no tourists have ever been forced into bad situations abroad." Houston laughed, but not as if he found the conversation particularly funny. "Keep dreaming, Chelsea."

"My plan is going to work."

"And every time a bell rings, an angel gets its wings."

"Seriously, do you guys need to go to separate corners?" Liz demanded. "Settle down!"

"It's not my fault that he's being a jerk."

"Ouch. You really told me off, Chelsea. Why, if I were a drug lord, I'd be *terrified* right now."

"All right." Ben stood up. "I can't listen to this anymore. If you need me, I'll be enjoying the lush scenery that this beautiful, beautiful country has to offer."

And with that he headed several rows away to a group of female tourists who were all wearing the thin cotton pants that I'd seen stall owners hocking in the marketplace. I thought the style made the girls look like bedraggled Shakespearean actors, but Ben appeared far more interested in the way they filled out their shirts.

"Amy, I wanted to ask you more about your independent study idea. Let's go talk. Y'know . . . not here." The accompanied jerk of Liz's head certainly wasn't subtle, but that didn't make it any less effective.

"Wha—oh. Right. We'll catch up with you two later."

They quickly booked it to the back of the bus, leaving me

sitting alone with Houston as the bus lumbered closer to Phnom Penh.

The silence that weighed down the air between us made even breathing feel unnaturally forced.

So closing my eyes, I pretended that once again I was moving gracefully across Ms. P's dance studio in a filmy pink tutu.

Houston cleared his throat, shattering my fantasy. "I, uh . . . overheard what you said. About your parents."

"Yeah." I glared at him. "Funny how that happens when you're *eavesdropping*."

He merely did one of his infuriatingly casual shrugs. "Did you mean it?"

I kept my eyes trained out the window because I knew that pity was the one thing I couldn't handle coming from Houston. He hadn't tried to sympathize with me when my parents shipped me off to Cambodia or when Jake's name first came up at the massage parlor. There had been no attempt to bond over the more painful parts of my life. No offered condolences or shoulder pats. And oddly enough, I wouldn't have wanted it any other way.

Even Houston's annoying habit of calling me "princess" didn't really bother me anymore. Coming from him it was just a nickname, not a subtle way of treating me like a doll whose only purpose was to be put on display. And I didn't worry that he was secretly trying to sweet-talk or manipulate me into his way of thinking because Houston didn't work that way. He had no problem confronting me directly.

Somehow that made the idea of him looking at me with pity even worse.

I crossed my arms defiantly. "Does it make a difference? My parents can think whatever they want."

Houston shook his head in disbelief. "So you do believe that crap then. Chelsea, your dad doesn't think you're stupid.

He worries that you'll make stupid choices. There's a difference."

"Wow, thanks. Next time I need a pep talk, I'll be sure to avoid you."

He looked disgusted, but I couldn't tell if it was with me or with himself. Probably both.

"Trust me on this one, Chelsea. Your dad just wants to keep you safe."

"Right," I scoffed. "And you know this how, exactly? Did the two of you have a long talk about his *feelings* or something?"

"He let something slip about a nasty ex-boyfriend of yours. Lyle, right?"

"*Logan,*" I corrected defensively. "And both of my parents loved him."

I did too.

Houston raised an eyebrow. "But Lawson's no longer interested, right?"

I pulled back, stung. Houston's blunt style of confrontation definitely felt less endearing now. I fought to keep my voice even.

"None of your business."

He continued as if I hadn't spoken. "It's time for you to move on, kid. I'm sure you'll have no trouble dating someone closer to your age."

"Logan *is* my age."

"Then who was the jerk at the Christmas party last year?"

Oh. My. God.

He knew about Jake. Not all the details—my dad couldn't share information that he didn't have—but Houston's reference to the dreaded annual Christmas party hit *way* too close to home.

"What, uh . . . what did my dad say happened?" I asked carefully.

"Nothing."

"Yeah, right," I shot back. "If he didn't mention the Christmas party, then how did you hear about it?"

"I was there. And I saw the whole thing." A chill crept into my bones as Houston lazily stretched out his legs. He looked as if we were chatting about nothing more personal than the last Portland Timbers game. "But feel free to fill me in on whatever it is you think I missed. I've already promised to keep my mouth shut."

"Tempting, but I'll pass."

Houston's palm touched my knee and I shot bolt upright. There was nothing sexual or even flirtatious about the feeling, but it was still too . . . intimate. He must have felt the same way because he quickly stuffed his hand into the front pocket of his jeans.

But if he was equally flustered his voice didn't betray it. "It's about time we cleared the air, don't you think?"

Much to my surprise the answer to that was finally *yes*.

"All right, cowboy. You're on."

Chapter 19

"So who was the Christmas crasher?"

I should have known Houston would prod straight at the heart of the disaster. He couldn't ease into the conversation with something relatively simple like, *Why were you drinking so heavily at your parents' annual Christmas party?*

Nope, he went right for *Jake the Mistake.*

"Somebody that I used to date," I said wryly, hoping to lighten the conversation.

Houston nodded thoughtfully. "He didn't seem to get the message that it was over."

I felt a quick surge of satisfaction as I remembered how surprised Jake had been to discover that I had grown a tougher skin since he dumped me. Jake had probably expected me to be overjoyed at the idea of picking up right where we left off during his infrequent visits home from college. He'd been so confident when he explained that we just needed to be mature about the situation. Monogamy wouldn't work for us. The whole concept was woefully outdated, practically guaranteed to end in disappointment and hurt feelings. An open relationship, on the other hand . . . well, all of his college buddies were enjoying them.

If you ever really loved me, you'll agree to do it too.

C'mon, Chelsea. Don't you remember how good we were together? Don't you miss it, babe?

You know that nobody will ever love you as much as I do.

I shook my head to dispel the memory of Jake's words and focused on Houston.

"He wasn't ready to accept that it was over." I mimicked one of Houston's shrugs. "Enough said."

"He nearly convinced you to ditch the party, Chelsea."

After downing way more than my share of wine, almost anything had seemed better than faking a functioning family. If Logan had been the one offering me an escape, I wouldn't have hesitated. If some random stranger had offered me a ride, it would've been a hard offer to resist.

It was no real surprise that even knowing exactly how capable Jake was at toying with me, I had almost accepted the offer.

"That's because I didn't want to stay there even a minute longer," I said defiantly. "Believe it or not, being paraded around like a show dog isn't exactly my idea of a good time." I pitched my voice higher in a spot-on impersonation of my mom. "Have you met my daughter? *Sit, Chelsea! Speak! Good girl.*"

Houston's fist tightened within his pocket. "Yeah, your mom is pretty . . . intense. I noticed that myself. So is that why you started drinking? Or did you pick the red wine because it matched the color of your dress?"

He remembered my outfit. It was such a ridiculously girly thing to get a thrill over. Especially because we were at a freaking *Christmas* party where all the women either wore a red dress and called it "festive" or pulled out a slinky black number for the occasion. For all I knew, Houston had just made a very lucky guess.

Except Houston didn't waste his time making up stuff.

He had seen me at the party and remembered the color of

my dress . . . but for the life of me I couldn't place him at the scene. I studied his face, hoping that any second I'd be able to connect his aquiline nose and dark green eyes with their tiny flecks of gray to a good moment from the party. Nothing came to mind.

Then again, I also couldn't remember enjoying myself at any point of the evening.

"You seem to remember an awful lot about that night," I observed.

Houston's eyes sparkled with humor. "Yeah, I wasn't the one drinking. That tends to help."

I laughed self-consciously, but I refused to let him get away with changing the subject that easily. "Seriously, though, cowboy. Why don't I remember you? Did you avoid speaking to me or something?"

The sparkle faded as he turned his gaze straight ahead. "Or something."

Releasing a frustrated breath, I nudged him with my shoulder. "Come on! What am I missing here?"

Houston smiled tightly. "Maybe this will refresh your memory: *Leave me alone, charity case. I don't want you here.*"

Oh crap.

"That was . . . *you?*" I couldn't believe that the student my dad had insisted on inviting to our Christmas party was *Houston*. It just didn't compute. From what I could dimly recall, the dork had been super-lanky, as if he'd recently spurted a few inches and didn't know what to do with the extra height. His cheap tweed suit jacket hadn't done him any favors either. Not that his looks had anything to do with my bitchiness.

My dad's insistence on inviting one of his most promising students had stung so sharply it burned. It had been one of the few times I'd actually seen my dad override my mom's objections. And was it to defend his only daughter? To encourage her to pursue ballet dancing, instead of casually dismissing it as a pipe dream?

No, it wasn't.

Thanks, Dad. Way to be supportive.

So I had avoided the scrawny college freshman because I was obviously going to feel every bit as intellectually inferior around him as I did near Mackenzie Wellesley. That's also when I started drinking my wine straight from the bottle.

I definitely hadn't made a good impression on anyone that night.

A vague memory slid into place. "Did you try to order me to my room?"

He shrugged. "You were acting like a petulant child."

No, I was acting like an insecure teenager who was sick of pretending everything was fine. And if I couldn't get my parents to notice the things I could do right, well, then I was going to find some other way to get their attention.

"You've got it all wrong."

"Really? Because I *wasn't* determined to get trashed. Let's see, you flounced around in a short red dress, tried to chug a bottle of wine, and then—and this part was everyone's highlight—you got into a screaming match outside with your boyfriend."

"Ex-boyfriend," I corrected automatically. "He had some trouble understanding the meaning of the word 'no,' so I needed to repeat it a few times. Loudly."

He stiffened, and once again his eyes locked on the front of the bus. "Your dad was really worried about you."

I laughed, but the sound was utterly without humor. "Yeah, he deserves a Father of the Year award for shipping me off to Cambodia. I'm so glad we got that all cleared up. You can stop prying into my private life now."

"It's not really a 'private' life if your ex publicly announces that all it takes to get into your pants is some tequila and a quick chat about your mom."

I reeled back as if I'd been slapped across the face. Those vicious words had haunted me for months, and there were still times I thought I'd never be able to rid myself of them.

Apparently, I had been right. They had followed me all the way to Cambodia.

"Sorry. I'm . . . I shouldn't have mentioned it." Houston raked a hand through his hair in frustration. "Look, I know I'm screwing this up, and you can hate me for it later, but I watched you nearly climb into that jerk's car. So if you've got some kind of a death wish or . . . I don't know, a self-destructive pattern, then I want you to get the help you need." He looked out the window before he continued uncomfortably. "Your dad isn't the only one who cares."

He thought I needed a shrink.

It was almost laughable. I had actually been thinking maybe we were becoming real friends—that despite my flaws and insecurities, Houston liked *me*—but what he really wanted was to send me to the nearest therapist's couch.

I straightened my spine because those last few words of his had made me feel dangerously weak. "I'll . . . consider your suggestion. But just for the record, Jake was wrong about a whole bunch of things. Including what it takes to get me into bed."

"I'm sure Ben will be very disappointed to hear it." Houston managed to keep a straight face for all of three seconds before we both starting laughing.

It was strange sharing an inside joke with him at first. If someone had asked me in the airport which scenario I thought was more likely to happen—that I'd accidentally steal a Buddha full of heroin or that I would *ever* feel comfortable around Houston—I'd have picked the drugs. I wouldn't have hesitated over such a no-brainer. Houston was practically the male version of Mackenzie Wellesley, and I wasn't exactly going to become besties with *her* anytime soon.

But even knowing that Houston was the brilliant student my dad had invited to the Christmas party . . . it didn't intimidate me. I didn't suddenly start worrying that he would dismiss my opinions as a waste of his time. And I knew he would never preface a dumb blonde joke with the always insulting words, "No offense."

He was still just . . . *Houston.*

"It's your turn to share, cowboy," I decided. "Why do you care so much about my dad?"

"I wouldn't necessarily put it that way."

I just shot him my best *oh, really?* look and waited for him to crack under the pressure.

"Besides the fact that he's a nice guy and a brilliant teacher? Your dad talked to the people in the financial aid office for me. He's the reason I'm not living at home and applying to my local community college right now."

I nodded and then forced myself to ask the follow-up question I probably should have already known. "Um . . . so where are you from?"

"Texas."

"Seriously?"

Houston took one look at my admittedly surprised face and burst out laughing. "Not even close. I'm from Colorado."

I crossed my arms but couldn't hold back an answering grin of my own. "So how did your parents come up with the name then?"

"Funny story, actually." He leaned back in the seat as his smile became smaller and yet somehow sweeter. "My mom went into labor three weeks early while my dad was away on a business trip. They had done all of these preparation classes together, and he had promised to be with her every step of the way. So when she went into early labor, she completely panicked. She actually called up my aunt Meredith and said, 'My water just broke, but I'm going to Houston. Book me a ticket, will you?' "

"What did your aunt say?"

Houston's smile deepened. "Meredith promised to drive her to the airport and took her straight to the hospital instead. Then she told her to just keep focusing on Houston."

"So you *were* named after the city!"

"Not exactly. My dad was in Toronto."

I stared at him in disbelief before I was the one to burst out laughing. "Um . . . what?"

"My dad is a freelance writer who specializes in agricultural issues. It's kind of hard to explain what *exactly* he does, but he travels a lot in the summer and . . . my mom got his trips mixed up."

"So what happened?" I shifted in my seat as I tried to get more comfortable, and my arm accidentally brushed against his.

Houston didn't seem to notice, or at least he didn't comment on it.

"My mom called him from the hospital, determined to play it cool, and said, 'Hey, honey! How's everything in Houston?' "

I giggled. "Let me guess . . . your dad let her know he wasn't there?"

"Yes, he did."

"What did she say to *that*?"

"I'm pretty sure there was some swearing involved. But she had already signed off on my birth certificate and didn't like the idea of naming me *Toronto*." He shrugged. "So the name stuck."

"Your parents sound pretty cool. I'm guessing you told them about, y'know, the whole Neal situation?"

Houston yawned. "Yeah, but I may have failed to mention a few things. My little brother has some serious anxiety issues, so I'd rather not have them worrying about me."

I knew he was exhausted; I was struggling to stay awake too. But I couldn't resist asking, "What did they name your brother?"

"Denver."

I eyed him suspiciously. "Are you messing with me again?"

"Maybe." He tried to stifle another yawn and failed. "Listen, I seriously need to sleep, so if you want to move somewhere else, now would be a good time to do it."

"I'm fine with staying here."

"I thought you didn't like sleeping around other people." The intense pressure of his stare had me quickly pretending to find the woven upholstery on all the seats absolutely fascinating.

"I don't."

He considered that for a moment and then shrugged. "Okay, princess. Just wake me before we get to Phnom Penh, please."

He closed his eyes and probably would have drifted off right then if I hadn't murmured, "Uh, Houston? One last question, I promise. Did you email your ex-girlfriend?"

Houston blinked as if he was having trouble processing the question. It had seemed fairly straightforward to me. "What's with the fishing expedition, princess?"

"I'm curious. You said you didn't want your family worrying, and I just wondered . . . did you email your ex-girlfriend?"

"Okay, I'm fairly sure there is some weird subtext to this question that I'm missing. But I don't get it, and I'm pretty sure I don't like it."

"That's not an answer," I pointed out.

"No, I didn't email Carolyn." He stated the words slowly to make sure there was no room for misinterpretation or any follow-up questions. "Now I'm going to sleep. Wake me at your peril."

I closed my eyes and tried to block out my hyperawareness of his body's proximity to mine by focusing on the jolting rhythm of the bus.

"Sure, cowboy. No problem."

Then I drifted off to sleep.

Chapter 20

Phnom Penh made quite a first impression.

Enormous colored umbrellas simultaneously protected baskets of produce and shiny tourist wares; people bustled and wove around stalls; motorcycles zipped in and out at breakneck speeds. Everywhere I looked appeared to be bursting with color, movement, and the sound of outraged tuk-tuk drivers honking their discontent.

It was nothing like Oregon, but it also made me feel . . . alive. I didn't even try to suppress my grin as I pressed my nose against the window.

"It's beautiful!"

Houston rubbed his eyes blearily. "Okay, who are you, and what have you done to Chelsea Halloway?"

"What do you mean?"

"You *hate* Cambodia."

"No," I corrected, "I *hate* being tossed around in a game of parental hot potato. Cambodia, on the other hand, is . . . growing on me. A little."

My parents were always so incredibly wrong, it was hard to admit that this time they'd actually had a point. Not about the program being a nonstop intellectually stimulating adventure—I'd nearly fallen asleep during all of Mr. Horny's lectures—but about admiring the strength of the country. It had taken a while for me to appreciate it; mostly because of the jet lag, humidity, and y'know, whole eating-gigantic-spiders thing, but the air had a vibrancy to it I'd never experienced before. Maybe because the temples stood as proof that when hundreds of thousands of people come together to create something beautiful, even decades of genocide, starvation, and the ever-present land mines couldn't erase it with one bloody streak. Cambodia had been kicked around and treated like crap for years, but judging from the view out my window, it was doing more than just surviving. It was thriving.

It made me feel like maybe I could figure out a way to do the same.

Although I quickly discovered it was a lot easier to enjoy the exotic atmosphere when a Plexiglas window was filtering the experience. Not quite as magical when I was part of the crowd, clutching my bags, and signaling for a tuk-tuk—only to be swarmed by four hollering drivers who each swore that *they* would give the best price.

Ben turned to me. "Where are we going, Chelsea?"

Change of plans, everyone. I've reconsidered. This is way too dangerous for us to try and handle on our own. Let's go to the American consulate and call in the diplomatic heavyweights to deal with it.

Maybe that's what I should have said. But I couldn't simply accept our failure before we had even tried to change the outcome.

"The Royal Continental Hotel, please," I instructed the two nearest tuk-tuk drivers before I climbed into one of them behind Amy.

"Are congratulations in order?" she asked me. "You sat next to Houston for a five-hour bus ride without attempting to strangle him even once. That seems like a good sign to me."

Liz slid into the tuk-tuk behind me, cutting off all means of escape. "Did the two of you finally work out your weird damage?"

"Weird *damage?*" I instinctively tossed my hair, only to find that with my shorter haircut it didn't produce the same effect. "I have no idea what you're talking about, Liz."

"Uh huh."

"As long as Houston doesn't start bossing me around again, we'll be just fine."

Amy rolled her eyes. "Sure. And there was no weird tension between the two of you whatsoever. Nope, not at all. Phew, glad we got all that cleared up."

I stared at Amy while I tried to process the implications of what she was saying. She thought Houston actually . . . liked me? And not just in a *hey, I think you should probably look into getting some serious psychological help* kind of way— assuming that was even a thing.

Interesting.

Usually, I had no trouble figuring out exactly where I stood with a guy. Then again, most of the guys who tended to approach me at parties weren't exactly subtle in letting me know that their interest was directly correlated to the amount of clothing I happened to be wearing. But I had yet to get a good read on Houston, which made it extra strange to think that *Amy* had a better take on the situation.

Not that this was really the time to obsess over whether some guy liked me.

That was way too high school. Even for me.

"All weird tension will just have to take a backseat," I said wryly as we drove through the very impressive gate to the Royal Continental Hotel. "This is going to be a working vacation."

The girls' jaws dropped as they soaked in their first views of the hotel I had researched back in Siem Reap. The pictures hadn't done it justice. Everything was sleekly perfect, from the stone wall outside with its gold lettering, to the cream-colored foyer with its mahogany furniture, to the immaculate cream-colored couches.

"What are we doing here?" Liz muttered nervously. "What happened to playing it safe and staying at hostels?"

"That plan got an upgrade. We're staying in the dragon's lair now."

I didn't give her a chance to demand an explanation. Instead, I sauntered over to the front desk as if I were simply strolling across the quad back at Smith High School. I learned a long time ago that if you look like you own the place, people will accept your authority without question.

Even if you smell like you've spent the past five hours on a Cambodian bus.

"Hello." I smiled confidently at the woman behind the concierge desk. "I'd like to book a suite for the next four days. What do you have in the way of availabilities?"

The woman tried ineffectively to hide her surprise as she typed my request into the system.

"Smoking or nonsmoking?"

"Nonsmoking," I answered readily, as Houston and Ben quickly moved across the lobby to join us. They both looked determined to pull me back before I could do something reckless.

Too late.

"And how many beds will you be wanting?"

"At least three. Ideally, four."

She nodded and added in that detail.

"Our deluxe suite is available. It comes with wireless Internet, access to the club floor, continental breakfa—"

"I'll take it." I slid the emergency credit card my dad had given me across the desk, without so much as a shred of guilt. Trying to rescue my professor from a Cambodian jail ought to count as an "emergency situation" by anyone's standards.

"What are you doing?" Houston hissed under his breath. "This is insane!"

I ignored him, accepted the key cards with my most gracious smile, pointed to our luggage for the bellman, and headed straight toward the elevators.

"I can't wait to discuss our sightseeing plans," I said pointedly to the group, "*once we've gotten settled into our suite.*"

Houston shut up, but he didn't look happy about it. Although when I opened the door to suite 17, everyone else started grinning broadly enough to make up for his blatant frustration.

"Holy crap." Liz hurried over to the windows that offered a breathtaking view of the city below. "This place is amazing!"

Amy flopped down on the nearest bed. "I can definitely get used to this. Maybe we should book it for a full week. You know . . . just in case our rescue takes longer than expected."

"We can't afford this place!" Houston pulled the credit card receipt out of my hand, looked down at the total figure, and blanched. "We *really* can't afford this place!"

"Nobody is asking you to pay for it. So just relax and enjoy."

"I can do that, Chelsea," Ben said easily as he prowled around the room. "*Hmm*, I wonder if the minibar is complimentary. . . ."

"Of course it's not!" Houston snapped. "Don't eat anything in there!"

Ben raised his hands in the universal gesture for "Don't shoot!" "Okay, man. Calm down."

But it didn't look like Houston would be capable of doing that anytime soon.

"Chelsea, you can't book a room like this on your credit card."

I couldn't help smirking. "Really? Because I'm pretty sure I just did."

"How are you going to pay for this?"

I briefly considered lying and then straightened my shoulders. He *definitely* wasn't going to like the truth, but I refused to let that stop me from saying it. "I'm not the one picking up the tab."

"The credit card belongs to your parents, right?" Houston's voice was one of hollow acceptance. "That's why you don't care about racking up a bill. Anything to stick it to them. Am I right, *princess?*"

The spacious suite suddenly felt unbearably small and claustrophobic.

"Listen up, *El Paso*. I'm trying to rescue a man from a Cambodian *prison* by making a deal with a *drug tycoon*. On the off chance that everything goes to hell, I'm spending my last few nights on earth sleeping on sheets with a high thread count."

Everyone soaked in that information for a painfully long moment before Amy broke the silence.

"Do you really think we're going to die?"

I shrugged. "Technically, we could all die in a tragic tuk-tuk accident. Or get blown up by land mines or something. But yeah, I'm sure the odds of things ending badly increases whenever drug dealers are involved."

Amy nodded, but the way she began worrying her bottom lip was a dead giveaway that she wasn't as comfortable with the idea as she wanted to pretend. I seized the opportunity to make eye contact with each of them.

"This is the last time I'm asking. Does anyone want out?"

Liz let out a disgusted sigh. "We're staying, Chelsea. You're not the only one who cares about Neal."

"Then welcome to our new headquarters."

Chapter 21

As far as top-secret lairs go . . . ours wasn't exactly state-of-the art.

We couldn't access military information off the television or watch the hotel grounds via a live camera feed. But it did come equipped with something else almost as good: room service.

After more than a week of eating nonstop Asian dishes, the first bite of hamburger was downright heavenly. I mainlined french fries with a low hum of satisfaction.

It tasted like home.

I'm not even usually a hamburger person, but that didn't stop me from keeping pace—bite for bite—with Ben and Liz. Everything on the room service tray tasted irresistible, and I wanted to do nothing more than gorge before sleeping off my food coma.

But that wasn't really an option.

So instead I cleared off a portion of the table and positioned my laptop so that everyone could see the screen before I began my impromptu presentation.

"This is Rithisak Sovann." I gestured with a ketchup-dipped french fry at the image of the dark-haired man. "He invested heavily in Cambodia right after the fall of the Khmer Rouge. Rithisak enjoys taking cruises and the finer things in life. He also has more money than even I could spend in a lifetime."

"Okay," Liz said around a large bite of lasagna. "So do you want to rob him or nominate him for the Cambodian version of *Dancing with the Stars*?"

"Neither. Rithisak Sovann happens to be Cambodia's most notorious drug dealer."

Ben grinned and cocked his head while he pretended to study the photo. "That doesn't mean he can't tango. I bet he could pull off some sequins too. A feathered boa would set off his shoulders nicely."

"You're hilarious, Ben. Now let's try to focus. Even if it wasn't his deal I accidentally derailed, he will definitely have heard the rumors about a missing drug shipment."

"And if you stole it directly from him?" Houston rubbed his forehead wearily. "What's your brilliant plan then?"

"Then we'll do some backpedaling. The last thing we want to do is anger Rithisak Sovann. His Wikipedia page practically comes with a warning. Especially since he's been known to start shooting when he doesn't get his way."

Amy's jaw dropped. "Explain to me again why this guy isn't already in jail."

"Because it pays to be disgustingly rich and have friends in the government. Oh, and it helps when you own the biggest newspaper in Cambodia. He's got that too."

Ben ruffled my hair. "Look at our girl—going into spy mode. I'm so proud."

I batted away his hand, but I couldn't conceal my smile. Back at Smith High School everyone had dreaded working on a group project with me because they expected I would be dead weight that they would have to carry. Most of the time they had been right too. Why bother trying when you can successfully do nothing?

Now it made a whole lot more sense to me why Jane and Mackenzie spent so many hours poring over all their assignments; knowing that you were fully capable of handling any problem felt really freaking good.

Still, I tried to play off the whole thing with a joke. "Looks like all those hours I spent cyberstalking boys in high school are really paying off now."

"Not funny, Chelsea," Amy said.

"I'm *kidding!*"

Mostly.

"So did your extensive research tell you where we could find this guy?" Liz asked. "The room service is great and everything, but I'd like to get a move on."

"Actually, uh, that's the other reason I booked us a suite. Rithisak Sovann owns this hotel."

"Nothing like sleeping with the enemy." Houston's voice remained steady and calm, but his eyes flashed fire. "Let me rephrase that: Nothing like being booked into the enemy's hotel room. Who else thinks a hostel sounds a whole lot better now?"

"He's not the enemy . . . yet. He's the target," Liz corrected. "And it's not like he has any idea we're here, so I don't see any reason for us to leave."

I was nodding in agreement when the words *Jane says . . .* began flashing across the tab of my email account, signaling that she had sent me an instant message. I quickly clicked on the tab, relieved to see one very welcome sentence waiting for me in the chat box.

Are you there, Chelsea?

I debated my response for roughly a nanosecond.

I'm here, geek.

"Chelsea?"

My head automatically bobbed in agreement before I realized I had no idea what anyone had said. "Sorry, what did I just miss?"

Houston raised an eyebrow. "Amy asked if everything was all right."

Jane is typing . . .

"Hold that thought," I said distractedly.

This better not be an elaborate prank, Chelsea. If Scott's dad staked his reputation as a journalist on a nonstory, I will find a way to kick your butt. He's working to get a news team out to you soon. You are still in Cambodia, right? RIGHT? *cracks knuckles menacingly* *books imaginary flight*

I laughed in disbelief as I imagined classic good girl Jane Smith landing in Phnom Penh and demanding satisfaction for all the time she spent worrying about me for nothing. It wasn't a particularly menacing image. After watching her barely manage to white knuckle her way through the singing part of the *Romeo and Juliet* audition, she didn't exactly scare me. Unless she started singing again.

I winced instinctively at the memory before I firmly pushed it aside.

Of course I'm still in Cambodia. How long do you think it would take to get a news team out here?

"Reading something good over there that you want to share with the rest of the class?" Houston asked drily.

Not until I had Jane's response.

I don't know how long it will take! Believe it or not, this isn't exactly my area of expertise! Now I need you to tell me where exactly you are in Cambodia. Actually, I have a better plan. . . .

A ringing sound instantly filled the air, and I found myself hesitating as I stared at Jane's invitation to video chat.

Part of me had wanted to keep my Smith High School life separate from my time spent abroad. Initially, I had thought it would help me pretend that my banishment had never happened. All that mattered was the narrative. So as long as I could dismiss the trip as nothing more than a temporary leave of absence, nobody would dare challenge me for the details.

The less information swirling around back home, the simpler it would be to sweep the whole thing under the rug.

But that plan definitely wasn't going to hold up now.

Houston pointed at the screen, which placed one very nicely corded male forearm in front of me in the process. "Are you planning on answering that anytime soon, princess?"

I straightened at the note of challenge in his voice and clicked to accept the call.

There was no going back now.

"Jane!" The sight of her familiar face filling the screen had adrenaline surging through me as if I'd just executed a perfect *grand jeté*. "How are you?"

She dismissed that question with a slight wave of her hand. "I'm fine, Chelsea. But . . . um, wow . . . just how many people have you killed?"

I stared at her in confusion. "Me personally? Nobody!"

"Oh," Jane grinned. "Really? Then maybe you haven't looked in a mirror recently."

I fingered the choppy ends of my much shorter—much redder—hair and tried not to squirm. "It's just hair. It'll grow back."

"Actually, I kind of like it. In fact"—Jane started laughing—"you're totally rocking it. Not that I should be surprised. This is *you* after all." She shook her head and was back to being all business. "But I still need you to give me an exact location for the press."

Amy reddened slightly before she stuttered, "The press? Does that mean we'll be giving interviews while we stay here? Wow. That's . . . wow. How did you manage that?"

I turned my attention back to an impatient Jane. "Good question. How *did* you manage that, Jane? Did you convince some big night news program to cover it?"

"*No!*" Jane said, shooting me one of her *you better be kidding me* looks. "Of course not! You do realize that the story isn't *that* groundbreaking, right? It's not like the Cambodian government has done anything illegal."

"They took Neal!" I protested hotly.

"Hey, innocent or not, if they busted him with drugs"— Jane shrugged helplessly—"it's hard to prove he's not guilty. That could easily happen in the U.S. with the exact same results."

"But he would've gotten a fair trial before being tossed into jail," I argued.

"Um . . . sure. Nothing *ever* goes wrong with our justice system. We don't have overworked public defenders or tainted juries or any problems ever. Keep telling yourself that if it makes you feel better."

"Hi. As much as I enjoyed your insightful take on our justice system, do you think we could agree to focus on the task at hand?" Houston drawled. "I would really appreciate it."

And just like that, Houston had gained the respect of Smith High School's most strategically goal-oriented student.

"Right. Absolutely. So where are you?"

"The Royal Continental Hotel in Phnom Penh," Liz answered as she moved behind me. "Suite seventeen."

"A suite?" Jane choked and then laughed. "How very . . . Chelsea."

"What is *that* supposed to mean?" I demanded.

"Oh, nothing." She swiveled in her seat and called out to someone in the room with her who had chosen not to be on-screen. "Chelsea booked herself a suite."

That's when I heard an all-too-familiar masculine laugh. "*Of course* she did. We should've guessed as much."

Jane turned back to me, and for the first time she looked a little apologetic. "Logan and Mackenzie are here with me. I probably should've mentioned that earlier. I asked them to help out. . . ."

What was gearing up to be an uncomfortable situation became so much worse when Mackenzie and Logan entered the frame together, especially when she began sheepishly waving at me. I fought the urge to slam my laptop shut.

"Hey, Chelsea," Logan said easily, then he did a double-take when he got a good look at my hair. He still knew better than to comment on it. "It's . . . uh, good to see you. High school just isn't the same without you, Chels."

Yeah. You must be relieved that you no longer run into your ex in the hallways.

I tried to take the words in the spirit in which they were given and forced myself to smile. "Thanks, Logan."

"Wait. *This* is Logan?" Ben hooted gleefully. I tried to silence him with a kick but connected only with the table leg. "You are *not* what I expected. I had you pegged as a whole lot preppier. I bet you don't actually own anything with argyle. I'm kind of disappointed." This time my foot did hit its intended target and he quickly added, "I mean . . . uh, it's nice to meet you."

It was pretty obvious from the obnoxious grin widening on Ben's face that he intended to find a way to tease me about this conversation every day for the foreseeable future.

And it was equally clear that Logan didn't particularly want him to elaborate on his expectations—or what they had been founded on. "Sorry, I didn't catch your names."

"We call him 'Nuisance' most of the time," I supplied quickly. "And Toronto is the guy currently doing an impression of a large-mouthed bass."

"You're Mackenzie *Wellesley*." Houston finally spoke although he looked positively tongue-tied. Maybe it shouldn't have bothered me that after everything we'd been through it was *Mackenzie* who successfully rattled his ironclad composure—but it did. "I—uh, I saw you perform with ReadySet a few months ago. You've got a great voice."

"Thanks . . . Toronto?" she said tentatively, as if she couldn't quite believe that was his name but didn't want to hurt his feelings.

She was just too freaking *nice* for me to even hate her properly.

"It's Houston, actually." I thought I heard his voice crack on his own name before he began gruffly clearing his throat. "It's, uh, nice to meet you, Mackenzie."

I glanced at Amy, Liz, and Ben, but they were all too pre-occupied trying to play it cool in front of a female YouTube phenomenon to notice Houston's starstruck behavior.

The whole situation was seriously starting to weird me out.

"Logan and I have been trying to help. But there's really not a whole lot we can do from here."

I gritted my teeth as I faked another smile. "Thanks for making an effort, Mackenzie. You really didn't need to do that. At all."

Logan met my eyes, and I knew that at least *he* realized that I wanted his girlfriend to back off. Too bad Mackenzie didn't get the message.

"Right . . . well, I'm glad Scott's dad was able to pull some strings. Media attention can make all the difference. In fact, during the Spanish American War—" Mackenzie's voice became increasingly animated as she warmed up to the subject.

"Save it, professor."

I couldn't take it anymore. I couldn't spend another second watching Logan, Houston, Ben, and even *Liz* gaze admiringly at Mackenzie as if they wished she had been the one sent abroad instead of me.

My laugh was brittle. "That came out wrong. Sorry, I meant to say that we've got to save *our* professor. Feel free to put that *fascinating* lecture on my tab with the rest of your tutoring sessions. Sound good, Mackenzie? Great. You take care, now!" Then I closed my laptop before anyone could protest.

The room momentarily descended into silence.

"That was real friendly of you, *princess*. Now I see why you're so popular."

I would've stormed out, but I had nowhere else to go.

Chapter 22

None of them would shut up about meeting Mackenzie. Instead of focusing on stuff that actually mattered, like saving our teacher from wrongful imprisonment in a third-world country, they kept asking about Mackenzie's sudden rise to fame. And they were pretty disappointed to hear that our interactions were limited to a handful of tutoring sessions that I'd crashed before she started dating my ex. End of story.

They weren't the only ones who thought I was holding back some details.

Everyone at Smith High School believed that I'd been behind Mackenzie's embarrassing moment hitting YouTube. I guess it made for a good story: Popular girl tries to humiliate geeky underdog by filming one seriously misguided attempt at CPR, only to have the whole thing backfire horribly when the video went viral. Too bad the entire story was a work of fiction.

At the time, I'd been focused on patching things up with Logan.

That's what I had been *trying* to do anyway. Mackenzie wasn't even on my radar until Logan turned me down because he was in love with her. And at that point I didn't really care what anyone was saying about me. In fact, I kind of liked being cast as the Wicked Witch opposite Mackenzie's socially awkward Snow White.

If I couldn't be wanted, at least I could be feared.

"If you're all done geeking out over Mackenzie Wellesley, can we please get back to work?"

Houston grinned. "Jealous, Chelsea?"

I rolled my eyes. "Yeah, I don't want to waste my time talking about my ex-boyfriend's girlfriend when I've got a Buddha full of *heroin* with me. Shocking, isn't it?"

My reference to the drugs snapped everyone's attention back to the task at hand.

"Shouldn't we just, uh, wait for the press?" Amy asked tentatively. "If this drug guy is so insane, I vote we let the media take the story public. That way *we* can stay out of it."

She had a point. It did seem kind of foolish to get overly involved when help was on the way. But there was no reason we couldn't do some of the groundwork to speed up the process.

I shrugged. "I only want to do basic-level surveillance. Find out if Rithisak Sovann is even in the building. That kind of thing."

Liz's expression was inscrutable. "Just surveillance?"

Probably.

"Of course."

"Then I'm in."

Ben opened his suitcase and started rifling through it. "Me too. I'll go scope out the pool area. Make sure there are no bad guys hanging around."

Translation: I'm going to be flirting with girls in bikinis.

Fine with me.

"Okay. Ben takes the pool, Liz can check out the ... gym?" Liz nodded in agreement. "Great. Amy stays here, and I'll cover the bar," I said.

"Actually, I'll watch the lobby," Amy volunteered.

"You sure?"

Her smile was one of irrepressible enthusiasm. "I have my needlepoint. Plus I spotted a book exchange in the lobby and I think they might have some romance novels. Trust me, sitting there isn't going to be a hardship."

Which just left Houston.

But, hey, if he didn't want to help, that was up to him. He could even stay in the suite and chat some more with Mackenzie. It didn't make a difference to me.

No weird tension there.

Houston stretched languidly. "Nice try, *princess*. You're not legally allowed to drink. Which means you'll be staying here while I go to the bar."

"Funny, I'm trying to recall asking for your permission, but . . ." I snapped my fingers. "Oh, that's right! I didn't."

"No time to fix that like the present."

I crossed my arms. "Look, if you think you can keep up with me, then you're welcome to come along, cowboy."

"Oh, I can keep up, princess."

Amy pointedly cleared her throat, and I knew that she wanted to make a big deal out of the fact that Houston had chosen the bar with me over the peace and quiet of an empty hotel suite. Except Houston's scowl wasn't exactly the type of body language he should be sending if he actually wanted our scouting expedition to take a romantic turn.

It should have left me totally unaffected.

Instead, my pulse was picking up speed at the idea of sitting across from one seriously annoying college student at a bar.

"You want me to join you guys?" Ben offered. "I could use a drink."

I shook my head. "No way. I don't need one chaperone, let alone both of you guys, going all caveman on me. No need for any chest thumping here, okay? Trust me. I've got this."

Liz nodded supportively. "Chelsea can handle it. So let's get out of her way and let her do her thing."

I nudged her with my shoulder. "Aw, thanks!"

Liz smirked. "Yeah, well, it doesn't take a psych major to figure out that you *enjoy* sticking your nose into other people's business. But if you think your amateur sleuthing can help Neal, then I'm fine with it." She turned to Amy. "*You*, on the other hand—no talking to strangers!"

Amy rolled her eyes. "Just for the record, I'm the oldest person here!"

Which totally proved my point about the irrelevance of the number on a driver's license.

Liz shook her head warily. "I stand by my earlier statement. No talking to strangers."

Amy looked thoroughly disgusted with all of us for doubting her survival skills, but she caved under pressure and promised to keep her mouth shut, her nose buried in a book . . . and her eyes peeled for Cambodia's most notorious drug tycoon. I couldn't help wondering if it was those big, innocent Bambi eyes that were preventing people from taking her too seriously, much in the same way that everyone acted as if the natural color of my hair debilitated brain function.

"She'll have her new prepaid cell phone with her in the lobby," I reminded everyone. "Amy can handle herself too. So, can we leave already?"

Amy nodded in agreement and then studied me closely. "You're not going to wear that to the bar, right?"

Oh yeah, if she was already thinking like, well . . . *me*, then Amy was definitely ready to handle a little reconnaissance mission.

"Good point. I definitely need to change out of these jeans."

Ben flopped down next to Amy on the bed, the swim trunks he'd just retrieved from the very bottom of his suitcase already forgotten. "I think I should wait before going to the pool. It's not a good idea to swim right after lunch."

He patted his stomach so unconvincingly that Amy, Liz, and I laughed. Houston didn't appear to find it funny, however. Instead he began pacing around the room.

"Yeah. You're *real* subtle, Ben." Unzipping my own suitcase, I rummaged through its contents, sorting everything into piles based on the level of sexiness. I briefly held up a sparkly black top for consideration before tossing it into the *maybe* pile.

"That one," Ben croaked. "You should definitely wear that one."

Liz shook her head. "Too obvious. She doesn't want to look desperate, and sparkles don't exactly scream sophistication."

I was willing to concede that point.

I held up a fairly conservative silk number . . . and then I remembered that my hair was now a matching fire-engine red. "Okay, that's not going to work." I tossed it onto the bed before anyone could comment and continued digging in my bag.

But the blouse caught my eye once again as Amy carefully began folding it.

"Want to try it on?"

"I, uh, don't know if it'll fit me." Amy's cheeks began to match the shade of the shirt while I mentally started to backpedal.

The last thing I ever wanted to discuss was weight.

It's one of those subjects that makes everyone feel awful, regardless of their body type. Sure, I've always been thin. That's just the way my body is built. Which is incredibly lucky because the one job I actually want—to be a professional dancer—demands a certain look. And I've got it.

But I've also got to deal with rumors that I'm secretly bulimic, even though the *only* time I've ever thrown up at school was after dissecting a frog in biology. Still, every couple of months I'm even called into the health office because a "concerned friend who prefers to stay anonymous" thinks I have an eating disorder. Then I get handed a whole bunch of pamphlets about body dysmorphic disorder while they insist that I'm in a safe space where I can share my problems.

Except my only real problem was knowing that my parents would be bickering when I got home. That at some point in their argument my mom would inevitably begin making dire predictions about my future—no college would accept me, no restaurant would ever hire me, etc.—and she'd insist that eventually my looks would fade and then I'd wish they had both pushed me just a little bit harder.

Not something I really wanted made common knowledge. So I took the pamphlets and kept my mouth shut.

"The offer still stands if you change your mind," I told Amy.

It looked like she rethought saying anything when Ben waved a hand at me to hurry it up.

"What else have you got?"

I held up a dark blue dress that featured a rather deep V-neckline, requiring a camisole underneath.

He wolf whistled. "Now, that's what I'm talking about."

Houston couldn't seem to find the humor in the situation. "She's *seventeen*. Let's just . . . not do this okay? There are too many things wrong with this situation."

It was kind of nice seeing him genuinely flustered. Especially because Mackenzie wasn't around this time. "By most people's standards this isn't even risqué. Loosen up, Houston. It's not exactly made out of mesh."

When his scowl only deepened, I couldn't resist teasing him a little. "Now that I think about it, I *might* have some mesh in here."

Ben perked up. "Really?"

"No!"

"What a shame." Liz pretended to leer at me. "I'd have enjoyed that."

"*Hey!* You've already got a girlfriend."

She winked. "Doesn't mean I can't appreciate a good show."

"Speaking of Sara," I interjected before Ben could say something beyond inappropriate, "what was her reaction to all of this Neal stuff?"

Liz began folding up the clothes I had tossed aside as a guilty flush crept up her neck. "I, uh, didn't tell her."

I definitely hadn't seen that coming. "Why not?"

Her shoulders lifted in a halfhearted shrug. "She's got enough to worry about right now. Her mom is giving her a hard time about her tuition money."

"What does that mean?" Amy asked softly.

"It means that it's none of our business," Houston interrupted. "So why don't—"

"I'm fine, Houston. Really. It's not all that hard to answer. Sara's mom is threatening to stop paying for college if she keeps dating me."

Dead silence met that announcement.

"Yeah, there was no celebrating in Sara's family when she came out of the closet. We've been together for *two years,* and they still won't admit that I'm her girlfriend. They spent the first six months of our relationship hoping that they could somehow pray the gay away. Since that didn't work, they're now trying to *pay* the gay away."

It actually made me miss my dad for the first time in years. Usually, I was so angry at him for hiding away in his office at Lewis & Clark, it didn't leave much room for me to feel anything else. Probably because underneath my anger was a pretty deep layer of hurt. And given the choice, I'd much rather be spitting mad. But at least my parents wouldn't threaten to stop paying my tuition if I brought home a girlfriend.

Granted, neither of them believed I could get accepted into college.

But *still.*

Amy nudged Liz's shoulder in a silent show of solidarity. "Well, that puts *my* problem in perspective."

We all turned to her and waited expectantly.

"I have to keep coming out to my family. As straight."

Liz's laugh was huskier than usual, but Amy still beamed with pride at her success. "You're kidding,"

"Nope. My parents hint at it every few months. You know: *How's your love life, honey? Have you met any cute girls? Or boys? We'll love and support you regardless of your sexual orientation. You know that, right?* And then I'm stuck going, *Uh, yeah. Thanks. That's really sweet but . . . um, I'm still straight. Just like the last time you called.*"

Ben stretched. "I've never had a problem convincing people of anything."

Amy rolled her eyes at Ben, while Houston stopped pacing and sat down next to Liz.

"I may know someone who can help with the financial aid office if Sara's parents follow through on their threat. So if she ever wants me to make some calls . . . well, just say the word."

Liz slung her arm around his shoulder. "Thanks, Houston. I appreciate that."

He shifted uncomfortably as he tried to play it off as no big deal. Just Houston being . . . Houston. His eyes connected with mine, and I could practically feel him begging me to create a distraction.

It was kind of cute.

Really cute, actually.

So I made a big production of grabbing my low-cut blue dress and sauntering over to the bathroom.

"I'll be right back," I promised coyly and shut the door on another one of Ben's wolf whistles.

Showtime.

Chapter 23

Creating massive amounts of stupidity is something of an art form.

You have to factor in the gender ratio of the room, the genre and volume of the music, the amount of skin on display, and most importantly, the availability of liquor, in order to get the conditions just right for poor decision making.

Good thing I'm something of an expert on the subject.

Which is why when I emerged from the bathroom after applying my makeup for maximum impact, I looked like my parents' worst nightmare. Houston wasn't exactly thrilled with the results either. His eyes barely met mine once before he quickly glanced down at his watch as if it was critically important that he monitor the seconds ticking by.

Probably because I had transformed myself physically into the girl from last year's Christmas party.

And I did it knowing that within five minutes I could make everyone at the bar underestimate me by slipping into the role of an empty-headed twit whose life ambitions were exclusively centered around designer labels and red carpets. A role I relished the chance to play if this time it could help Neal. I flashed the group my most devastating grin as I twirled for inspection.

"Go knock 'em dead," Liz told me.

"Oh, I plan on it." I turned to Houston. "As for you, when we're at the bar, don't talk to me. Don't talk to anyone near me. Don't—"

"I get it."

"Good."

We rode the elevator in silence while I mentally ran through my plan one last time. Not that I needed to stress over it. This was one of the few areas in my life where I trusted my instincts. Sure, trying to create drug contacts in a third-world country might be significantly more dangerous than getting dirt on fellow high school students. But the technique wasn't all that different.

And I'd been inadvertently preparing for this moment since middle school.

The hotel obviously catered to wealthy travelers, and there were plenty of tourists at the hotel bar, which allowed me to simultaneously blend in and stand out. That's the trick to getting noticed for all the right reasons: You never want to be the only person in a crowd who looks different. If the dress code calls for a slinky black dress, a hot-pink, sparkly number is a risky move. The safer course of action is to make sure that the black dress draping *your* figure is the most flattering one in the room.

Except the large quantity of corporate guys in dark suits meant I was going to have to tweak my normal approach. So I whipped out my cell phone and hastily brushed off the fine coat of white powder that clung to the surface, before I aimed one last warning look at Houston and sauntered over to the busiest part of the bar.

"What do you mean ReadySet isn't here?" I demanded, mimicking my mom's irate voice of authority. "What am I supposed to do? Waste my time waiting for some wannabe rock stars who have barely left puberty behind them?"

That definitely caught the attention of half the guys at the bar. Well, that and the V-neck of my dress as I played the role of frustrated, high-powered businesswoman to perfection.

"You know what? Fine. But I'm charging my bar tab to the company." I thrust my cell phone back into my purse while I slid onto a barstool next to the youngest-looking guy without a wedding band.

Then I mentally began counting.

One. Two. Th—

"Having a rough day?"

The stranger's cologne smelled overwhelmingly of citrus, but it fit with his preppy Harvard brochure looks. He seemed like the type who was used to trying a little bit too hard. Which meant that he would be too thrilled with a reversal of fortunes to risk blowing it by asking the wrong kind of question. The rush of a performance heightened my every sensation as my target was officially acquired.

"The worst," I admitted with a soft sigh. Then I gave him a warm look that said I was more than willing to let him try to make it better.

"Why don't I buy you a drink and you can tell me all about it."

Oh yeah, redheads can definitely have just as much fun as blondes.

"Are you sure you really want to hear it? I just got off the flight from hell." I made a face that I hoped would come across as endearingly charming instead of unsophisticated. "I kid you not, four screaming babies."

"Ouch," he winced, while I ordered a glass of red wine. Not my preferred drink of choice, but I thought it added a classier touch.

"No kidding. It gets worse too. Apparently, my *Rolling Stone* interview depends on the whims of a boy band." I took a sip of wine before flashing a grateful smile. "Enough about me. What brings you to Cambodia?"

He tugged at his tie self-consciously. "I'm here with a team from Brookes and Merriweather."

I laughed delicately. "I'm sure I'd find that *very* impressive if I was familiar with the company."

He flushed. "I'm part of a team of lawyers."

I surreptitiously glanced around the bar and counted at least five other guys in his pack of suits who appeared curious about the redhead chatting up their geeky coworker. In fact, the only guy within a twenty-foot radius *not* tracking my every movement was Houston. Apparently, the football game playing above the bar was far more interesting to Houston than watching me work my magic. Although at least he wasn't brooding or scowling at anyone whose gaze lingered too long on my cleavage. That would have been a whole lot harder to explain away.

I leaned in closer toward my intended target. "So if the band never shows up, should I get you to represent me in court?"

He laughed self-consciously. "Not yet. I'm actually still an intern."

It didn't make a difference to me. All that I really needed was a good excuse to linger in a bar for a few hours. One that didn't seem likely to protest loudly if I had to leave suddenly, because his expectations had been fairly low all along.

"So does that mean you'll be stuck under a mountain of paperwork here?" I asked conversationally while I surveyed the room once more in the hope of seeing something . . . not quite right.

Nothing jumped out at me.

Then again, my eyes had developed a terrible habit of lingering on one particular person sitting on the other side of the bar.

"Worse, I'm going to be stuck in meetings. Get twenty lawyers in a boardroom and—"

His words were cut off as one of his cheerfully intoxicated

colleagues draped an arm around his shoulder. "Who's this, Wesley? Can't keep the pretty girl to yourself."

I didn't hear any slurring, but that didn't make me any more comfortable with an unexpected third-party intrusion.

"Ignore him," the guy who was apparently named Wesley murmured in my ear. "Aaron thinks he can handle his liquor, but two drinks in and he's like this for the rest of the night. But he's totally harmless, I swear."

Aaron smiled, and I noticed the red flush in his cheeks that was a dead giveaway that he had exceeded his limits.

"Wesley, huh? I'm glad I finally caught your name. I like it." I maintained my flirtatious body language as I evaluated his buddy: Asian American, judging by his accent, or lack thereof, with dark black hair and an attractive smile. "Nice to meet you too, Aaron."

"Y'know, I think we may have real chemistry together. What's your name, babe?"

Apparently, it was possible to have a more patronizing nickname than *princess*.

I took an extra-long sip of wine while I racked my brain for a good fake name to help keep me in character. Something that would make me feel strong. Something that would remind me of just how much power I'd been able to wield at Smith High School. A dim memory of Jane's nicknames for Ashley and Steffani back at the Portland Airport began to take shape. I could feel it percolating to the surface despite the nice buzz slowly building from the wine.

Fake and Bake. Which meant that I had to be—

"Lake. My name is Lake Scott."

"*Lake,*" Aaron hiccuped. "I could just drown in you."

Wesley shook his head and mouthed the words, *I am so sorry,* while I did my best to play the whole thing off as a joke. Of course, I found it *hilarious* when guys who were one beer away from passing out started hitting on me.

Even the fictional version of myself wanted to get out of

there before the situation could become really uncomfortable.

There was an empty suite only an elevator ride away. And it was entirely possible that I could flip through channels until I found an episode of the *Real Housewives of Somewhere-other-than-Cambodia*.

Instead, I tried to subtly glance around the room again.

"My mom's a total hippie," I lied, because it would seem suspicious not to say anything. "She's a vegan peace protestor who sells crafts at Portland's Saturday market. I'm just lucky she didn't name me Rainbow Trout."

Wesley clinked his beer bottle against my wineglass with a shy smile, but the mood was broken by Aaron's loud chortle. "Rainbow Trout! That's hilarious. Dude, the hot chick is *hilarious!*"

Somehow I had been upgraded from a babe to a chick.

My parents would be so proud.

"So have you guys been able to see the sights? I'm thinking about booking a tour tomorrow."

Hint, hint.

"Absolutely. There's an amazing pagoda on top of a hill called Wat Phnom. Have you heard of it?"

I shook my head.

"Well, back in the thirteen hundreds it's believed that the Lady Penh retrieved a tree from the river and found four statues inside."

"Don't bore her, Wes." Aaron lowered his voice, but it was still loud enough for everyone around us to hear him. "Cuz if you do that then we'll *never* see her again!"

"I'm not bored," I promised, letting my fingers travel closer toward the ring of condensation Wesley's drink had left behind on the bar. "I'd love to hear more about this temple."

Wesley shot Aaron a look of superiority, but his buddy was so focused on trying to flag down the bartender that he missed it entirely.

"The Lady Penh has a shrine at the temple where people bring her offerings."

"Pretty nice gig, if you can get it," I mused. "Find some statues and then enjoy centuries of presents. Sounds almost too good to be true."

Then again, in my experience, finding Buddha statues where they don't belong only served to create a world of trouble.

Some people have all the luck.

Aaron scooted closer to me, and I began trying to breathe exclusively through my mouth just to block out his cologne. "Some things you just have to see to believe, Lake."

Well, that was forward of him.

"Sounds like I will have to see that temple for myself. Although I wouldn't necessarily say no to a little company."

"I can take you," Wesley said eagerly. "I make a really great tour guide."

"*So* true," Aaron seconded. "Wes is just like the History Channel except he's *real*."

This was getting me nowhere. It had been crazy of me to expect anything else out of the situation. I mean, what? I thought I'd instantly spot both an exclusive VIP table corded off from the rest of the room and a framed picture behind the bar proclaiming it the finest den for drug dealers since 1989?

As if *anything* had ever come that easily to me.

For all I knew, I wasn't even scouting out the right hotel. Rithisak Sovann might prefer even swankier accommodations during the downtimes when he wasn't actively expanding his drug territory. It was still entirely possible that he had nothing to do with Neal's situation.

That my desperation for a lead had me lunging at shadows.

I lifted my glass in an ironic mock salute, while I tried to suppress my sudden surge of panic. "To keeping it real, then."

"I like the sound of that."

I glanced over my shoulder to see yet another member of what I assumed was the Brookes and Merriweather team giving me a slow once-over. The newest addition pulled off a bold red power tie nicely and looked like he would have no trouble following Ben's *What happens in Cambodia stays in Cambodia* rule.

All I wanted to do was slide off the barstool and call it a night. Instead, I cranked up the megawattage on my smile. "I take it this is another one of your friends?"

"Joel, this is Lake. She writes for *Rolling Stone* magazine."

I fought the insane urge to laugh in Joel's face at the ridiculousness of the situation.

A high school girl walks into a bar with three lawyers . . . It sounded like the setup for a bad joke.

And yet there I was, sipping my wine at the counter and looking for any sign of trouble while the guys engaged in some good-natured ribbing. Well, most of it was good-natured. There was definitely some tension as they each fought to monopolize my interest. As the evening progressed, I was regaled with stories that ranged from perfectly thrown spirals and game-winning touchdowns to brilliant legal maneuvers.

"So, what have you guys been working on here?" I asked lightly, hoping to steer the topic of conversation away from Aaron's fifth-grade spelling bee. "Is there a top-secret lawsuit or something?"

"No," Wesley laughed. "I wish! We're all assisting on a fairly standard merger right now."

"It's not *standard*." Aaron reached for another beer, only to have Joel intercept him. "*Hey!* Not cool, man."

"What do you think, Joel?" I asked, as though I actually cared about his opinion of some merger that had *nothing* to do with me. "Have the negotiations seemed unusual to you?"

His mouth spread into a broad grin. "You mean *more* unusual than conducting our business here instead of in the U.S.

because the guy who owns this place is on the no-fly list? Something like that?"

Something *exactly* like that was what I had been hoping to hear.

It all made so much sense too. Of course anyone infamous for their ties to the drug trade would not be welcomed into America with open arms. Rithisak Sovann's reputation for waving around firearms probably hadn't helped the situation either. And since the lawyers at Brookes and Merriweather couldn't bring the drug tycoon/hotel owner to the U.S., Mr. Sovann was enjoying his home-court advantage.

Probably.

My theory was definitely based on conjecture . . . but that didn't make me wrong.

It just meant that I needed to score an introduction to a drug lord and finally get some definitive answers.

Luckily for me, I knew three guys who would all happily jump at the chance to do me a solid, even if a certain high school boy—like, oh, I dunno, *Houston*—started yelling about how we'd be taking crazy risks for no good reason.

I just needed to do a little more sleuthing before sharing my plan with the gang.

Which was why I took one deep breath before I really got the party started.

Chapter 24

I wasn't drunk—I'd barely even touched my second glass of wine—but something was definitely wrong with me.

The adrenaline rush from playing the part of sophisticated Lake Scott should have peaked hours earlier. I couldn't figure out what had me feeling all warm and bubbly on the inside. But I wasn't sure I cared. Some dim part of my mind kept screaming that I needed to raise my guard and get the hell out of there, but the *why* remained unclear.

Why leave when tugging Wes out onto the dance floor by his tie felt so right?

Years spent fighting for control had never seemed so exhausting. Daunting. Meaningless. The music pulsed through me until I felt positively electric. The urge to dance had never been so strong as I writhed to the vibration of the bass.

This was what I had been missing, the freedom to move my body the way *I* wanted. Not because it was a staged performance for the benefit of others.

Just for me.

Grinning foolishly, I gave myself over to the music. It didn't matter that Wesley hadn't mastered anything beyond the awkward middle-school-level sway that should barely qualify as "dancing." It didn't bother me. I kept right on gyrating even when he mumbled something about needing a drink and moved away.

I didn't need anyone.

It should have seemed so obvious to me. I had lost count of the times I'd thought those exact words over the past few years. But they had never been true before.

There had been plenty of nights when all I'd wanted was to have my parents tell me that they loved me, without any endgame or elaborate point-tallying system in mind. *You know I love you, Chelsea. . . . I just wish you would try to meet your potential.*

Your mother and I both think sending you abroad is for the best.

Nobody will ever love you as much as I do.

I shook off the jumble of voices from my past and blinked in surprise at the guy dancing with me. I didn't remember him. I couldn't have picked him out of a police lineup if my life depended on it and yet his limbs were entangled with mine.

And I had no idea how that had happened.

Stumbling away from him, I accidentally jarred a woman who looked to be in her mid-thirties.

"Sorry, I have to . . ." My words dried up as I realized that nobody was listening.

Most of the strangers crowded around me seemed like perfectly friendly travelers who were just hoping to collect stories about what a good time they'd had on their vacation. They probably wanted to tell all their friends that in Cambodia you didn't even have to leave the hotel to find a crazy party. The rest happened so quickly, it felt like a blur of movement. Couches and tables were pushed aside as the crowd thickened and the bartender was slammed by drink orders.

Half of the people waiting in line were probably looking only for plausible deniability before they joined the fray.

The whole thing was insane.

Somehow the sophisticated hotel bar had been transformed into a nightclub that had already hit full capacity with no sign of quieting.

None of which had been part of my plan.

As I twisted away from yet another stranger, I desperately searched the crowd for a familiar face. In that moment I would have even welcomed a vision of Logan walking toward me so that I could dismiss it as another one of my seriously messed-up dreams. Even waking up in a bathtub to Houston's dire threats about girls who oversleep their alarm clocks sounded pretty good to me.

No such luck.

There were too many people blocking my view of the bar for me to catch even a glimpse of Houston; I could only assume that he was still doing his best bodyguard imitation. Then again, it was entirely possible that this new mess of mine had irritated him into bailing once and for all.

I craned my neck for a better look and gasped as cold beer sloshed my neck, trickling down the front of my dress and soaking into my bra.

This wasn't even remotely fun anymore.

Not when I could feel strange hands touching me, my shoulders mostly, but someone grazed my stomach before trying to cop a feel. I couldn't make it stop. There were too many people pressed against me. Too many laughing faces everywhere I turned. Too many memories.

I couldn't even distinguish the flashbacks from a haunting sense of déjà vu.

The high school parties I had once crashed with Logan, Ashley, and Steffani had started this way too: drinks, flirting, dancing, and then an overwhelming sense of panic when the crowds pressed too close. But I hadn't wanted the girls to think I was intimidated by *anything* so I had lied.

Oh yeah, I'm fine! I love this song! I just need to get another drink. . . .

Half of those beverages had been discreetly tipped into potted plants and bathroom sinks.

But the other half I had sipped and swallowed down.

I had needed my boyfriend to pull me into a secluded corner and focus on making everything a bit better, one meltingly slow kiss at a time . . . but Logan had usually been too busy helping everyone else to realize that his girlfriend was coming unraveled.

Then one night I started wondering if my boyfriend preferred confiscating car keys from drunken strangers because he was no longer interested in me.

By the time I had downed a couple of drinks, I was convinced that he wanted to break up but couldn't say the words to my face.

Jake had started grinding with me when I was staring at the bottom of my third drink. From there the night got a little fuzzy. I remember thinking that I wasn't doing anything wrong, not when Logan had practically ignored me the whole evening.

And being flattered that an older high school guy would be interested in *me*.

Now I lurched unsteadily toward the bar, no longer even trying to apologize as I attempted to escape the crowd, the memories, and an overwhelming sense of shame that I'd been so determined to make someone—anyone—love me that I had lost myself.

That it could still happen to me again.

Sweat dripped down my back, and all I wanted to do was shower away the stickiness of the spilled beer and chug water until I felt clean inside. But I couldn't seem to find a way out.

Not with a throng of flailing bodies surrounding me, blocking me in. I only grew increasingly claustrophobic when the world started spinning.

Oh yeah, something was definitely wrong.

Panic flaring, I raised my arms as if I were playing a drunken version of Marco Polo and tried to stumble my way to freedom . . . only to be halted by two strong hands that gripped my shoulders. I couldn't manage more than some feeble thrashing.

"Calm down, Chelsea. Breathe!"

The familiar voice had my arms going all tingly and my knees weakening. It was the alcohol, a distant part of me reasoned. A dangerous combination of alcohol, adrenaline, claustrophobia, and flashbacks.

That had to be the reason.

"Houston." I gasped for breath as he forcibly pulled me away from all the flailing limbs and sweaty bodies. "I don't feel so good."

Although the way he cradled me against his chest and began gently stroking my back, as if the wet material wasn't entirely disgusting, that felt beyond good. My panic began to ebb away because I knew that I was safe. Houston wouldn't let anyone hurt me.

Even if he wanted to strangle me himself on a semi-regular basis.

"Hey, man, take your hands off Lake!" Aaron pushed his way out of the crowd behind us and succeeded only in jostling me forward.

Houston stopped walking and cupped my face with his hands, but I didn't think it had anything to do with following Aaron's instruction. Not when he stared even more intently at me than usual. Some emotion swirled around in his eyes but vanished behind a cold, hard mask before I could figure it out.

"I'm making sure she's okay," Houston replied coolly.

"Yeah? Well, keep your hands to yourself!"

Which seemed a little over the top to me considering that Houston's hands hadn't strayed anywhere all that interesting. Much to my chagrin.

"Is there a problem here?" Wes asked, finally making it through the crowd and appearing at my side. "Is this guy bothering you, Lake?"

My head felt heavy, but I forced myself to mumble, "Fine. Sleepy."

"No, she's *not* fine." Houston's voice held barely contained anger, but his hands remained gentle. "She nearly collapsed out there."

"From one glass of wine?" Aaron said skeptically. "I doubt it. Buzzed maybe, but unless she's allergic, she shouldn't be more than that."

Houston frog-marched me over to an empty chair before he turned to the two lawyers. That's when reasonable, rational, intelligent, Student of the Year, *let's think this through* Houston? Yeah, he punched Aaron right in the face.

It was epic.

His fist connected with Aaron's jaw, snapping back his head just like in an old-time western. Except in the movies, the hero usually doesn't start shaking out his hand and yelling, "Damn, that *hurt!*" And usually the bad guy doesn't glare and say, "I'm going to sue you, asshole," before lashing out with a left hook of his own.

I started yelling for help before Houston even hit the floor.

Nobody appeared willing to intercede. I caught a few people taking photos of the brawl on their phones and shouts of "Fight! Fight! Fight!" rang throughout the bar while Aaron and Houston rolled around in a tangle of thrashing limbs.

I grabbed desperately at Houston's jacket, but he refused to release his grip on Aaron's leg.

"Houston! Knock it off!"

"Not. Now. Chelsea," he grunted. "I'm busy."

I tugged again and very nearly got an elbow in the stomach for my efforts. "Somebody help me!"

Wesley stared at the three of us on the floor in confusion. "Chelsea? You said your name was Lake."

Because it was really important for us to get that *cleared up in the middle of a fistfight.*

"It's a nickname," I snapped angrily. Houston no longer had the advantage of surprise working for him, and Aaron was starting to get into the swing of it. *"Help me break them up!"*

Wesley clearly didn't want to intercede, but through more luck than skill he managed to pull Aaron back a few steps. "How do you even know him?"

"He's my photographer, okay?"

"Oh."

That's when he actually put some muscle into separating the two lunatics. Typical. Wes didn't want to run the risk of getting caught in the crosshairs of a right hook if he didn't think he had a shot with me. I had a feeling that wouldn't last if I happened to mention the illegal age gap separating high school from *law school.*

The words "statutory rape" would effectively squash any interest the lawyers had in me, which made the prospect of blurting it out awfully tempting. If I hadn't suspected that Wesley was my ticket in with Rithisak Sovann, I would've marched Houston right over to the elevators without so much as a wave good-bye.

Instead, I maneuvered it so that the parting shot Houston kept trying to throw at Aaron would have to go through me.

"Out of the way, princess!"

"Earth to Houston," I hissed, grabbing onto his shoulders. *"Snap out of it.* You're better than this!"

The words weren't part of some kind of bizarre attempt to flirt him out of prolonging his fistfight. They were the truth. But then I noticed the way the muscles in Houston's shoulders contracted and strained against my hands. No wonder he kept himself so controlled all the time: When he actually let loose, he was all pulsing anger and jagged frustration.

And then he snapped.

I'm not sure what happened. One second, his scorching green-eyed death glare was focused solely on Aaron's face, and the next, his eyes had widened in near panic while his arms instinctively slammed me against his body.

And then he was kissing me.

Chapter 25

I went all gooey.

Instead of shoving him away, I let my fingers go on a little expedition, moving upward from his shoulder blades until I felt the silky ends of his hair. Which may have been when I started kissing him right back.

There was no easing into it, no meltingly slow anything. This kiss contained an edge of insanity that had me fervently hoping it would never stop. That he wouldn't think about any one of a dozen reasons why we wouldn't make a good couple, and pull away.

Because with his lips against mine, I thought I could come up with just as many reasons to give it a shot.

Houston didn't pull away.

Instead, he bent to my ear and whispered, "Keep your head down, princess. We've got company."

No kidding. Right before his tongue had investigated my mouth, he'd personally sucker punched some of that company in the face. If he'd wanted to avoid a scene, he should have rethought that one. I just hoped Ben wasn't among our witnesses or neither of us would ever hear the end of it.

"You really need to back off, man!" Wesley's timing couldn't have been worse. I was in no mood to deal with any more male ego competitions.

Especially when I was starting to feel slightly nauseous.

Houston didn't let go of me entirely, but I could feel the barrier between us go right back up.

"You're going to lower your voice while we walk out of here. Otherwise I am going to make sure everyone knows that you drugged my friend," Houston growled.

Oh god.

Now I really needed to hurl.

Except . . . it didn't make any sense. I had watched my glass of wine the whole time, and it wasn't like there were that many other ways to secretly drug me.

Wesley rubbed his forehead as if he were fighting back a killer migraine. "Holy shit," he murmured under his breath, almost like a benediction.

He'd better hope that the patron saint of wimps was feeling charitable toward him because I certainly wasn't.

"We didn't drug her. I swear, I'd never do something like that, and neither would Aaron or Joel."

Aaron nodded dumbly, but let Wesley do all the talking. Probably because he didn't want any more punches thrown in his direction.

"Look, we can't afford any trouble during our merger with Rithisak Sovann. You may never have heard of him, but believe me, he's a really big freaking deal."

Houston stiffened, and I wasn't sure if it was because Wesley had mentioned the drug dealer we were trying to track down or because of the handful of guys in dark suits heading toward us across the lobby, but either way he kept his voice low.

"I'm seeing her back to her room," Houston informed Aaron and Wesley as he not-so-gently shoved me toward the exit. "Come near her again and I will make your life a living hell."

"Ignore him, Wes," I put in. "Suite seventeen. Anytime. Sightseeing."

"Shut up, Chelsea." Houston looked as deranged as the guy on his "No edge!" shirt as he picked up the pace. "For the love of everything holy, *keep your mouth shut.*"

"That's—"

"*Shut!*"

I harrumphed, but with Houston's arm pressing tightly against my stomach, that was about the extent of the protest I could manage. So I kept my silence all the way to the elevator, where he finally released me and jabbed angrily at the button for the sixth floor.

"Can I talk n—"

"No."

Okay, that was taking his protector-y alpha-man stuff too far. I mean, the caveman approach back in the bar had been kinda nice, but I hadn't expected it to last this long. Yanking me into a blisteringly hot kiss? Awesome. Treating me like a misbehaving toddler? Not so much.

And yet I couldn't stop myself from hoping that as soon as we reached the privacy of our now-deserted hotel suite, he'd start kissing me again and we'd . . . pick up where we left off. Except when we got inside, Houston didn't appear even remotely interested in reliving any part of our bar experience.

He just handed me a bottled water from the overpriced minibar as I slipped out of my heels.

"I thought you said you could take care of yourself."

I stared at him in confusion. "I'm fine."

"Oh *right*," Houston snorted in disgust. "I forgot. Chelsea Halloway is *always* fine. Thugs open fire at her? She's fine. Strangers spike her drink? No big deal. Well, guess what, princess? Everything is not fine!"

"They didn't drug me, Houston."

"Then do you want to explain to me why after one drink with them you nearly collapsed on the dance floor? Why your eyes are still dilated? If you have any handy explanations, I would really love to hear them right about now."

"I had a panic attack, okay? My claustrophobia kicked in big-time, and I kind of freaked out. But I really am fine now."

Houston raked a hand through his hair while I pretended not to think about how soft it had felt to touch. My fingers itched to toy with the strands by the nape of his neck again. "And the dilated pupils?"

"I don't know!" I crossed my arms. "It was fairly dark in there. Maybe that affected them or something?"

He looked fairly unconvinced but seemed willing to temporarily table the issue. "You know that water will hydrate you a whole lot faster if you actually drink it."

I took a large gulp just to keep the peace. "I thought you didn't believe in using the minibar."

"I also don't believe in putting you in harm's way. Looks like I've done all sorts of compromising lately."

It was strange thinking of Houston as willing to bend on anything, especially since his words had such a sarcastic bite to them. But truthfully, he'd been a much better team player than I had.

It was way past time for me to reciprocate.

"Everything is going according to plan, Houston. In fact, it's coming together even better than I could've hoped—your bar fight being the one notable exception. We *know* that Rithisak is right here! We're halfway home already. We make the trade and get out. End of story."

"Oh, is that all? I'm so glad everything I've ever said to you has fallen on deaf ears. Really. That's just"—he punched his right fist into his left palm and winced at the jolt of pain—"freaking perfect."

My anger spiked. *Deaf ears?* "Just because I don't always agree with you doesn't mean I don't *listen!*"

"So you heard the part about this being a suicide mission, and you still made a scene in the bar? I'm sure the thugs that kicked the crap out of Neal really enjoyed your show, princess. I'm pretty sure at least one of them saw you with me. So congratulations: You just made their job a whole lot easier. Hell, you even shared our *room number!*"

And that's when the very last bit of my happy *he kissed me* glow disappeared. Because what I'd mistaken for passion was nothing more than his anger and frustration over the situation. Actually, maybe there was a bit of panic thrown into the mix too. The fear that we would be identified at any moment seemed like strong motivation to me.

I had just been kidding myself into thinking it was some-thing different. That he enjoyed the odd tug of attraction be-tween us because we challenged each other. I had stupidly dared to hope that this amazing guy who had seen me at my very worst still accepted me.

Still wanted to kiss *me*.

But Houston had only planted one on me because he needed to shield my face from a thug. There had been no af-fection involved. No real attraction either. Just his way of ful-filling a promise to my dad that he probably continued regretting even as our tongues tangled.

And once again, I'd been too stupid to see it coming.

Stupid, stupid Chelsea.

I sucked in an unsteady breath before raising my chin in defiance. "My plan is working. And the last time I checked, disagreeing with you wasn't a crime."

"Want to know what is illegal, princess? Possession of nar-cotics. Drug trafficking. If anything goes wrong with your plan, those are the charges we could be facing!"

"What is this really about, Houston?" I asked quietly. The silence following his last outburst made my words resonate through the room. "I told you my plan. I didn't hide it. You know I'm here to get Neal so . . . is this about the kiss?"

His face became an expressionless mask, but I refused to take the question back. I had to hear it from him that there was absolutely nothing between us. That it had all been in my head. That once again I'd recklessly developed feelings for yet another unattainable guy who wanted to be rid of me.

"Is this about the dancing?" I persisted. "Or the flirting? Or the fight? You're acting like I deviated wildly from the plan, but I *didn't*. I kept my word. So . . . what is this about?"

Houston's green eyes bored into me, and for a second I thought my first instinct was right. That I'd finally found someone who didn't just see the glossy image I tried so hard to present but the girl underneath that layer of swagger and makeup.

"Nothing."

That one word from Houston landed like a direct blow. My rib cage ached fiercely as the pain in my heart radiated outward until it consumed my whole body.

I nodded slowly. "Nothing. Fine. When we get back to Oregon we can both pretend that you didn't kiss me when you thought I was drugged."

Houston looked away. "I didn't think I had a whole lot of choices, Chelsea. I needed to get you out of there unseen. But . . . I'm sorry. It never should have happened."

The satisfaction I felt in being right about something didn't even begin to soften the sharp sting of rejection.

"You won't get any objection from me, cowboy. I thought we might be able to make it through this thing as friends but . . . well, so much for that plan. Now if you don't mind, I have a suite to enjoy."

Then I headed straight for the bathroom and tried to shower off the sticky remnants of beer and sweat along with the awful sensation that no matter how hard I scrubbed, I would never be clean.

Chapter 26

I couldn't avoid Houston.

He kept handing me bottled water and insisting that I take it easy. It might have annoyed me how easily he was able to put aside our seven-minutes-in-heaven moment if he hadn't been so *nice* in the immediate aftermath. He even handed me the television remote and didn't snatch it back when I settled on some really terrible reality shows.

The kind that not even Jane would be willing to watch with me.

And when I started laughing at his snarky running commentary, he leaned back and seemed to honestly start enjoying himself as well.

If that was an act too, he had a much brighter future in Hollywood than I did.

Then again, Houston probably thought that our one measly kiss had messed with my head. On the list of things *not* to do with your favorite professor's high school daughter, kissing her while she might be under the influence had to be ranked pretty high up there.

Telling her that the whole thing meant nothing, however . . . yeah, he didn't seem to have any regrets on that score.

Still, if he wanted to pretend that we had shared nothing more than a few minutes in a crowded bar, he wouldn't hear any complaints from me. I played it cool as the others began returning to the room because I had significantly bigger problems to occupy my time than deciphering a kiss-and-run college boy.

Just off the top of my head, oh right: *I had a gun-toting drug tycoon to bribe.*

"So I think my trip to the bar paid off. I've got a lead," I announced when Ben finally strolled into the room, towel dangling around his neck, looking ridiculously good in his damp board shorts. Amy dropped the book she had borrowed from the book exchange downstairs.

"Oh, really?" Ben plopped down in the empty sofa chair right near where the book had landed. Without bothering even to glance at the cover, he handed it back to a blushing Amy, who quickly tucked it into the crook of her arm. I had no doubt the English major would have her nose buried back in the pages the instant our meeting was over.

Might as well get right to the point.

"Yeah, I went to the bar and found a great source. There's a guy who—"

"Found a source?" Houston crossed his arms in annoyance. "That's your euphemism for flirting with total strangers and then nearly collapsing in a crowd of people? Good to know."

Ouch.

I kept my expression neutral. "I flirted. It worked. I'm fine. Get over it. And now we know that there are a bunch of lawyers here planning a merger with, drumroll please—Rithisak Sovann."

Liz streaked gold nail polish on top of her already colorful manicure. "That's more than I was able to get. Everything was pretty boring in the gym. Just your basic hotel full of tourists." She blew delicately on her left hand before turning to Ben. "What about you?"

"I met several rather extraordinary travelers." Ben's quick-fire smirk left little doubt that he'd been amply entertained by his time spent poolside. "I didn't learn anything Neal-related though. Can we go back to Chelsea? I think we all need a more detailed account about this source of hers."

I wasn't sure if Ben realized that he was riling up his best friend, or if he was purposely overlooking that fact. Either way, Houston tensed.

But there was no reason I couldn't talk about it.

Since "nothing" had happened, I had nothing to hide.

Although that didn't mean I wanted Ben prying too closely into my private life, especially since it was so obviously going nowhere. And the last thing I needed was for someone to forget the whole *What happens in Cambodia stays in Cambodia* rule and mention my not-so-little panic attack to my dad. So I merely shot him my most cryptic half-smile.

"A lady doesn't kiss and tell."

And neither does a gentleman. I hoped Houston was picking up on the subtext written in my steely-eyed gaze. If he told *anyone* about the kiss, which meant exactly nothing to him, I'd have to kill him.

"Um, Chelsea? You still with us?" Amy waved her hand in front of my face, and I tried to play off my absentmindedness with a dreamy smile.

"Sorry. I was just thinking about Wesley. I think you guys are going to like him. He's very sweet. And he's got this whole experienced-older-guy thing going for him." I would have sighed gustily, but I didn't want to oversell it.

I didn't think any further embellishments were necessary either.

Houston's gritted teeth made it pretty clear that he had no trouble understanding my message: *Plenty of other fish in the sea for me to choose from. I don't need you.*

Maybe he would think of *that* the next time he felt obligated to stick his tongue in my mouth.

"Yeah, he's a real keeper," Houston growled. "Too bad you didn't get his number. Such a shame. Oh well."

"I'm pretty sure Wesley still wants to show me the temples here." I winked at Amy just to see if I could make her blush. "We had a real, um . . . spiritual connection."

Amy burst out laughing. "Of course you did, Chelsea. Why does that not surprise me at all?"

Maybe because I was an even better actress than most people thought.

"Weasel isn't showing you anything."

"I don't think that's your decision to make, cowboy."

Liz coughed. "I thought you guys were finally getting along. Using your words. Playing nice. Do you want us to leave the room again? We can hang out in the lobby until you clear the air."

"Or the pool," Ben suggested. "There might be some potential sources of information that I've overlooked there."

"Houston and I don't have a problem." Ben snickered, and I realized that once again my words were a little too close to *Apollo 13*. "Seriously. Everything's fine, guys."

Liz never glanced up from her fingernails. "Doesn't look that way to me."

"Well, looks can be deceiving. Isn't that right, Houston?"

He stared at me in silence, and for one achingly long moment I imagined how it would feel if he actually shooed everyone out and agreed to discuss the Cambodian-sized spider in the room.

Good. It would feel so freaking good.

"Yeah," he said at last. "Looks can be deceiving."

Or not.

"There you have it: We agree on something. My date with Wesley probably won't happen anyway, because none of us are going to be in Cambodia much longer. All we need to do is send Rithisak Sovann a message during the merger meeting, and we can be on the next flight out of here."

Ben tilted his head and began whacking his ear as if it was waterlogged. "You want us to pass a note to a known drug lord in the middle of a private meeting? We're not exactly in middle school anymore, Chelsea."

"So what? It sounds like fun to me!" Amy's enthusiastic smile never faltered.

"Oh, Amy. If that's your idea of fun, we need to get you out more often. A lot more often."

It was *my* idea and even I wasn't looking forward to it.

"What? I liked passing notes in middle school. Except for the ones with the check boxes to find out if someone liked you back. Those were brutal. But since we don't care if a drug lord *likes* us, I think it'll be fun!" Amy said. "Plus I'm kind of curious to see what a merger looks like in real life. Probably not all that different from the search committee to find a new professor for the history department, but—"

"We get it." I couldn't resist teasing her a little. "You're a geek extraordinaire with the credentials to prove it."

Amy seemed to consider that for a moment before nodding. "Well . . . yes."

"So how do you feel about taking the lead with this one?"

Her eyes widened, and for one second I was sure she'd stutter out an apology. Something short and sweet along the lines of *Thanks, but I'd much rather not.* Amy was all Bambi eyes and friendship bracelets and needlepoint and romance novels—the last thing she wanted was to be the one in charge of contacting a drug lord.

Or so I thought until I saw steely determination underlying the softness. "What do I have to do?"

I grinned. "Just be yourself."

The rest of us could take it from there.

Chapter 27

I half expected Amy to have changed her mind by the next morning.

But not only was she determined to take charge of the situation, she actually burst out laughing when I called it a "high risk" scenario that warranted backup and asked which action movie I was quoting now.

Apparently, I'd lost my intimidating edge.

I didn't think that was a good thing. Maybe Amy's resolve hadn't weakened overnight, but that didn't mean I wasn't desperately searching for a better alternative. Something that didn't involve any of my friends going within one hundred yards of Cambodia's most notorious drug-dealing psychopath.

I never should have mentioned the idea in the first place. Not when there were so many ways for everything to go horribly wrong. Considering the way my simple bar excursion the night before had included both a full-blown panic attack and a brawl, I should have insisted that we sit tight. We knew for a fact that Rithisak Sovann was in the building. There was no reason we couldn't wait for the team of reporters Jane insisted were en route to break the story.

I didn't have to keep scheming.

Amy didn't have to carry out one of my riskier plans.

Except I couldn't shake the feeling that time was running out for Neal in prison. Even if the promised reporters magically showed up within the next few of hours, their hands might still be tied. A group of American students abroad holing up with a Buddha full of drugs while they waited to prove their teacher's innocence didn't exactly scream Pulitzer Prize material. They needed actual *news* to cover. Something a lot more conclusive than our speculation that Rithisak Sovann was up to no good.

And since I didn't want that story to include Neal's death, Amy was our best bet.

We needed someone who could pass for a hotel employee interrupting the meeting to discreetly slip Rithisak Sovann a note before hightailing it out of there. Liz's multicolored hair was a dead giveaway that she didn't belong, and Ben's muscular physique tended to catch a few too many female eyes. Maybe Houston could have pulled it off if he hadn't started a fistfight with Aaron the night before.

Somehow I doubted Aaron or Wesley would forget about that anytime soon.

So it had to be Amy.

"Are you sure you want to do this?" I asked her for what had to be the millionth time.

Amy glowered at me, which didn't really produce the intended effect because even irritation looked cute on her. "Absolutely. Now zip it, Chelsea."

"But—"

"I'm fully capable of making up my own mind, *thank you very much!* I don't need babying any more than you do, Chelsea."

That finally shut me up. Amy was right. I hated to admit it, but I was acting even worse than Houston. She didn't need me giving my best impression of a worried mother hen clucking over her baby chick. And I was the last person to be denying anyone an opportunity to face down their fears.

To prove to herself that she was so much more than the handful of descriptors other people applied to her.

"It'll take me fifteen minutes to slip into the meeting." Amy grinned at Liz. "Maybe less. Time me, okay?"

And then with a last cheery wave, she trotted off to the elevator as if she didn't have a care in the world . . . or a blackmail letter for a drug lord.

It was the most stressful fifteen minutes of my life. The knot of fear in my stomach clenched tighter with each passing second as I imagined what Amy was doing.

By now she should have found the conference door.

I ran through the basic ballet positions five times before I allowed myself to glance at my watch again.

Okay, she should be opening the door and heading straight for the man at the head of the table. A simple "Excuse me, Mr. Sovann. I was asked to deliver this to you," should do the trick.

First position. Third position. Fifth position. *Brisé.*

Amy was heading swiftly for the exit. She wasn't running, not even speed-walking. She just kept moving with a deliberate sense of purpose toward the door . . . then she pushed it open . . . closed it behind her . . . and maintained that speed until she spotted the nearest elevator.

Grand plié. Fifth position. Third position. *Coupé.*

That's when she finally started running.

She sprinted into the elevator, pressed every single button, but only rode up one floor before taking the stairs the rest of the way up.

Any minute now she would be knocking on the door, her face flushed from exertion, adrenaline, and an overwhelming sense of achievement. She would grin up at us and say the most annoying sentence ever spoken, "I told you so!"

Any minute now . . .

"You're making me even more nervous, Chelsea!" Liz

twirled a strand of blue hair around one of her fingers. "Do you think you could . . . stop?"

Not really, but I was willing to give it a shot.

"Fine, do you have a better way to pass the time, Liz? Anything. I'm open to suggestions."

"Not really, no."

"I've got an idea. Why don't we play seven minutes in heaven?" Ben suggested.

None of us so much as batted an eye. "That's not helping, Ben."

"Are you sure? I think it's a brilliant idea. What about spin the bottle? That one's a *classic*."

"Shut up, man," Houston advised.

Ben threw his hands in the air. "*Seriously?* It's like a freaking morgue in here. Amy's delivering a message in the middle of a business meeting, not trying to infiltrate Al-Qaeda. Let's keep things in perspective here, people."

Liz and Houston both ignored him and focused on me instead.

"Do you think it's going to work, Chelsea?" Liz asked in the same low, husky voice that I'd only heard once before when she'd mentioned Sara's parents.

I resisted the urge to say something snarky like *You think I know the answer to that? I don't know anything. Just ask Houston, he can confirm that for you!* There was absolutely nothing to be gained by confessing my fears. I would only succeed in freaking out the group, and since I was betting that even Ben was secretly worried, that didn't seem fair to anyone.

Houston looked like he was nearing his breaking point. The last time I'd seen him this on edge he had kissed me like the world was ending. So I wasn't exactly sure what to expect. Especially since his bruised hand kept clenching into a fist, only to be forcibly relaxed when he caught himself.

"She should be here by now." Houston growled as he made himself comfortable in one of the sofa chairs and claimed my laptop from a nearby table.

"Hey! That's mine!"

He ignored me entirely and clicked on the most recent item in my email account. "Oh look. Jane says that there are *definitely* reporters headed our way. Apparently, they'll be here by tomorrow evening at the latest. She doesn't want us to do anything rash before they arrive. If Amy doesn't get here within the next five minutes, I think we should probably go ahead and tell Jane that her warning came a little too late."

"You're reading my emails now?" My blood began to boil. "*Seriously?* That's an invasion of privacy!"

"Yeah? Feel free to ask Weasel to sue me after your date."

"Okay, I'm sick of this," Ben said, cutting through the tension in the room. "Houston, you're acting like a jackass. Chelsea . . . you're not helping matters either. Now could you both *please* deal with your crap and move on?"

I opened my mouth to point out that *I* wasn't the one poking around in anyone else's business, but I was cut off by a hesitant series of knocks on our hotel door.

Everyone froze before we collectively breathed in relief.

Amy was back. It had taken her exactly twenty-three minutes to safely deliver the message—1,380 excruciatingly long seconds during which we'd been going out of our freaking minds.

But everything was going to be fine now that she was back.

Still, I had expected her to play it up. At the very least, I thought she would hiss, "It's me!" or go for a dramatic, "I'm baaaack!"

Considering that this was her big moment of victory, she wasn't making much of an entrance. So instead of unhooking the security chain, flinging the door open, and launching myself at Amy, I went up on tiptoe to spy through the peephole. Better safe than . . . well, dead.

Not Amy.

I didn't even have time to register my disappointment because Liz knocked me out of the way. "What are you waiting for? Let her—who are *you?*"

Aaron smiled sheepishly and then winced in pain. The bruise Houston had given him the night before was a vivid shade of red. "Is this a bad time, Lake?"

Oh yeah, he could say that again.

"You don't have to call security," Aaron continued quickly. "I'm not here to make any trouble, Lake. I just came to apologize for last night. I have no idea how you could have been drugged, but I swear nobody at Brookes and Merriweather had anything to do with it."

"Lake?" Ben murmured questioningly in my ear.

I barely jerked my head in assent, knowing that Ben would accept my new nickname without comment as long as Aaron was in the vicinity.

"I know you guys didn't, Aaron. I had . . . well, let's just call it an intense moment of claustrophobia, and my colleague jumped to the wrong conclusion. That happens more often than not with him."

I could feel Houston's glare burning into my back from where he stood behind me.

Luckily, Ben blocked him from Aaron's view.

"So you weren't drugged then?"

I shook my head and felt an absurd urge to smile at the look of relief that suffused his face.

"Not that I know of, Aaron. I'm fine."

His shoulders instantly relaxed. "Good. I was worried that you might not be safe with the guy who dragged you out of there."

I restrained from commenting that it had certainly taken

him long enough to actually check up on me, while Liz peered down the hall in search of Amy. "How did you even find me here?"

"You, uh . . . mentioned your suite number to Wes. So I just thought . . . I'm sorry, this is a bad time, isn't it?"

"Yes. If you don't mind, we're expecting someone," Liz said sharply. "Visiting hours are over."

"Of course. Sorry. I just thought I'd check in while I had the chance."

I watched him turn and begin heading for the elevator, apprehension niggling at me with every step he took.

Something wasn't right. All my instincts were screeching at me to figure it out, because this wasn't a minor inconvenience like driving halfway to Steffani's house only to realize I'd accidentally left my sunglasses at home. This *mattered,* and yet I was totally drawing a blank.

I wondered what Amy would have to say when I told her about . . .

My stomach dropped.

Oh crap.

"*Aaron!*" I yelled, halting him right before he stepped into the elevator. "I was just wondering . . . um, why aren't you holed up with all the other lawyers at your merger? It sounded like a pretty big deal last night."

He shrugged. "The guy we're meeting here requested that we postpone while he handles some other matter. Although *request* is understating it, if you know what I mean."

Liz froze next to me. "Did anything weird happen during the meeting?"

Aaron looked suspiciously at the two of us as he approached our door once more.

"Yeah, I guess. He left shortly after he received some message. Why? What's it to you?"

Oh crap. Oh crap.

I grabbed on to his suit jacket and yanked him inside the

suite before he had time to protest. Liz locked the door and Ben stepped forward protectively.

"Hey, buddy. Good to see you again. How's the jaw today?" Houston's words sounded civil enough, but there was no missing the ice-cold glint in his eyes.

Aaron instinctively drew back. "I'm still pressing charges against you!"

Houston leaned casually against one of the walls as if he didn't have a care in the world. "No, you're not. Because then you will have to explain what exactly you and your buddies were doing buying that second drink for a minor."

Aaron's mouth dropped open comically as he gave me another once-over. "No way."

"Actually . . . this time he's right. It does happen on occasion."

Liz pushed her way forward until she was right in Aaron's face. "We don't have time for this garbage right now. Where is she?"

"Where is *who?*"

"The girl who interrupted your meeting! Brown hair. Brown eyes. Medium build. *Where the hell is she?!*"

Ben interceded before Liz could strangle Aaron with his own tie. "We'll get her back, Liz. I promise," he said gravely.

Aaron stepped back and raised his hands as if he could ward off the craziness. "I have no idea what you guys are talking about, and I hereby state, for the record, that I want nothing to do with any of it. Now if you'll excuse me—"

The guy was already practicing his testimony for the stand. Un-freaking-believable.

"Okay, I need you to listen to me very carefully, Aaron. This—right here—is one of those defining moments in your life. Today you're going to find out whether you're the kind of man who will sit idly by while an innocent girl is killed." I intentionally left out all mention of Neal because I thought my words might have more impact if he pictured the nervous girl who had poked her head into the boardroom only a handful of minutes earlier.

"*Killed?*" Aaron stared at us in disbelief before he burst out laughing. "Good one. Okay, did Joel put you up to this because of the whole email-attachment prank I pulled on him?"

Liz couldn't hold back any longer. "Listen up, dumbass. This isn't a joke. You just negotiated a merger with a *drug dealer.*"

Not the most tactful way to put it, but she definitely got the point across.

Aaron still looked as if he was expecting us to admit the hoax at any moment. "Right. Nice try."

My palms were sweating, and a small voice in my head kept screaming the same sentence.

He has Amy.

He has *Amy.*

He has Amy . . . and it's all your fault.

I numbly forced myself to move toward the closet where I'd not-so-inventively decided to stash the Buddha statue. My lips twisted into a tight smile as I held it out for Aaron's inspection. "See that white powdery stuff at the bottom? That's the heroin my friends' *lives* depend on getting to a whacked-out drug lord. Now let's see if you can use your fancy law degree to figure out how to help us."

He paled noticeably. "This isn't the kind of law I practice."

"And this isn't exactly our idea of a great study-abroad program, but that's life," Houston pointed out drily.

"Although we did get to Skype with Mackenzie Wellesley. That was pretty cool."

Houston, Liz, and I stared at Ben in disbelief.

"*What?* Does she make up for the extreme crappiness we've been through? No. Was it cool getting to talk with her? Hell yes! That's all I'm saying."

Aaron looked at Ben with renewed interest. "You actually spoke to her?"

"Yeah, man. She's Chel . . . *Lake's* best friend."

Okay, so *that* was the biggest lie I'd ever managed to hear with a straight face. But I didn't see any point in correcting Ben when he might have stumbled on a way to motivate Aaron into doing the right thing.

Not that he should need any extra incentive.

Aaron straightened his tie. "Do you, uh, think you could introduce me to her? Mackenzie, I mean."

Not happening in a million years.

"Sure." I gritted out the word. "But first you're going to do a few things for me."

I didn't have too much confidence in my plans anymore.

But I had to try *something*.

Amy's life might depend on it.

Chapter 28

"It's not entirely your fault."

Those were the very last words I ever expected to hear coming from Houston. The guy had practically been going for the world record of times that one person could reasonably say, "I don't think that's a good idea." But instead of rightly blasting me for our current disaster, he was cutting me some slack.

Maybe someone had declared it Opposite Day when I wasn't looking.

"Yes, it is," I said bluntly. "It's *absolutely* my fault. It was my idea, my plan, and if it had worked, I would be taking full credit for its success right about now. Just because it blew up in my face doesn't make it any less mine."

He looked momentarily taken aback, probably because he expected me to embrace anything that made me less culpable for what had gone wrong. But I was done putting on my game face to hide my insecurities. Sure, I could convince most people to fear me, admire me, desire me . . . or at least not want to directly oppose me. But when it came to actual friendships, I only had a handful of real ones. And I'd knowingly just put one of my friends directly in the way of danger.

There was no ignoring that, even if I wanted to try.

"You didn't see this coming," Houston said firmly.

"Well, no kidding. I'm not a psychic, but that doesn't make this any less my fault. I told her to do it."

"*Amy* agreed to go, even knowing the risks. I'm not saying it wasn't stupid. But it's not entirely your fault."

"I made her do it."

Houston's green eyes narrowed. "Let me get this straight: that's no to being a psychic, yes to mind control?"

"This isn't a joke, Houston."

"Oh, I know it's not. It's an unmitigated disaster. But Amy made a choice, and you shouldn't beat yourself up over what happened. You're acting like she's incapable of making up her own mind."

"But—"

"But nothing. Listen up, Chelsea; I'm only saying this once: Maybe I took the responsibilities your dad gave me a little too far."

"*Maybe?*" I crossed my arms. "*That's* your big concession?"

Houston ignored my interruption. "You're not the girl he described or the one I remembered from that party. And I didn't give you the benefit of the doubt, so that part is on me. But I'm not taking the blame for your decisions. You made your choices—hell, we *all* made our choices, and now we've got to deal with the consequences. Together."

But it had to be my fault.

That's the way it worked. Ask anyone. If Chelsea Halloway was around, she was the source of the trouble. I regularly overheard whispers in the hallways about feuds that didn't exist. If someone's boyfriend inexplicably dumped them, within minutes someone was claiming that I'd had a hand in it. The whole thing was absolutely insane. And yet somehow that had become . . . normal. Just part of the price I had to pay for my position as Queen of the Notables. The rationale behind blaming me even started to make sense; when people think you hold all the power, they also think you hold the blame for *everything*.

And maybe somewhere along the way I had bought into my own myth just like everyone else at my school.

Except Houston didn't think Amy's abduction was entirely my fault. I had spent so many years fighting to preserve a fake image of perfection, I had always assumed it would be devastating for anyone to see through the cracks. Instead it came as a relief to know that he didn't expect me to have everything under control. He didn't blame me for being scared and confused.

He just wanted us to deal with the consequences together.

"I have a new idea," I said softly. "It's a risky move, and we don't have to make it. We can sit here and wait for the reporters to show up tomorrow, just the way we all originally agreed. I'm sure they will love getting the details about Amy's disappearance from a lawyer at a prestigious firm. But that's not going to guarantee Amy's safety. This new plan of mine might be reckless, but I still think it's the right call to make for both Amy and Neal. So do you trust me?"

His mouth quirked wryly. "Do I have a choice?"

"Do. You. Trust. Me?" I repeated obstinately. "It's a simple yes or no question, Houston."

He looked right past me as if I were invisible, and I felt my stomach lurch.

"Guys, you might want to come over here. Chelsea has a new plan she wants to share with the class."

Liz glanced up at me from the table where she and Ben had been stress-eating french fries ever since Aaron had left the room with the understanding that we'd be in touch. "What's that?"

"I want to be the hostage negotiator."

The room descended into silence, and I struggled not to fill it with promises I might not be able to keep.

"I know I've screwed up plenty of times before, but I'm asking for one more chance to make this right," I said at last. "I think I need to do this."

Ben spoke around a mouthful of fries. "Better you than me."

Liz nodded in agreement. "I'm with Ben on this one. What do you think, Houston?"

"I think Chelsea's the right pick for the job."

The warmth of those words jolted my system as if I'd just drained a cappuccino in one swallow, but I couldn't allow it to go to my head. Not when I had Amy to focus on. Wiping my sweat-slick palms on my jeans, I reached into my pocket and pulled out my prepaid cell phone. Everything I had heard about this guy suggested he had an aggressive streak and liked to play with guns. If he had shot Amy . . . I shut my eyes and tried to block out the unwanted mental images.

Somehow I would just have to convince him that it was in his best interest to leave her unhurt.

Unless it was too late.

The life might be seeping out of my friend while I waffled over my approach. Her blood could be staining a bathroom floor somewhere in this very hotel and I'd be helpless to stop it. If this panic was what Amy had experienced when she saw the mess I made in the Happy Wonder Hostel, I owed her a billion more apologies.

I closed my eyes and pictured what my mom would say if she could see me panicking over a phone call right now.

You created this mess, Chelsea. So why don't you act like an adult and fix it?

Deep breath in and out.

Okay, I could do that.

Fingers trembling, I dialed Amy's prepaid cell number and put the call on speaker. The ringing filled the room while I forced myself to keep breathing steadily. Any second now . . .

Ring.

Or now . . .

Ring.

Why wasn't anyone picking up?

Ri—

A brusque, heavily accented voice interrupted on the third ring. "Speak."

Okay, so drug dealers didn't waste time on pleasantries. That was fine with me.

"I have an important message to relay to Mr. Sovann," I replied calmly, grateful that my shaking hands couldn't be seen over the phone. "Is he available?"

"Who are you?"

"I'm simply someone trying to fix an accident I believe happened to one of Mr. Sovann's shipments. I'd like to speak directly to him."

There was a brief pause before an even gruffer voice filled the room.

"Who are you? How dare you toy with *me?*"

Oh, snap. That was one very unhappy drug lord I had on the phone.

"Mr. Sovann," I said carefully as my heart rate tripled. "It is an honor to speak with you, sir. My associates mean no disrespect, and we apologize for disrupting your busy schedule."

His voice didn't soften in the slightest. "I do not believe you mean no disrespect. Why else would you send this pathetic *child* to do your bidding?"

There was no mistaking the sound of a palm connecting with flesh and the muffled cry that filled the air.

Amy.

I didn't think it was possible for Liz, Ben, and Houston to look any more panic-stricken, but hearing Amy's pain broadcast into the room did the trick. A distant part of my brain started screaming that I needed to do *something* to stop him. Beg. Plead. *Anything.* But I couldn't let him know just how deeply I cared about Amy without playing right into his hands.

Houston's palm clasped mine as I stared at the phone in horrified speechlessness.

If that simple display of affection had happened a few hours ago I might have tried to analyze whether it indicated friendly support or a more romantic type of interest.

Instead, I just gripped it for all I was worth and focused on keeping my voice steady.

"We meant no disrespect, Mr. Sovann," I repeated. "We needed a way to communicate with you and thought our messenger would draw the least attention to a sensitive matter."

"You thought to threaten me!" The uncontrolled anger in his voice had me clutching Houston's already bruised hand even tighter. He winced slightly but gave me a quick squeeze back.

"Never. We only wish to help you correct a mistake."

My words dangled unanswered, leaving me terrified that he might have grown bored and hung up on us. If that happened, I might as well message Amy's parents so that we could start making funeral arrangements.

"And what of this 'Neal' in your note? Do you not demand that I release him?"

Part of me wanted to tell him to forget it. That I had changed my mind and we only cared about reclaiming our captured messenger. But I couldn't do that to Neal. Not when I had already come this close to gaining his freedom. If I backed off now, it might be too late by the time more official diplomatic efforts were attempted, and Amy's mission would've been for nothing.

Two lives depended on what I said next.

But, y'know, no pressure.

"We simply hope that with your considerable influence, we can free an innocent man."

An appeal to his pride, vanity, and any sense of honor he might possess. If my victory hadn't been so far from assured, I would have been damn pleased with my quick thinking. Mackenzie Wellesley probably could have rattled off some drug-related statistics, but for the first time I was confident that if we failed, it wouldn't be because I wasn't smart enough.

"If I free him, you will return my shipment," Rithisak Sovann murmured thoughtfully, while I did my best not to get ahead of myself . . . or him.

He was considering my proposal, but he hadn't agreed to my terms yet.

"Absolutely."

There was another long pause.

"And what will you give me for the return of your messenger?"

A panicked mewl of terror on the other end of the phone sent my ragged pulse racing even faster. Houston's hand instinctively gave my hand another supportive squeeze.

"Surely," I croaked, "a man of honor would never shoot the messenger."

Oh crap. I didn't need Liz's sharp kick in the shins to remember belatedly that one of the basic rules of hostage negotiating was probably: *Never remind the crazy man with a gun that he has a freaking gun!*

"Your note was for the release of one man. It never said anything about this girl." There was something even more terrifying about his sudden calmness than his blatant anger and hostility. I had absolutely no doubt that a man who had lived through the horrors inflicted on his country, who might have witnessed firsthand the deaths of thousands of his countrymen, had a very different idea of what constituted fair play than I did.

He also didn't appear to have any scruples when it came to getting what he wanted. You don't become a well-known drug dealer and the owner of one of the most luxurious hotels in Cambodia by being nice.

I forced myself to swallow some water so my voice wouldn't crack like a pubescent boy's. "You could release her as a gesture of goodwill."

He chuckled. "She's too fat for most of my customers, but many men like having white women in their collection."

Another loud *smack* and an answering cry of pain rang clearly through the phone.

I froze. I could either call his bluff or fold . . . either tactic ran the risk of leaving Amy equally dead. But something about the cold way he calculated his decisions reminded me of the way I had ruled the Notables at Smith High School. If any girl had the nerve to spread rumors behind my back, I would've decimated her social standing through a whisper campaign of my own creation.

But challenge me head on . . . and I just might have caved.

"Hurt her and the deal is off," I told him clearly. "Half of your package will be found in *your* hotel courtesy of an anonymous tip. That won't be good for your image, right, Mr. Sovann? Particularly with a potential merger in the works. Who knows? The drugs might even be discovered in the very conference room you've been using."

I didn't need a Cambodian translator to understand that I had one seriously pissed-off drug dealer swearing at me.

"I'll call you with further instructions," I said, interrupting him mid-diatribe.

And then I hung up on him while the others looked at me with a mixture of shock, fear, and . . . respect.

Uncomfortable with the intense scrutiny coming at me from every direction, I glanced down at my watch.

"Time for phase two."

Chapter 29

The prepaid cell phones were without a doubt the best purchase I'd ever made, beating out the sea-foam-green jeans that had previously held that distinction by a landslide.

Although there's nothing quite like a great-fitting pair of pants to increase your confidence . . . even when your *to do* list includes meeting up with a renowned drug lord/kidnapper at a holy Buddhist temple.

Okay, so *technically* I was only scouting out the location in preparation for the meeting. But delaying the inevitable until we were ready to make our move didn't magically alleviate my stress, no matter how beautiful the atmosphere or how historic the architecture surrounding me.

It was strange knowing that if Neal had never walked into the wrong room at the worst possible time, the syllabus would have brought us to this very spot. Amy would've been breathing in the heavy scent of incense and laying down offerings like all the other tourists while a new guide with another unpronounceable name showed us around. Liz would have made some crack about orange robes not really being her color; Ben would've inevitably come up with a wildly inappropriate response that would make even Houston laugh in spite of himself. And the whole time Neal would have been encouraging us to take notes for our upcoming final.

Then he'd have taken each of us aside to make sure we weren't struggling with life abroad.

A few weeks ago that would have been my definition of torture, and now I was daydreaming wistfully about imaginary history lectures when I needed to be prepping for my face-off with a drug cartel. Somewhere buried in this mess I suspected I had a really great college admission essay just waiting to be written.

You know, on the off chance that I survived.

The warm pressure of a hand on my shoulder halted my inspection of every nook of the temple that I intended to memorize inside and out in case one seemingly insignificant detail could give me an advantage during an escape. Pasting a warm smile on my face, I looked up expectantly at Wesley.

"I'm, um, glad you came here with me, Lake." He spoke haltingly, as if he wasn't exactly certain how he had ended up giving me that promised tour after the unmitigated disaster of a date we'd shared the night before. "Surprised that Aaron of all people has now suddenly decided to play matchmaker, but really, *really* glad."

I tucked my arm through the crook of his so that we looked like just another couple of tourists strolling around the popular destination, which was part of the reason I'd asked him to join me there: Nobody pays much attention to obnoxiously happy couples. Although keeping him away from Aaron so he couldn't ask any nosy questions like, "Why are you calling the corporate jet pilot and asking how quickly he can go wings up?" had definitely played a part in our outing as well.

It had seemed like a perfect solution at the time. We needed to get Wesley out of the hotel, and since Ben was busy flirting his way into information about Mr. Sovann from his various female employees, Liz was messaging with Jane in an attempt to keep the press apprised of the situation, and Houston was out buying emergency medical supplies in case

Rithisak Sovann ignored my threat, I was the only one available to keep him occupied.

The task of playing carefree tourist would have been significantly easier if I wasn't carting around five pounds of heroin in my tote bag. Simultaneously, I was scouting out areas public enough to make Mr. Sovann reconsider pulling out his gun but private enough to make the switch without getting caught. Not to mention, I was expected to bat my eyelashes charmingly at a guy who didn't exactly set my pulse racing.

"I'm glad you still wanted to be seen with me after the way my colleague overreacted last night." I released a short, self-deprecating laugh. "I can't believe he thought I'd been drugged. I swear, sometimes I don't think photographers can see what's right in front of them unless it's being filtered through a lens."

Liar, liar, low-rise jeans on fire!

"I'm just glad you're okay."

I pushed back my red hair so that I had an unobstructed view of his earnest face. The guy was really pretty sweet, which probably meant I should feel guilty about leading him on . . . but I didn't.

Maybe because Amy still had a chokehold on my guilty conscience.

I smiled and moved the conversation onto safer ground. "Me too. This place really is incredible. I could spend hours just soaking it all in."

At least those words were the truth. I was avidly studying the golden Buddhas that glowed majestically in the midmorning sunlight. In a way, I was using the temple just as selfishly as the tourists who complained bitterly about the heat and the Cambodian children who were trying to support their families by selling travel guide books to the tourists.

Except instead of looking for the best angle for a Facebook photo, I was trying to figure out how best to avoid getting shot.

I sort of hoped that would earn me at least a handful of karmic bonus points.

One arm still entwined with Wesley's, I strolled down a semi-secluded pathway and tried my best to discreetly check my phone for missed calls. I had copied down everyone's numbers and taped the list to the back of each cell so that if *anything* happened, help would be only a phone call away. That was the theory anyway; I wasn't in a position to rush back to the hotel if anything else went terribly wrong.

The distance separating the hotel from the temple was actually something of a relief. I could see why the others hadn't wanted to do the negotiating: It was hard knowing that if something went wrong, you were the one who had been unable to fix it. That you'd be forced to spend the rest of your life what if–ing yourself straight to the therapist's office, which Houston already thought I needed.

Please ring with good news.

"Wat Phnom is the tallest religious structure in this city," Wesley told me as he tugged me flush against his side.

"That's fascinating." I glanced down at my phone.

Please, please ring.

"We're only a few miles away from Wat Botum. We could go there next, if you want?"

"*Mmm,*" I murmured noncommittally.

Ring, damn it! I'm going insane here!

"Pol Pot lived there for a while as a kid. Apparently, he was really well liked. Creepy, right?"

"Definitely."

"Or we could go back to the hotel and have wild monkey sex?"

"Uh, sure," I said vaguely. Then I registered his words. "I'm sorry. I know I'm a bit . . . distracted."

"That's one way to put it."

I looked sheepishly up at Wesley. "It's a work thing. I'm

expecting a call and until I get it—" I shrugged. "Let's just say I'm having trouble staying in the moment."

"I know a great way to fix *that*." He leaned in close and kissed me.

It wasn't bad.

In fact, I would even categorize it as solidly decent.

Most of my girly parts that usually take notice when an attractive guy kisses me responded. I felt . . . warm, or at least *lukewarm,* but not exactly all hot and bothered. And it was nothing compared to the jolt I had felt only yesterday when Houston had kissed me right on the edge of the makeshift dance floor. *That* had been . . . unreal.

Although Houston definitely could've taken a lesson from Wesley about the proper way to end a kiss, which was with glazed eyes and a grateful smile.

"Um, *wow*."

Oh yeah, I hadn't lost my touch.

Wesley grinned at me. "So does this mean we don't need to talk about the guy from last night? Your work buddy, right?"

My phone finally rang.

I never expected I'd be relieved to get an update on the status of an evil drug lord.

I didn't even let it reach the second ring.

"What's going on?" I demanded into the phone while my heart finally began to pick up the pace. "Is everyone okay?"

Ben's voice crackled into my ear. "You're not going to believe this, but I just caught a glimpse of Neal being frog-marched through the lobby. He looks like he's been through hell, but at least he's here and he's breathing. That's all that matters right now."

"I completely agree." I glanced up at Wesley and chose my words carefully. "Any idea what caused such a sudden shift?"

"I guess your threat rattled Mr. Sovann into acting faster

than anyone expected. The guy is mega-wealthy, so maybe he keeps the private plane around just for this reason. You know, the trusty *in case I'm blackmailed and need to fly someone to Phnom Penh* plane."

I struggled not to smile. "Of course. I guess we should have considered that possibility."

"I think we should move up our whole timetable. Call him right now and see if you can catch him off guard."

"But . . . you do realize that we need to make sure this thing goes off without a hitch, right?" I blurted. "Our team isn't even in place yet!"

I had just enough presence of mind to stick to vague pronouns, because no matter how entrancing my kissing skills, Wesley would probably start paying attention if I dropped the name of the hotel owner into my conversation.

"You mean the reporters Jane promised would get here today? Funny story, they got in early too. I did just tell you that you weren't going to believe me."

Only Ben would waste time making jokes in the midst of a hostage crisis, but his tone lost its lightheartedness when he said, "It's time for you to make your move, Chelsea. We need Sovann out of the hotel for as long as you can manage. Starting right now. So when you get him there . . . stall."

"I understand." My mouth turned painfully dry as if I had just tried to eat five saltine crackers. "I'll make the call right now."

"Good. Give him hell, Chelsea."

Ben hung up, and I tried to hide my panic by pretending to have found the disturbance annoying instead of life threatening. I tossed up my hands in mock disgust.

"Work crisis. I'll only be a minute."

I started dialing before he could suggest that we both try to kick back and take the day off work . . . or something equally ridiculous. It was funny because Wesley struck me as a workaholic type, but he wouldn't stop talking about how lucky we were that the hotel owner had asked for a temporary recess in the middle of negotiations.

Yeah, not so lucky for me, actually. Or Amy.

"Hello, sir," I formally greeted the drug lord when he picked up on the third ring. I found myself missing the feel of Houston's hand squeezing mine, but I forced myself to stay on task. I couldn't afford any distractions when I needed to be at the top of my game. So I glanced skyward one more time for good measure so that Wesley would know that I'd *much* rather spend the day exclusively with him.

And I tried incredibly hard not to let Rithisak Sovann sense my fear over the phone.

The accented voice that replied was going to haunt my nightmares for years. "I have the man. You want him in one piece, we meet now."

I nodded like a demented bobblehead. "Shall we meet at Wat Phnom temple in, say, thirty minutes? Does that give you long enough to get here?"

Wesley stiffened, and I hoped that Aaron didn't need any more alone time to make those phone calls of his. I couldn't bring my fake date with me to a hostage exchange with a brilliant psychopath.

"We conduct our business at the hotel," Rithisak insisted hoarsely.

"Neutral ground is so much better for everyone. Less room for either party to renege on the arrangement."

Silence. God, his silences were effective at rattling me.

At that moment I wanted to agree to anything he said rather than risk piquing his anger, except Ben had specifically told me to lure him away from the hotel. Probably because getting him away from his base of operations was the fastest way to split up his forces.

The only downside was that it left me dangling in the wind too.

Still, Ben had sounded determined, not scared, on the phone. This time it was my turn to go on blind faith and take the plunge.

It helped knowing that Rithisak Sovann had wanted to make the exchange badly enough that he'd bribed the Cambodian police and dragged Neal out from whatever cell he'd been rotting in. He wouldn't back out now over the inconvenience of meeting a few miles away from his precious hotel.

"Let's meet by the shrine for the statue-finding lady." I probably would've sounded a lot smarter if I had remembered the woman's name, but details like that tend to allude me even when I'm *not* negotiating with people who probably want me dead.

"Fine. Be ready to make the exchange."

"I look forward to seeing you soon, sir."

He disconnected, leaving me in the decidedly uncomfortable position of having to explain to my date that my work-related crisis required my immediate attention. Oh, and that I would *completely* understand if he didn't want to stick around.

If I happened to leave out the little detail that I was about to become an international drug dealer, well . . . some secrets are better off kept that way.

Chapter 30

He was right on time.

Apparently, punctuality was one of the few values this particular drug lord was a stickler for upholding. And here I'd assumed that anyone who made their living in less-than-legal enterprises would have an equally flexible relationship with deadlines.

Not so much.

It unnerved me to realize that we hadn't even exchanged pleasantries and I had already underestimated him once. It didn't exactly inspire much confidence in my ability to proceed with our swap, especially when I saw that the few photos I had found of him online hadn't done him justice. They had all been portraits that featured him smiling in a "Welcome to Cambodia, foreign investors!" kind of way.

He wasn't smiling now.

Instead, he was bearing down on the relatively secluded shrine with a scowl firmly entrenched on a face that didn't betray his age. His jet-black hair was cut with razor precision, and I knew even from a distance that his watch alone could pay ten times over for our stay at the Royal Continental Hotel. Even more impressive than the obvious display of wealth was the way he radiated power—a *don't mess with me* air of authority.

And I didn't want to mess with him. I really, *really* didn't.

Especially when I caught sight of Neal being shoved forward by the thugs on either side of him. The vicious blows he'd taken back in Siem Reap clearly hadn't been the only ones he had received; Neal's normally expressive face was swollen red and mottled black and blue.

The beaten, run-down man in front of me didn't look foolishly optimistic anymore . . . but when he saw me, standing only a few feet away from a statue of the Lady Penh, he yelled out a hoarse warning.

"Run!"

My stomach clenched as one of the thugs delivered a stunningly powerful punch to Neal's gut, but I couldn't bring myself to meet the professor's eyes. That would be the fastest way for me to entirely lose control of my emotions. Neal needed me to keep it together . . . and so did Amy.

I just hoped the others were doing a much better job of rescuing her.

And that someone would be hurrying this way to provide me with some desperately needed backup.

"Hello, sir." I bowed my head respectfully the instant Rithisak came close enough for us to speak without drawing attention to ourselves. "It's an honor to meet you."

Then again, I'd be even more honored if you would just hand over my friends.

He examined me closely before speaking, his gaze lingering on my every attribute like I was a thoroughbred horse being scrutinized before a big race. I half expected him to demand to see my registration papers.

He also didn't appear even mildly disconcerted by Neal's pain-filled wheezes. "I fulfilled my end of the arrangement. I hope you were also true to your word."

I nodded and gripped my tote even tighter. "I have it stashed nearby."

A lot closer than you might think. Now I simply need to stall until the cavalry arrives.

"You appear to have overlooked part of our arrangement. I don't see my messenger with you. Where is she?"

Neal gasped and tried to lurch forward. *"Run, Chelsea!"*

I desperately shook my head, hoping that signal would be enough to keep him from speaking again, but the fist that plowed into his rib cage was probably a more effective deterrent. The resounding crack of broken bones only ratcheted up the noise inside my head until it became a hot, twisting mess beyond my control. The keening scream that barely escaped through Neal's swollen lips shredded me. I felt empty. Strung out.

Terrified.

A tourist nearby gasped in horror, but she quickly ducked out of sight so that she couldn't be pulled into my mess. I didn't blame her for not sticking around. She hadn't signed up for hero duty, and since this wasn't the kind of adventure abroad she could brag about to her quilting group I doubted she would be returning with help.

"I know what I'm doing, Neal." I tried to infuse my words with a confidence I didn't feel. "Mr. Sovann and I have an understanding."

We both understand that I might not be making it out of this alive.

Ben better have had a good reason for asking me to stall.

"However, I *am* confused about the absence of my messenger. Did I not make myself clear enough on that point?"

It was hard to tell because of all the swelling, but I thought Neal's eyes became even more frantic as he tried to mouth the question, *Amy or Liz?*

"Give me the Buddha and then we can negotiate for her." Rithisak Sovann's lips twisted upward at the ends into a rough version of a smile.

"That's *not* what we agreed!"

His expression didn't waver as his hand disappeared in his suit jacket only to reemerge with a handgun that looked fully capable of shutting me up. Permanently.

"I'm keeping the girl." Rithisak took three confident strides toward me and then ran one long, elegant finger down my cheek and hooked it beneath my chin in a dispassionate examination. "I may even keep you. Now give me the package."

This would've been a *really* great time to utilize some sneaky maneuver I had been holding back in reserve. In the Hollywood version of my life, my ballet training would allow me to gracefully execute a perfect *grand jeté* to the evil drug dealer's face.

Too bad real life never works out that way.

Instead, I stood there frozen. And the only thing I could think was a resounding *Holy crap!*

Seriously.

Nothing profound about the meaning of life or the importance of family or all the things I should have said or done but hadn't. No regrets about Logan. Or Jake. Or even Houston, for that matter.

Just . . . *holy crap.*

"Uh, okay. Fine. Keep her!" I said desperately, my eyes never straying from the barrel of his gun. "Would I like her back? Yes. Finding good help isn't easy. I'm sure you can relate to that in your line of business. But she's not worth this much trouble. So . . . whatever. All yours."

Okay, so now *that* was the biggest lie I had ever told. No way would I calmly accept letting that creep get his hands on Amy again. Ben, Liz, and Houston were going to ensure it for me. But Mr. Sovann seemed to have no trouble believing that the panic-stricken girl in front of him would willingly sell out a glorified assistant if it meant saving her own skin.

"Why don't you, uh, put that down so we can talk?" I said hopefully.

He lowered his gun only slightly, but I didn't doubt for a

second that he could have it jammed against my throat before I sucked in the breath to scream. He may have wanted the drugs badly enough to fly Neal into town, but nothing was valuable enough for him to allow someone else to call the shots. Especially if that someone else was a seventeen-year-old ballerina-in-training. I was just lucky he hadn't decided to lodge a bullet into some "non-essential" part of my body in order to teach me a lesson about interfering with other people's affairs.

Although I couldn't shake the horrible suspicion that my current lack of bullet holes was probably a calculated decision based on the profit margin between uninjured sex slaves and their crippled counterparts.

That thought didn't exactly help me keep it together.

"No more talking. Give me the package." Rithisak flicked the gun at me like a composer leading his orchestra with a baton. "Now."

But I couldn't . . . not when Neal was alive and two feet away from me. All I had to do was keep him that way. To trust in Ben and keep stalling.

"You release him, and I will make sure you get the heroin. Simple."

"He'll kill you!"

I couldn't handle it.

Neal and I both knew exactly what was coming. He even braced himself for the thug's retribution, but that didn't make it any easier for me to watch him crumple under the force of the blow. To see it coming and be absolutely unable to prevent it from happening . . . that's when I completely lost it.

It was like some essential part of me snapped.

"He's not wrong," Rithisak said calmly, as if he'd politely told Neal to raise his hand before speaking next time. "I can't let my rivals think a silly little girl can undermine me. Especially now that I'm handling a new product."

Then he chuckled, not in a supervillain *I shall plot world domination while I twirl my mustache* kind of way—that at least would have allowed me some room for levity in the midst of this completely un-funny situation. No, this laugh was legitimately terrifying because it didn't sound even remotely calculated. The man was actually taking *pleasure* in watching my face blanch with every strike Neal received.

He was enjoying this twisted game with me because he saw it as a temporary amusement. I was just a little bit of sport to him. A fleeting diversion that would never become a serious threat because I wasn't going to leave our little meeting alive.

Whatever plan Ben was using sure had one enormous flaw in it.

There was no backup on the way for me. I was screwed. Damned if I handed over the drugs and equally damned if I didn't.

My fingers slid into my tote and clutched the Buddha that had landed all of us in this mess. A sense of inevitability settled over me. I was going to die. That much had become painfully clear when I had first looked down the barrel of the gun. Rithisak Sovann was going to have no moral reservations to prevent him from pulling the trigger. He wouldn't start making exceptions based on my age and gender.

I tipped my face up toward the sun I saw so infrequently back in Portland and tried to accept the situation.

It was a beautiful place to die. I could almost taste the incense that saturated the air around the temple. Idly, I wondered if my funeral would be held in this very spot or if my mom would insist on having it back in Forest Grove. It didn't matter much to me either way. No doubt somebody would point out that my tragic fate could've easily been avoided if I hadn't tried to coast through life on my looks. If I had only been a little more interested in textbooks instead of tutus. I had no trouble imagining my mother standing above my grave, wailing, "This is all your fault, Paul! If you hadn't coddled her—"

She might not be able to directly inform me of her disapproval, but I seriously doubted that would stop her from publicly expressing it. At least she would have the satisfaction of being right about her only daughter's ineptitude to keep her warm at night.

Except that was such *bullshit*.

The more I thought about my impending death, the more pissed off I became until I was inwardly seething. I didn't deserve this. Okay, so maybe my reign as the Queen of the Notables meant I had some bad karma stockpiled with my name on it back at Smith High School. But even at my bitchiest I hadn't done anything to merit *this*. Even the psychopathic drug dealer had no reason to criticize my behavior considering that *I* had contacted *him* trying to return his missing merchandise. And what did I get for all my effort?

Most likely, one shallow Cambodian grave.

The cool wooden body of the Buddha felt right clutched in my fist. Maybe I wasn't going to make it out of this particular mess alive, but it wouldn't be for nothing. And I was going to drag out every second for as long as was humanly possible before I enacted my very last act of revenge.

Mr. Sovann was in for a big surprise if he thought I would docilely await my death sentence. Maybe it was the young-high-school-girl thing I had going for me, but he was seriously underestimating just how much hell I could raise when cornered. A misconception I had every intention of using to my advantage.

I wasn't going down without a fight.

"So how do you see this playing out? I hand you the drugs and you sell me as a sex slave? That doesn't seem like a fair deal to me."

Another one of those low chuckles was his only immediate

response. The sound didn't bother me as much this time. The more he snickered at my naïveté the less he would expect of me.

But that didn't mean I'd expect any less of myself.

For the first time I really, truly, swear-on-whatever-holy-book-you-want, didn't care that I was being dismissed as nothing more than an ornamental object. Maybe I wouldn't become a Rhodes scholar anytime soon, but at that moment I wouldn't have traded my ability to keep cool under pressure even for all the answers to the redo SAT test my mom would have undoubtedly made me take back in Oregon.

No textbook could teach that particular skill.

And maybe it was petty and vindictive to make destroying Rithisak Sovann's precious Buddha my very last mission in life . . . but I was surprisingly okay with that. Just as long as I could get Neal out of there first.

"I have a better punishment in mind for you."

I raised one sardonic eyebrow. "You want me to stick around as a devoted ass-kisser? Oh, right. I forgot. You already have a pair of those."

As long as he planned to hurt me, I saw no reason to be polite to the jerk.

"Seriously, guys, I don't care how much he's paying you. So not worth it."

The disdain radiating from his eyes would have been petrifying if I'd had any spare room for fear. My anger did such an excellent job of insulating me from every other emotion, I gave him my sunniest smile.

"You foolish little idiot!" he snapped. "You don't even know what you carry, yet you dare to lecture *me!*"

Some distant part of my brain registered that there was something seriously off about his little rant—something besides the way his ego was spinning out of control. I didn't know what I carried? Sure I did.

Heroin.

I had Googled it and everything.

Except that didn't explain why Rithisak Sovann had been so bent out of shape over reclaiming half of his shipment. Sure, nobody likes to lose a profit, but according to Wikipedia, heroin is the most common drug available in Cambodia. It didn't make sense for Rithisak to go through the trouble and expense of paying for a private plane, bribing the police to release Neal from prison, hiring thugs to escort him every step of the way to Phnom Penh, not to mention the delay to his precious merger to regain something that he could so easily replace.

It wasn't worth the effort.

Which led me to one sickening conclusion: I had something else entirely.

Something that could easily have been impairing my judgment ever since Houston and I sprinted out of the hotel. I had just assumed that my weird dreams were stress-induced, even though I had never experienced anything nearly as vivid as my bizarre middle school reenactment with Logan.

Even the night before my SAT test I had slept like a baby.

It was almost funny; my parents had shipped me off to another country to stop my partying ways, and I'd inadvertently started sampling the latest in Cambodian narcotics. I didn't think they would appreciate the irony.

Houston would enjoy being right though. Nobody had slipped anything into my drink, but that didn't mean I hadn't been drugged. I quickly tried to replay the events of the night before to figure out how I could have accidentally dosed myself. I had gotten dressed in the bathroom, but none of the others seemed affected by anything. Then I had pretended to make a phone call . . . and wiped away the white dusting of powder on my phone before I had sauntered over to the bar.

I couldn't have inhaled more than a handful of airborne molecules of the stuff.

No wonder Rithisak was so eager to get his hands on it. A gram would probably be worth five thousand times its weight in gold.

It would also be enough to incapacitate a full-grown man.

I tossed my hair, but this time I paid close attention to the direction the slight breeze moved the short red strands. Edging forward slightly so that the wind was to my back, I nodded in Neal's direction. "Why don't we try this again? You let him go, and I'll hand over the package."

Rithisak's scowl deepened. "You lied to me earlier."

I reached into my purse and pulled the damn thing out. I was careful to keep my finger plugging the crack in the side so that no loose particles could blow into my face.

"I sure did. Release him. Now."

Rithisak nodded at the bigger of his two thugs, who proceeded to shove Neal hard enough to send him sprawling across the pavement. Neal barely managed to lift his bloody face high enough to meet my gaze. No amount of swelling or bruising could disguise his panicked look of desperation— and he was still trying to look out for me. "Chelsea, don't!"

I wanted to tell him not to worry, that I had one last move up my sleeve. But I didn't have the chance to utter more than a single word as Rithisak strode toward me.

"Duck!" I yelled.

That's when I either made the smartest decision or the biggest mistake of my life, as I channeled every ounce of the anger still coursing through my veins into smashing that butt-ugly statue on the cobblestones.

Right at the drug lord's feet.

Unfortunately, it was right at my feet too—and even with my mouth and nose buried in the crook of my non-pitching arm, I knew it was too little too late. The white powder plumed the air, licking up Rithisak Sovann's suit as if he had tried making cookies and accidentally put a blender on a high speed with nothing but baking soda and flour in the bowl. But the mysterious drug that had dragged me into this mess now coated me too.

A lethal amount of it.

I was vaguely surprised that I wasn't already high as a freaking kite.

And I was struggling to remember why exactly it mattered. I stumbled backward and did my best to suppress a giggle as I saw the thugs' mouths drop open in horror. As far as final moments go, it was rather satisfying to watch it sink in on Rithisak's face that some foreign brat had just completely destroyed his shipment. It didn't last long, only a handful of seconds, but I relished each one of them. It felt like time lengthened so that I could suck out every last drop of enjoyment from the little snippet of life that I had left on earth.

But it still ended too soon and I felt cheated, like a kid hustled back inside the house right before the Fourth of July fireworks begin their grand finale. The world tilted as I staggered once more, hoping to find Neal before the darkness creeping at the edge of my vision closed in entirely. I wanted to make sure he hadn't experienced the full force of the blast zone. To feel his pulse beating while mine slowed . . . and then stopped.

I couldn't even manage that one final task before everything went black.

Chapter 31

I was dead.

And *this* was hell.

There were no flames roasting the soles of my feet, no devil cackling in the corner, no giant pustules breaking forth or anything, but there was no worse punishment than for me to open my admittedly gritty eyes and see . . . Mackenzie Wellesley.

Mackenzie *"ex-boyfriend nabbing"* Wellesley.

Oh yeah, this was hell, all right.

"Uh, Logan." The figment of my tormented afterlife spoke warily. "I think she's looking at me. Or . . . glaring at me. Same thing, right?"

I blinked and, sure enough, there was my ex-boyfriend, looking every bit as perfect as I remembered with those piercing gray eyes staring searchingly into mine.

"Hey, Chelsea. You always did know how to make an entrance."

That sounded suspiciously normal considering that I was dead. I sort of expected my divine punishment would be a lot more painful than making awkward small talk. At the very least I expected to be forced into watching them make out for all of eternity.

Now *that* would make anyone start repenting their sins.

"Logan?" His name emerged as a croak from my dry mouth, and Mackenzie quickly slid a straw into my mouth. The tepid water trickling down my throat was almost enough to make me forgive her presence in my afterlife, until I realized that nothing could possibly feel this good in hell. And since I definitely hadn't earned a spot beyond the pearly gates ... I wasn't dead.

Although *not dead* wasn't all that comforting when everything else was a blank.

I tried to push myself into a sitting position, but my chest ached fiercely and my arms refused to work properly, probably because there were a million plastic tubes attached to me.

That's when I started screaming bloody murder.

"Chelsea, calm down!" Logan ordered, cupping my face in his hands while Mackenzie darted out of sight. "You're safe, okay! You're in Oregon and you're safe."

"You don't understand! He wanted to *kill* me, so I smashed the Buddha and—"

I trailed off because I didn't have the foggiest idea what had happened next. *Nothing happened next.* That's what my brain kept insisting. It went black and time stopped.

The end.

Except, apparently, I had missed something since I was definitely lying in an ugly hospital room surrounded by drab beige walls and my *ex-boyfriend.*

Nothing made sense. I had accepted my death the moment I chucked the bloody statue—maybe even a little before that. Sure, I'd been pissed off about it. I hadn't *wanted* to die. Then again, I hadn't *wanted* to be sent to Cambodia in the first place.

I had accepted it though.

That's why I had gone in alone—negotiating for Neal,

stalling for Amy—I had wanted my death to mean something, but apparently I couldn't even correctly pull off a grand sacrifice. Every inch of my body was aching, while the others were . . .

I didn't know.

"*Neal! Amy!*" I didn't care if I screamed my throat raw. I rounded on Logan. "*NEAL!*"

"No, Chelsea." He looked absolutely panicked. "I'm Logan, remember? *Logan.* Just . . . take it easy, okay?"

Except I couldn't.

Not when my last memory of Neal involved him bloody, beaten, and sprawled out like an offering near the base of the Lady Penh's shrine. Not when Amy might still be locked away in some hotel room getting the same treatment herself.

"What happened to them, Logan?" I snapped, unable to hide the fear surging through my system. "Amy and Neal. Are they *here?*"

"Both of them are expected to make a full recovery." Logan's mom stood in the doorway, wearing her doctor's coat and holding a thick chart. *My* chart, I realized slowly. "But let's focus on you for the moment, all right? Let's see, you've got a concussion, a cracked rib that was sustained during your CPR in Cambodia, and some mild dehydration. Now the next thing I'm going to say will sound really scary, but take a deep breath and hear me out, okay?"

I did as she instructed and nodded.

"The drug that was in your system is known as 3-Methylfentanyl, and it's incredibly dangerous stuff."

"No kidding," I croaked.

Logan's mom placed the straw back between my lips and waited until I sipped some more water before she continued.

"It's actually classified as a chemical weapon that's now being widely sold on the black market. Since it's also estimated to be between four hundred to six thousand times stronger than morphine, your survival is nothing short of a miracle, especially because of your resulting respiratory depression."

I felt myself sinking into information overload and the room kept spinning so I squeezed my eyes shut.

"You want to say that again in English?"

"It appears that you hit your head, passed out, and then stopped breathing entirely. If you hadn't received CPR, we wouldn't be having this conversation."

I didn't have any idea what I should say to *that,* so I repeated the question that was most important to me. "Neal and Amy are okay?"

Logan's mom settled her hand warmly over mine as she assured me, yet again, that everyone was going to be just fine. That we had all made it out of the nightmare alive.

I cried.

Stupid, really. I had stared down a notorious drug leader and brokered a life-or-death deal—all without shedding a tear. The entire time I was in Cambodia I had kept a tight hold over my emotions because falling apart wasn't an option. But now that I was safely tucked away in a clean hospital, away from maniacs and firearms, I started sobbing like a baby.

Right in front of Logan.

I doubt he liked being saddled with the job of reassuring his concussed ex-girlfriend. Still, he gently stroked my hair and repeated, "You're fine now, Chelsea. You're safe," as if there weren't an airport carousel's worth of baggage between us.

It felt like . . . home.

Of course, Mackenzie had to go and ruin it by opening the door and sticking her head inside. "Oh, uh . . . never mind! I'll just, uh, tell the others that Chelsea's not ready for company yet. Okay. Uh . . . 'bye!"

The girl had to be applying for sainthood or something because nobody is *that* nice when they see their nemesis bawling her eyes out. Instead of gloating or snapping a quick picture to hold over my head, she made a hasty exit while I wiped away the dampness on my cheeks with a tissue that Logan handed me. That small gesture from him nearly got the waterworks going all over again. It felt nearly impossible to process my emotions when my sturdy, dependable Logan was right freaking *there*.

So I stopped trying to process them altogether and instead I finally started telling him the truth.

"I want to hate her."

Logan's mouth curved into a smile, and for a second I thought he had misunderstood me. That he was so in love with Mackenzie he couldn't fathom anyone wanting to hate her.

"I know you do."

"No, but I *really* want to hate her, Logan. And her ability to spout useless trivia."

"What part of this is supposed to be coming as a surprise, Chelsea? You haven't exactly been subtle when it comes to my girlfriend."

I nestled farther into the pillows and briefly considered keeping my mouth shut until I knew for certain that this sudden need for total honesty wasn't some weird side effect of the drugs. Except I couldn't seem to keep anything bottled up anymore. Not when part of me still expected that the next time I opened my eyes I would be back in Cambodia with Rithisak Sovann.

"You don't understand, Logan. She's too freaking nice for me to even hate her properly! It's obnoxious." The words tumbled out on top of one another. "And whenever she does something awkward I just feel guilty about wanting to hate her in the first place!"

Logan's whole face sort of lit up with an open affection as he thought about Mackenzie. "I happen to love her bouts of awkwardness, so I'm not exactly impartial here."

I ignored the increasingly loud sounds of an argument building outside my hospital room door as I grabbed Logan's hand and concentrated solely on him.

"I miss you, Logan."

And there it was—out in the open—the one thing I had been unable to say before leaving for Cambodia.

"Uh," Logan said articulately. "Chelsea?"

"Just hear me out. I miss you, okay? I've been missing you for years."

He cleared his throat and jerked his head over toward the hospital door, which now had an audience that included Logan's mom, his girlfriend, his girlfriend's best friend, his girlfriend's best friend's boyfriend . . . and Houston.

Oh yeah. I've always had impeccable timing.

"I, uh, think they need a few more minutes," Mackenzie mumbled, before she turned around stiffly and walked straight out of the room. Jane hesitated, clearly uncertain whether she also should storm out, or if my recent trauma gave me a temporary pass for hitting on her best friend's boyfriend. Scott solved her dilemma by nodding to me with a wry grin.

"Good to see you, Chelsea. Things were getting dull around here. Now if you'll excuse us—" He didn't bother even finishing the sentence as he took Jane's hand and left in pursuit of Mackenzie.

Somehow, I'd managed to make a complete mess of things without leaving my freaking *hospital bed*.

And yet my mom didn't think I had any natural talents. Go figure.

"I'll come back later too," Mrs. Beckett informed me, scooping up my charts as she aimed one last parting look at her son that said clearly, *If you toss aside Mackenzie for your ex-girlfriend, you will be making a mistake. A huge mistake.*

She closed the door behind her, leaving me alone in the room with my stunned-looking ex-boyfriend and one seriously rumpled Houston, who must have spent the entire plane ride doing his stressed-hair-raking thing with his fingers because it had reached a whole new height.

He looked absolutely wonderful.

"I'm glad to see you're okay, *prin* . . . Chelsea. I'll just let you"—he waved a hand to indicate me and Logan—"get back to your regularly scheduled programming. Don't worry, I get it. What happens in Cambodia stays in Cambodia."

He didn't slam the door behind him. Oh no, that would be too much of an emotional display for Houston. Instead, he shut it decisively behind him with a resounding *click,* while Logan struggled to process my ill-timed confession.

"No offense, Chelsea, but you've got a nasty habit of destroying my life. I should probably go check on my *girlfriend* now." Logan put an extra emphasis on the term, as if he thought the concept of a committed relationship might be foreign to me. "Thanks for that, by the way."

"She has nothing to worry about from me," I told him honestly.

Logan laughed, but there was little real amusement in the sound. "Oh, I know that, and usually, so does she. But sometimes I think she expects me to realize I'm dating the biggest . . . how did you put it, Chelsea? Geek. That I'm dating the biggest geek at school and dump her. Well, it isn't going to happen. Not for you. Not for *anyone!*"

"Wow, simmer down there, Romeo. I didn't ask you to *date* me. I told you I *missed* you. Two very different things."

He looked at me skeptically. "Uh huh, *sure,* Chelsea."

"You were my *best friend,* you idiot! And, yeah, I screwed up. I hurt you. And I'm sorry about that—more than you know. But I want my best friend back. The one who was there for me when my parents were yelling and . . . well, I've missed you." I glared at him and couldn't stop myself from adding, "*Dumb-ass.*"

His lips twitched into a grin, in spite of himself. And then he reached out to deliver a soft punch to my shoulder, careful not to disturb any of the tubes in my arm.

"I can do friends, Chelsea. *Just* friends. If that's all you're looking for, we can give it a shot. But if you're messing with me, I swear—"

I rolled my eyes and cut him off before he could come up with a threat. "Yeah, no ulterior motive here. I have my sights set higher this time. No offense."

"None taken." He looked at the door again, as if weighing whether my battered physical condition obligated him to stay with me when we both knew he wanted to be chasing after the geek of his dreams.

"I know half a dozen guys who will happily comfort Mackenzie if you don't go after her."

Logan instantly started moving toward the door, pausing only briefly when it was half opened. "I've missed you too, Chelsea. Now let's see how long you can make it without pissing someone off."

I closed my eyes sleepily, as once more the darkness threatened to pull me under. "I make no promises."

Logan's laughter was the last thing I heard before slipping back into a dreamless sleep that was only disturbed when I heard two very familiar voices bickering in my room that weren't going to be lowered just because they were in a hospital.

"It was *your* idea, Paul! *You're* the one who thought it was a good idea to send her to Cambodia! This never would've happened if you had even considered the all-girls' boarding school I showed you."

Wow. I didn't know it was possible to make me *grateful* I'd been shipped off to Cambodia, but I was willing to believe the popular girls who ruled the undoubtedly prestigious boarding school my mom had looked at could have given Rithisak Sovann a lesson in how to terrorize people.

"No one could have anticipated *this,* Suzanne."

"It's *Cambodia,* for god's sake, Paul! The country must be *full* of criminals!"

Funny that the crime rate in Cambodia was only occurring to her now. Not, you know, *before* she had lectured me about what a great opportunity it was for me, and how I should be eternally grateful they were letting me go. I also wanted to point out that there were plenty of honest, hardworking Cambodians like Mr. Horny too.

Just because I'd had the misfortunate of tangling with a drug lord didn't mean she had to blame the entire *country.*

"Let's focus on who she's going to stay with when the hospital releases her, Suzanne. I think she should stay with me."

My mom made a scandalized sound. "*You?* So you can just coddle her forever. I'm not letting that happen to her."

"Suzanne!"

"Paul!"

"*Leave.*"

My parents stared at me in surprise, probably because they'd been so absorbed by their arguing that they had forgotten that their own daughter was recovering in a hospital bed right in front of them. Of course, my presence had never prevented them from snipping at each other before. I guess it was too much to hope that my near miss with death could have brought the two of them to a cease-fire.

"I'm so glad you're okay, princess." My dad brushed a strand of red hair off my forehead, and the protectiveness of the gesture almost made me close my eyes and let them stay shut. Part of me wanted to sleep forever if that would keep the throbbing pain in my chest at bay. But I knew that if I didn't deal with my parents now, they would continue squabbling over me.

No amount of Advil would be able to ease my parent-related migraine then.

"Thanks, Dad. But if you two are going to argue, do it far away from me."

Neither of them looked comfortable hearing their only child point out one of their shortcomings, so they both pretended I hadn't spoken.

"Chelsea, you scared me!" my mom said accusingly, as if that had been my plan all along. "I never should have let your father talk me into sending you abroad. You'll come back home with me, of course. We'll get you registered back at Smith High School right away. And maybe then we'll look into getting you an SAT prep tutor or something. How does that sound, sweetie?"

Awful, actually. But thanks for the offer, Mom.

"I want to stay with dad in Portland."

"*What?*" she squawked, turning swiftly on my dad. "What did you say to her, Paul? I *knew* you would make me out to be the bad guy in the divorce!"

"I didn't do—"

"*Stop!*" I cleared my throat, but neither of them thought to offer me any water. "I'm going to try living with Dad, and if that doesn't work, then I will come up with a different solution. Which might include filing to become an emancipated minor."

That shut them up . . . for all of a second.

"You're not ready to live on your own, princess," my dad informed me, while my mom launched into a rant about rebellious teenage years and how she hoped someday I had a daughter *just like me* because *that* would show me.

I closed my eyes and let them vent for a few minutes before I held up the remote attached to my hospital bed.

"My turn to talk. If either of you interrupts, I'm paging for a nurse to escort you out."

They definitely didn't like the sound of that, but I wasn't about to back down now. I hadn't defied a drug dealer only to allow my own parents to tear me down. My mom stiffly crossed her arms as I fought to find words for the jumble in my head.

"You wanted me to leave. You wanted Cambodia to be my wake-up call. And you know what? It worked."

"By associating with a drug dealer? *That* was your wake-up call?" my dad asked dubiously.

"Absolutely. I handled a deadly situation. Not every decision I made was a good one, but do you want to know what I learned? I *really* don't need you. Either of you."

"Right," my mom scoffed. "Those not-so-good decisions landed you in the hospital. Honey, you need to be reasonable right now."

"I got everyone out alive."

"I saw your father's colleague. I wouldn't be bragging about that quite yet. The man looks half-dead to me, and your other classmate isn't much better."

My stomach clenched painfully and my cracked rib began screaming at me in protest. I nearly pressed the button for a nurse just so I could see if I could get anything to help with the pain.

"I know that Neal and Amy had a really . . . rough time."

Understatement of the freaking century.

"And maybe I'm partly to blame for it. But did it occur to either of you that four of the smartest people I know—whose SAT scores probably doubled, maybe even tripled, mine—were all in that situation with me? That we made mistakes together and did our best to deal with them?"

My mom shook her head. "Chelsea, I know this has been awful for you, but you can't use it as an excuse for your shortcomings. You can't go through life thinking, *Why bother studying if it won't save me from a drug dealer?*"

I clenched my teeth, which only worsened the migraine that was gaining force. "I'm not making excuses. I'm just trying to point out that test scores aren't everything. They don't measure the important things. And my low SAT score doesn't make me *stupid*. I don't ever want to hear you imply that it does again."

"Chelsea—" my dad started, but I cut him off.

"You're not much better, Dad. Because you heard her say it, and you still chose to hide in your office like a coward. Every. Single. Time. So there will be no Father of the Year nominations for you. You both wanted me to leave and find myself. Well, I did. I'm not going to let either of you treat me like that again."

"So this is how things are going to be from now on?" my mom demanded dramatically. "The two of you teaming up against me?"

"I love you, Mom." The words tore more painfully from my throat than any of the others. Somehow saying those four words made my entire conversation with Logan look like child's play. They eviscerated my heart because I knew it was the truth even as every fiber of my being wished that I was lying. That I could somehow find a way to stop loving her so that she could never hurt me again.

"I love you," I repeated. "I just don't like you very much."

Her lips whitened as she pressed them tightly together. She didn't spare me another second of her time. Instead, she turned on her heels and strode out of the room with as much poise and dignity as ever. It was as if she had merely been attending a business meeting and, having found the terms unsatisfactory, had no other recourse but to leave, secure in the knowledge that *she* at least had been reasonable.

The stiffness in my shoulders slowly began to ease as I faced my dad. "I'd like you to enroll me at the high school closest to Lewis & Clark. That should make things easier for both of us."

"Are you sure you want to do that, princess?" he asked me seriously. "Leave all your friends behind when you've only just come back?"

I laughed hoarsely. "I want a fresh start. Besides, I think I can figure out a forty-minute commute with the people who cared about me when I was halfway around the world."

And just maybe I'd be able to start something with someone even closer.

Chapter 32

There's nothing fun about having enormous holes in your memory that you have to ask other people to fill in.

And there's no super-casual way to bring it up either. Hallmark hasn't exactly created a card that says, *Thanks for throwing that great party last night. Any chance you could fill in a few details sometime soon?* Even knowing that I had probably spent most of that void in a hospital or in transit to a hospital didn't exactly sit well with me. I wanted details.

"Hey, buddy," I said casually the first time Ben came to visit me in the hospital. "Perfect timing. I was hoping to hear a bedtime story. Something exotic. Here, let me start you off: *Once upon a time, there was a beautiful princess who went to meet a very wicked drug dealer.* . . . Why don't you take it from there?"

Ben laughed and flopped down into the chair beside my bed. "I don't know if you really want to hear my version of that story. The beautiful princess was super-close with this very handsome knight who enjoyed staring at her luscious—"

"Seriously, Ben," I interrupted. "It doesn't feel real to me. You know, just waking up in Oregon after everything faded to black. That may work in the movies, but it's creeping me out."

"Okay." He nodded. "The handsome knight screwed up and let the princess down. That's the story. It has a happy ending to it though. The princess lived, and the knight was magically transformed into a jackass. The end."

"Ben, I have absolutely no idea what you're talking about."

He scrubbed his face with one hand and then closed his eyes. "I'm just . . . so sorry I told you to set up that exchange with Rithisak Sovann. I wasn't thinking. Obviously. It honestly never occurred to me that you would be going to meet him alone." He peeked at me through his fingers. "Any chance you could forgive me?"

"Hold up, what do you mean, *you didn't think I was alone?* None of the others were with me! Isn't that the definition of alone?"

"I thought you would have a new plan or an army of Chelsea's helpers or . . . something."

I tried not to laugh because my rib hurt like hell anytime I so much as snickered. "You have got to be *kidding* me!"

Ben couldn't even bring himself to meet my eyes. "I'm so sorry, Chelsea."

"I'm actually . . . oddly flattered. Don't get me wrong, you *definitely* should have told me that I was flying completely solo *before* I arranged a private meeting with a drug lord. But I kind of like the badass version of me you've got floating around in that pervy head of yours. She's not real, but she's pretty freaking cool."

"Chelsea, you waited until Neal was low on the ground before you used a *chemical weapon* against three enormous men who wanted to kill you. I don't think you have to worry about not living up to anyone's hype."

And yet I hardly recognized the scene that he was describing. I hadn't intentionally waited for Neal to hit the pavement before dropping the Buddha because I thought it would increase his chances of survival. That just happened to be when three big, scary guys all started walking toward me. . . .

It had been mostly luck, whether or not Ben wanted to see it that way.

"So what happened, Ben? I hit my head, passed out, *and . . .*"

"I guess some lady saw them beating the crap out of Neal earlier and she tracked down a security guard. By the time they got there, all of you were unconscious except for Neal."

I mock glared at him. "Are you taking dramatic pauses now? Come on, spill!"

Ben shrugged. "Everyone was rushed to the hospital, and thankfully one of the nurses there answered your prepaid phone because otherwise we still might not be sitting here right now."

"You called me?" I asked, feeling oddly touched.

"Just for the record: We all called you. When you didn't pick up the third time, we also panicked." Ben grimaced. "Houston almost killed me when I told him about our last conversation."

I tried to sit up straighter, but my aching body quickly vetoed that idea. "What did he, uh . . . say?"

Ben rolled his eyes. "It wasn't so much the words he used as it was the decibel level at which he hollered them." He glanced guiltily at his shoes while he scuffed them on the linoleum hospital flooring. "So, uh . . . you do forgive me, right?"

"You've won me over with your brilliant storytelling," I quipped. "So how did Houston react when he found out Neal and I were in the hospital?"

He shook his head in disbelief. "Oh no, we are *not* doing that whole girl thing where you dissect some guy's every move to figure out if he likes you. Not happening. Take that junk to Amy's room. She'll love it."

I opened my mouth, but Ben cut me off before I could ask the next question on my mind. "*Yes!* Amy is still doing just fine. She perked right up when your dad brought her all those romance novels from you. She wanted me to deliver some message to you, but there was no mention of anything even remotely sexual, so I'm afraid I can't remember a word of it."

"You're ridiculous," I informed him.

Ben was shrugging his acceptance when a knock on the door interrupted us and a familiar multicolored head peeked in. "Good, you're both here. I need a break from Neal. He keeps trying to cram lectures on the history of Cambodia into my visits." Liz perched on the side of my bed and gently patted my leg. "Admit it, Chelsea; that's the real reason you're still lying here."

I smiled wryly and gestured at the source of my constant pain. "It's not everything that it's *cracked* up to be."

Liz rolled her eyes. "That answers my question about whether or not they've got you on morphine. Just let me know when the real Chelsea Halloway comes back, okay?"

"She was just asking me to fill her in on our epic escape from Cambodia."

Liz grinned and briefly traded a knowing look with Ben before her focus shifted to me. "How far did he get into it? I think my personal favorite moment was when Houston went completely berserk and rushed over to the hospital with me to make sure that we wouldn't be bringing any corpses home with us. Now *that* was pretty epic."

"He really freaked out over me?"

"Big-time."

Ben stretched and began to edge his way toward the exit. "Well, I'll leave the two of you to talk everything over while I drop in on Neal."

"You'll be singing a very different tune once he gets going on the rise of Pol Pot," Liz predicted darkly.

"I'll risk it. Get better soon, Chelsea." Ben hesitated at the door and then swore under his breath. "Houston's ex-girlfriend Carolyn is dropping by our new dorm room tonight so that they can have a talk. But this is *not* me getting involved, do you understand?"

I nodded wordlessly, torn between laughing at Ben's obvious discomfort and crying because . . .

"What happens in Cambodia stays in Cambodia," I mumbled to myself.

"Here's the thing about that saying: It couldn't be any more wrong." Liz jerked her head toward the door that had already shut behind Ben. "Not too surprising, considering the genius who came up with it."

I managed a smile, but it felt wobbly around the edges, as if the expression knew it had no business being on my face. "What do you mean, Liz? We all agreed to it."

"We agreed to that before a lot of things happened, Chelsea. Just off the top of my head . . . before you confronted a notorious drug dealer and Buddha-bombed yourself. Before the boys and I teamed up with those journalists Jane promised were on their way and pressured the hotel staff into leading us to Amy. Before your buddy Aaron made a few calls and scored us seats on the Brookes and Merriweather corporate jet in exchange for the promise of some *very* flattering press coverage—it's really a shame you were so out of it during the flight. Are you noticing a trend?"

"Not really."

"You're the person who made it very clear that no one would be left behind. Now you're stuck with us. Forever." Liz crossed her arms. "Deal with it."

"Yeah, I'm not sure everyone in the group sees it that way." My words came out raspy, and Liz reached to fill up my water glass and hand it to me.

"You mean Houston, right? I'm not exactly an expert when it comes to guys, but I'm pretty sure it is generally considered a bad idea to tell your ex that you want him back in front of someone else. Even in a hospital. *Especially* when that someone else is a guy like Houston. But that's just my advice."

"I was actually referring to Amy."

Liz snatched the water glass out of my hand, sloshing some of it on my arm in the process. *"How did you manage to sneak alcohol into a hospital!"* She dramatically lifted it up to her face. "Hmm . . . it smells like water. It looks like water. And yet, you're clearly under the influence of something. . . ."

"Amy was kidnapped and *beaten* because of me. I don't think that's the kind of thing she's going to forget overnight."

I didn't see Liz's finger coming until she was jabbing me in the shoulder. "Amy was beaten because *insane drug dealers* don't usually like it when people pry into their business. And, yes, I am sure she's going to have more than her fair share of nightmares. But she's way too strong to let it destroy a friendship."

"You mean she's too nice."

"No, actually, I had it right the first time. You want to hear what Amy's first words were for me when we boarded that private plane back home?"

I nodded my head mutely.

"She said, *I've got this great idea for a romance novel. It's about this group of college students studying abroad in Cambodia who accidentally anger a drug lord. . . .*"

I burst out laughing, and it was worth every sharp spike of pain radiating from my rib.

"A *romance* novel? Right after being abducted and tortured she wants to start writing a book about it?"

Liz's smile was tinged with awe. "She told me that every time they hit her, she promised herself to use it as research. Then she mentioned something about Navy SEALs coming to the rescue, so I don't think it's going to be all that autobiographical. Oh, and she's convinced that one of us needs to die."

I shot her a skeptical look. "And you're sure she isn't mad at me?"

"Positive. She's thinking that Ben would make an excellent victim. I'm not sure what exactly she means by that, but she seems excited about it."

I tried to stifle a yawn, but Liz wasn't fooled. "Okay, I'm out of here. Any messages you want me to relay, now that we don't have to worry about any drug lords abducting us?"

When I just stared at her incredulously she smirked. "Too soon?"

"Um . . . *yes!*"

"Probably for the best anyway. I think Houston deserves to hear how you feel straight from the source." Liz winked at me before she disappeared.

Now all I had to do was scrounge up the courage to do it.

Chapter 33

My dad didn't let me linger in Amy's hospital room for long the next morning.

In fact, he didn't give me a chance to do much more than plant a quick kiss right in the center of her forehead. It was one of the few places where she wasn't bruised. Still, it was a relief watching Amy's infectious grin spread across her face when I tentatively entered the room.

"We did it, Chelsea!" she crowed victoriously.

"I couldn't have done it without you, Amy."

Her smile only widened, and I found myself hoping that someday I would have one ounce of her unshakable optimism.

Screw SAT scores. I wanted to see colleges take *that* strength into consideration.

Then again, that probably still wouldn't improve my chances of gaining admission.

That's when my dad looked pointedly at his watch, wished Amy a very speedy recovery, and shooed me out to the parking lot. He didn't even give me a chance to peek in on Neal myself. Instead, he kept insisting that what Neal really needed was all the uninterrupted rest he could get.

If I hadn't suspected that my dad was right, I would have dug in my heels and insisted on visiting my former professor before seeing this great surprise my dad insisted he had in store for me.

Okay, so maybe I was a little curious to see what had my dad so excited.

I've heard about kids getting outrageous gifts when their parents divorce; apparently getting a car with a big, shiny, red bow on the top was supposed to make all the pain go away. But considering that *my* divorce gift had been a thoroughly disastrous trip to Cambodia, I was also a tad apprehensive about it.

All of that faded away when he pulled up into the driveway of a house in northeast Portland. The paint color matched the gray cloud cover that overshadowed the city for three-quarters of the year. The flowerbox on the deck was barren, and a tree with some crabgrass around it was the closest it came to a yard.

Once more there was a suitcase sitting right outside the door.

Except this time it was *mine,* and I wasn't going anywhere.

I had never seen anything more welcoming.

My dad dropped a copy of the key into my palm. "Welcome home, princess. I've been moving in stages so it's kind of a mess right now. Our dishes are still boxed somewhere in the living room. So . . . it's definitely going to take some work. I figure it's nothing you can't handle putting to rights, though."

I raised an eyebrow at him. "Seriously? You're making *me* unpack an entire house worth of stuff?"

"You're the one who said she thought she could handle life as an emancipated minor," my dad pointed out. "I thought you might see this as an opportunity to get a feel for what that means."

I narrowed my eyes. "Uh huh. I seriously doubt that's the reason you want me doing it."

My dad kissed my forehead. "Oh right, and there was this

call I received from my bank letting me know about some of the charges placed on your emergency credit card."

I was so busted.

"Right. I forgot about that." I nodded agreeably. "You make an excellent point. Why don't you show me your office. That's got to be the messiest room here, right?"

He chuckled but gave me the grand tour before heading into the kitchen to place an order for pizza.

And while he was preoccupied with that, I slipped into his office and typed out an email I'd been mentally composing ever since Liz had left my hospital room the day before. I paused only to double-check my dad's event calendar, which was conveniently lying right next to his computer.

> *Houston,*
> *I would love to discuss your experiences in Cambodia at your earliest convenience. Are you available to meet in my office between 5 and 7 pm today?*
> *~Paul*

I clicked send before I could lose my nerve.

With every passing minute as I waited for his reply, I regretted sending it more. Liz was wrong; the last thing Houston wanted from me was an explanation. As far as he was concerned, I had been delivered back to my dad, officially fulfilling his sense of obligation. The princess was safely in the castle. Mission over.

> *Sure. See you at 6 pm, Paul.*
> *~Houston*

I had to fight the urge to do a victory dance. Instead, I deleted all traces of the email so it wouldn't get back to my dad, and reminded myself that Houston and I had never actually been a couple. Not officially. No kiss—no matter how staggeringly great—equals a relationship, especially under such crazy extenuating circumstances. So if he wanted to get back together with the girl Ben insisted was about as interesting as oatmeal, he didn't owe me an explanation.

Although I couldn't help feeling kind of pleased that the years I had spent pining after Logan hadn't been a complete waste. They had given me a whole new appreciation for the blunt approach.

Do you like me or not?

Are you back together with Carolyn, or do you actually want to give this thing between us a chance?

And if Houston honestly wanted to stick to the whole *What happens in Cambodia stays in Cambodia* thing, I would respect his decision and move on with my life too.

Just as soon as I heard the words directly from him.

The rest of the details were almost *too* easy to arrange.

I simply smiled at the receptionist and told her that my dad wanted me to wait in his office until his department meeting had finished. Then I tested the locked door and rolled my eyes with amused exasperation as I said that once again he'd managed to lock the key inside his office. And since the receptionist had experienced that scenario firsthand with my dad far too many times to count, there was no reason for her to suspect me of lying. She simply pulled out her emergency key and left me to settle in.

I couldn't stop pacing the room while I mentally rehearsed my speech.

Hey, Houston. I don't know what you think you saw between me and Logan in the hospital, but it's over. Really. I don't love him that way anymore. I haven't for a while, I think. It just took some time for my brain to catch up with my heart. So ... uh ... are you back together with Carolyn or what?

Unless I should let him bring up Carolyn and their talk for himself. . . .

Hey, Houston. So we never did discuss that kiss in Cambodia. In hindsight, I was tripping on 3-Methylfentanyl the whole time. But my memories of it are still spectacularly good, so do you think we could try it again? Maybe after a date this time?

Then again, maybe reminding him that our only kiss had taken place while I was under the influence *wasn't* necessarily the best approach.

I thunked my head down against my arm and began seriously considering canceling on him. A simple three-sentence email and I could pretend that nothing had happened. Except . . . I had to clear the air once and for all. Even if I didn't like what he had to say. Even if he didn't like what *I* had to say. There was no way I had faced down a freaking *drug lord* only to turn to jelly because some guy might not like me back.

No way.

"Hey, P—" Houston's face turned stony when he realized which Halloway was in the office. "Chelsea."

He was wearing the same ridiculous *No edge!* shirt and a pair of beat-up sneakers, just as he had been that first day I met him in the airport.

"He's . . . on his way." I quickly pointed at the chair on the other side of the desk. "My dad, uh, asked me to have you wait in his office. So take a seat."

Houston hesitated, then, clenching his jaw tightly, he lowered himself into the chair. Not much of a victory, but at least he hadn't instantly stormed out of the room. I was willing to count that as a marginal success.

"So how have you been?" I asked, nervously pushing back my red hair from my face. A small part of me couldn't help wondering if Houston had noticed that the blond girl who was furious with her parents had been transformed into someone a whole lot stronger.

That's how I now saw myself anyway.

"I'm fine."

Two whole words. I braced myself and tried again.

"I haven't seen you since I first woke up two days ago."

Houston raked a hand through his hair, but I couldn't tell if it was a good thing that I had him on edge. "I've been busy. Is your dad going to be here soon? Because otherwise I should—"

So he really wanted nothing to do with me.

The pain blasted me as I stood, scooping up the mounds of paperwork into a rough pile simply to give my hands something to do.

"You don't want to see me ever again? Fine." I shrugged but managed to keep my voice even. "Have a nice life, Houston. Let me know if you ever change your mind. In the meantime, don't let the door hit you on the way out."

He didn't move. Instead he narrowed his eyes and leaned back in the chair. "You made it *very* clear in Cambodia that you didn't want to see me after the trip. Pretend to be strangers, remember? That was *your* idea."

"I said that stuff before we became friends, Houston! I'm allowed to change my mind."

"I'm not interested in being one of your toys, Chelsea. I don't work like that. You can play your games with Lerman or find someone else. I'm sure you'll have plenty of offers."

I crossed my arms and glared at him. "I'm *not* playing any games right now."

Unless luring him there under false pretenses counted. . . .

He raised an eyebrow skeptically. "So you don't think you'll keep leaping at any opportunity to get away from your parents?"

"Let's get this clear: When I was in middle school I dated a guy who didn't care about me. At all. And some part of me—

maybe *all* of me—knew it even at the time and went along with it because *anything* seemed better than going home. It was a mistake but one I needed to make at the time. And I *refuse* to be ashamed of it." I glared at him and would have employed one of Liz's finger jabs if Houston hadn't looked so confused.

"I'm not trying to shame you, Chelsea. I'm just not interested in taking a number and lining up with all the other guys."

"Okay, you understand how ridiculous that sounds, right? There is no freaking line!"

He didn't exactly look convinced. "I've seen you in action, Chelsea. You meet a new guy roughly every ten minutes."

"I *flirt*, Houston. And yes, if a guy actually seems interested in anything beyond looking down my shirt, I'll go out on a date. But that's not why you didn't swing by my hospital room yesterday. Not the real reason, anyway."

"Okay, I'll bite. Tell me your theory, *princess*. Why do you think I've been avoiding you?"

"I think you're jealous."

The words lingered there between us, and even though he folded his arms stiffly, I didn't shut up.

Because I was right.

"You're jealous because you like me. And that scares you because, unlike boring Carolyn, who you'd better not be dating—I'm a little . . . unpredictable. And I know that's not always fun, but I can promise you there is no line of guys. Even if there were . . . they wouldn't stand a chance."

That last part was the hardest for me to say, and I stared down at the papers in my hand as I waited nervously for him to say something. *Anything.*

But he waited until I forced myself to look him in the face again before he spoke.

"In Cambodia, you said you were in love with Larson."

My heart started pounding faster as I nodded. "I think a

part of me will always be in love with Logan. But mostly that's because he was my best friend long before anything else developed. That's all there is between us now."

"It didn't look like just friendship in the hospital."

"Well . . . I don't know what to tell you. Beyond the fact that you really shouldn't jump to conclusions when a concussed girl tells someone she misses him from her *hospital bed*." I propped my hands on my hips. "Now will you just admit it already?"

"Admit what?"

"That you like me!"

It wasn't a question I had planned to blurt out, because demanding a yes-or-no answer has rarely worked out well for me. Taking the forward approach meant that my heart was dangling right there in front of him . . . ready for anyone to whack like a piñata. And yet taking charge of the situation so that I would finally know where we stood . . . it felt right to me. Better than right.

"I—" Houston seemed temporarily at a loss for words. "I can't do this, Chelsea."

My heart plummeted, but I forced myself to act like an adult about it. "Okay. Can you tell me what's holding you back?"

"You're too young for me."

"Okay, there are three years between us," I scoffed. "Hardly unsurmountable. Try again."

"You're in *high school*."

"And yet I totally held my own on a *college* study-abroad program."

As I continued shrinking the distance between us, Houston held up his hands as if that would ward me off. "You're my *professor's daughter!* It's just . . . inappropriate."

"Actually, it's not. If you were dating my dad, *that* would be a problem. Me? Not so much."

His fingers began clawing at his hair in a now-familiar gesture. "You're a self-centered ballerina and you drive me absolutely crazy!"

I grinned.

"You're a geeky know-it-all and you drive *me* absolutely crazy too. But I still like you. And I think you like me back." I tried to ignore the doubt that kept sinking its claws in deeper. Maybe I had entirely misread the situation? Maybe he wanted nothing to do with me after all?

Maybe—

He kissed me.

And this time I wasn't reeking of cheap beer, or overwhelmed with flashbacks, or worried about lawyers and drug lords—and I *definitely* wasn't drugged.

At least not by anything other than a rush of endorphins that had everything to do with the way Houston's lips moved over mine. My insides felt like they were liquefying, and I leaned against my dad's bookcase since my knees weren't entirely steady. Feeling the book spines press against my back while Houston's arms formed a kind of cage around me was . . . hot.

Maybe Mackenzie and Logan were onto something with their make-out meetings in quiet corners of the library. Definitely something to consider at a later time when the guy I was ridiculously, illogically, and completely crazy about wasn't running a gentle finger down my jawline.

"I like you."

Three simple words that had me grinning foolishly back at him while I ran my fingers over the hair at the nape of his neck.

"I take it that's a *no* on the whole dating-Carolyn-again thing?"

He laughed and I grinned up at him. "We both agreed that we were right to break up."

"What a shame." I wrapped my arms more tightly around him.

"Tragic."

Sliding up on tiptoe, I leaned in for another kiss before I murmured, "Her loss."

But Houston stepped back slightly so that he could meet my eyes. "We're taking this slow, okay? I know you don't think our age difference should be a problem, but I don't want to be one more guy who . . ." He suddenly looked vulnerable. "I'm not going to be like him, Chelsea."

If anything, my heart sped up faster at his words. "I can do slow."

"Yeah?"

I grinned and then glanced at my watch. "Absolutely. We can even hold hands and take long walks in the rain. But right now we've got an hour of prime kissing time before my dad's faculty meeting ends. Get back here."

He raised an eyebrow. "Long walks in the rain?"

I smiled wickedly. "We can negotiate the terms later."

Something I had a feeling wouldn't happen for a solid fifty-five minutes.

Not that either of us would be complaining.

A Notable Playlist

Since Chelsea is stuck in an airport on her way to Cambodia, she thought she would share Jane's travel soundtrack with you!

With some additional snarky commentary, of course . . .

"You Don't Know Me" by Ben Folds

Well, Jane got that part right: Nobody here knows anything about me. Although that doesn't appear to be stopping Walker Texas Ranger from spreading rumors about me.

Whatever.

Who cares what they think anyway?

"Boys with Girlfriends" by Meiko

Subtle, Jane. That's really subtle. I get it. You don't think I should have anything to do with Logan now that he's in a relationship with Mackenzie.

But, maybe, friendship isn't entirely impossible. . . .

"Gonna Get Over You" by Sara Bareilles

I thought that this was supposed to be a travel mix, not a breakup soundtrack. Of course I am going to get over Logan. Eventually. It took me a long time to stop constantly thinking about Jake the Mistake too! And that relationship was—

Next!

"Gives You Hell" by All-American Rejects

I haven't heard this song in ages! I'm not entirely sure who Jane thinks I should be giving hell. But Dallas might make an excellent target. . . .

"Monster Mask" by Pomplamoose

It's a weird song, but I actually really like it. Go figure.

"Shine" by Laura Izibor

I'm definitely going to be experiencing a whole lot more sunshine in Cambodia than in Oregon. So I guess that's a small perk.

"Unbroken" by Missy Higgins

This song is ripping my heart open. And yet I can't stop myself from listening to it over and over again.

"Go Places" by The New Pornographers

Yeah, it wasn't exactly my choice to go places, Jane. Nice song though.

"You, Me and the Bourgeoisie" by The Submarines

A song about the wasteful practices of first-world nations while I wait for my flight to Cambodia! Jane and Scott probably had a good laugh when she added this to the playlist.

"Something Good Can Work" by Two Door Cinema Club

I agree, Jane: Something good can work. It can also become something else entirely.

And look at that, time to start boarding my flight. . . .

Don't miss prom at Smith High!
Awkwardly Ever After is coming next July.

Chapter 1

Love is in the air at Smith High School! Tuxes are being rented. Dresses are being fitted. The magic of prom is only one month away . . . and the question on everyone's mind is "Will that special somebody ask me to the dance?"

—from "Preparing for Prom,"
by Lisa Anne Montgomery
Published by *The Smithsonian*

There's no good way to tell your friend that you've got a crush on her little brother.

It's not the kind of thing that I could imagine easily slipping into a casual phone conversation with Mackenzie.

"Hey, it's Melanie. Listen, is Dylan around? Because I was kind of hoping the three of us could hang out together. Why would I want to do that? Well, you know how you just see him as your annoying little brother? Yeah, nothing about him seems brotherly to me."

Oh yeah, *that* wouldn't get weird or anything.

In fact, mentioning Dylan at all seemed downright dangerous for my health. It's generally considered a bad idea to provoke an overly protective person, and beneath the thin layer of insults Mackenzie and Dylan enjoyed slinging at each other, there was an intense sibling loyalty. All it would take for Mackenzie to go into full mother-grizzly-bear mode was the vaguest rumor that some high school girl was interested in dating her middle school brother.

I doubted she would care that there was only a one-year age gap. That next year he would be a freshman and I'd be a sophomore. Or that the year after *that*, he would be a sophomore and I'd be a junior.

Perfectly normal.

Except for the whole little-brother factor, which I couldn't imagine Mackenzie Wellesley *ever* overlooking, the two of us would barely raise eyebrows as a couple by next year's prom.

Thirteen months from now.

"Um, Melanie? You do realize that you're staring at my boyfriend's butt, right?"

Actually, I hadn't. My mind had been wandering again, and apparently my eyes had made a little side trip of their own. Mackenzie's eyes were glinting with amusement, so instead of trying to deny it, I leaned back in my chair and took another sip of hot chocolate before I gestured to the rink in front of us where the Smith High School hockey team was practicing.

"Not my fault. It's . . . wow."

"Yes, it is." Mackenzie's smile only broadened as Logan skated past with a look of pure concentration on his face. "But if *he* sees you staring, it might get a little awkward and . . . oh no!"

I turned just in the nick of time to catch Patrick Bradford checking Logan hard, sending him sprawling across the ice. My nose wrinkled in contempt; the standard expression whenever I was forced to share the same room with Patrick. Thankfully, it didn't happen all that often because he doesn't exactly associate with lowly freshman. He's far too busy trying to climb the Smith High School social ladder to spare a second for someone who won't propel him up a rung.

Patrick's delusions of grandeur wouldn't have bothered me if I hadn't seen Mackenzie's devastated expression when she had finally figured out that he was more interested in her sudden rise to YouTube celebrity than he was in her as a person. She had looked absolutely shredded. I still felt a twinge of guilt every time I thought about that night. Because while Mackenzie was drinking to the point that she couldn't walk in a straight line, I was flirting with her little brother.

To be fair, he had started flirting with me first.

Although that still didn't make him any less off-limits.

So even now that Mackenzie was obnoxiously happy with Logan Beckett, I still blamed Patrick for the way it had gone down. Maybe I would have tried harder to let bygones be bygones if Patrick would stop taking cheap shots against his own team captain to prove some kind of stupid guy point.

But probably not.

Mackenzie let out a quiet breath of relief as Logan picked himself up off the ice, and his best friend, Spencer Heath, skated over and glowered at Patrick. There was no doubt in anyone's mind that Spencer was more than ready to throw a few punches if it turned into an outright brawl.

"Okay, all good." She smiled at me. "You were saying?"

I decided to test whether she would actually be able to focus on me with a testosterone-fueled display only a few feet away on the ice. "Um . . . that your boyfriend is cute?"

"Right. Yes. That's undeniably—oh *seriously!*"

Logan said something to Patrick that had the other boy glaring and moving within striking distance.

"So I take it things are still kind of awkward there."

"Uh huh . . ." Mackenzie nodded absentmindedly. She jerked upright in her seat as Patrick tossed his stick aside and launched himself at Logan. "If he gets a concussion, I'm going to kill him. It's hard enough getting him to concentrate already."

"You sure that doesn't have something to do with you

being more than just his tutor now?" I asked wryly. It wasn't exactly a secret that Logan Beckett hated his AP U.S. History class. Something that had actually brought the two of them together before Mackenzie's embarrassing YouTube video launched her into fame. Now that they were dating though, I had a feeling he was trying to find new ways to distract her from the books.

And judging by the blush that crept up her neck, his efforts weren't entirely unsuccessful either.

"Nope. I'm sure that has nothing to do with it."

I rolled my eyes.

"That's my story and I'm sticking to it."

"Sure, Mackenzie. And that hickey I see peeking out under your shirt is a coincidence, right?"

"Absolutely."

I laughed until I saw Logan haul off and slug Patrick in the stomach. "Okay, yeah. Coincidence. Don't sic your boyfriend on me, please."

She laughed. "We both know that Logan's totally harmless."

It didn't look like Patrick would agree with that statement as the rest of the team rushed over to surround the two boys. I barely caught a glimpse of Spencer grabbing a solid handful of Patrick's jersey and cheerfully pulling him away from his friend. From where Mackenzie and I were sitting, I couldn't be certain if Spencer had tripped Patrick up in the process. But I definitely enjoyed watching the jerk slide five feet across the ice . . . on his face.

"Um, okay. *That* was impressive."

Mackenzie swiveled and stared at me. It didn't take a genius to figure out that her brain had jumped to the wrong conclusion. "Really? Because I happen to know that Spencer is very single."

"Uh . . . good for him."

"And I happen to think the two of you would make a cute couple, Melanie. Kind of a *Beauty and the Beast* thing."

I glanced over at Spencer, who had taken off his helmet and was explaining the situation to the coach while Patrick sulked and Logan scowled. Spencer's blond hair flopped charmingly across his forehead while he gestured animatedly from one boy to the other. It looked like the guy honestly *enjoyed* breaking up fights. Although I had a feeling he would've enjoyed it even more if he had gotten in a few blows of his own.

"In this scenario, I'm guessing I'm the beast?"

"You're right, Melanie. I took one look at you and thought, *Wow, that girl needs a total fashion makeover.* Oh wait, nope. That's what you gave *me.*"

To be fair, it was Mackenzie's friend Corey who had been most adamant about giving her a fashion makeover. I just happened to tag along, the lone freshman resident in the Geektopia they were forming.

"Okay, so it would be a Beauty and the Beauty scenario." Mackenzie rolled her eyes. "I still stand by my earlier statement."

I flipped a page in my textbook, which I should've been concentrating on from the very beginning of our "study session" instead of staring out at a rink full of hockey players.

Next time I crashed a practice session, I needed to make sure I didn't actually have to accomplish anything. That way I could keep watching the action for as long as I liked.

"So about this whole Boston Tea Party thing . . . did anyone actually drink the tea, Mackenzie? Or make crumpets to go with it? Because that sounds delicious."

"You're trying to use American history to distract me."

"Yep."

"That's pretty nefarious of you."

I grinned, willing to bet that a true history nerd like Mackenzie would combust in a matter of minutes if she didn't answer my questions. "Scones, maybe? With, uh . . . clotted cream. That was a thing, right?"

Mackenzie's smile widened as the team began filing off the ice, and she closed my textbook with a faint thud before she began packing up. "You're not going to distract me that easily. I think you and Spencer would be cute together. He might act like he only cares about partying, but he's actually a really great guy once you get to know him. And he's loyal to a fault."

"Riiight," I snorted. "That's why he gave you all those tequila shots at his party. Because he's such a stand-up guy."

"He was trying to make my night a little better."

I remembered the panic that had sharpened Dylan's soft brown eyes when he realized how trashed his older sister had gotten while he was preoccupied dancing with me. The anxiety had vanished when Mackenzie started drunkenly rambling about their dad.

That's when his face had turned stony and unreadable.

He had barely spoken a word to me for the rest of the night, even after we'd successfully hauled Mackenzie's drunken butt into Logan's passenger seat. Instead, Dylan had mumbled some lame excuse and disappeared into the crowd.

Leaving me alone at the party until Corey picked us up on the way home from a date of his own.

Not that I'd been on a date with Dylan.

It doesn't count as a date if the other person avoids you for hours on end.

"Yeah, Spencer really made your night special. If he had 'improved' it any more, you would have needed to get your stomach pumped."

"That was totally my fault," Mackenzie protested. "I'm the one who kept drinking even after he tried to cut me off. And I learned my lesson. Tequila and I will never be on speaking terms again. But that doesn't make him a bad guy. In fact, I'll prove it to you."

I eyed her suspiciously. "Just what do you have in mind for—"

"Nice skating, Spencer. Hey, have you met my friend Melanie?"

Well, I had walked right into that one.

My cheeks felt unnaturally warm, as if I had been the one exerting myself on the ice instead of sitting on the sidelines with a cup of hot chocolate. But it was hard to act cool when I had one of the most popular guys in the junior class sizing me up.

"Well, hello again, Pocahontas."

I winced at the assumption that I had Native American roots just because my skin happened to be *slightly* darker than the average Oregonian's—not much of a feat in a state where pale is the norm. Back in elementary school I had landed the role of Sacajawea while everyone else got to be part of Lewis and Clark's expedition every single year. The fact that my ancestry is primarily Italian with a bit of Greek thrown in made it more than a little awkward.

"Hello, jock."

Mackenzie kicked me under the table again as I smiled innocently.

"What? I thought we were giving each other cute nicknames based purely on first impressions."

Spencer at least had the good sense to meet my eyes directly. "Okay, not my best opening line. Doesn't it help if I admit that I had a thing for her as a kid? I mean, that 'Colors of the Wind' stuff was hot." His smile quirked up at the side, and I began relaxing in spite of myself.

I shrugged. "Yeah, I'm still not thrilled with the comparison."

"It's the long brown hair," Mackenzie pointed out.

"And your eyes."

"And my skin tone. Not exactly a secret here, guys."

"I think mainly it's your eyes." Spencer leaned closer as if an intense examination was required to settle the matter. "They're almost the same shade of dark chocolate as your drink."

I blinked up at him. "Okay, I get it. You weren't *trying* to be a jerk. Message received. You can tone down the flirting now."

He laughed and glanced over at Mackenzie. "Does she give everyone such a hard time?"

Only when I suspect a guy might want more than I feel comfortable giving. Yeah, then I have no trouble speaking up. That's the only way to make sure nobody takes advantage. I learned that lesson a long time ago. That's why I only truly relax around a handful of people that I trust not to push me too far.

A selective group that happens to include Dylan.

"Um, actually she never has be—"

"Hey, Mack," Logan Beckett interrupted, stopping Mackenzie's words with a quick kiss. Not that she appeared to mind, judging by the way her fingers gripped his hockey jersey. "Did you catch the show?"

"Nah, I hardly noticed you at all." The foolish grin plastered all over her face gave her away. "Melanie and I were discussing the Boston Tea Party."

He groaned. "No more American history, I beg of you."

"Actually, I was thinking the four of us could get together to watch *Pocahontas*."

Oh crap.

Logan glanced over at his best friend, whose face I now found impossible to read. "Um . . . I'm not so sure Spencer enjoys discussing historical accuracy, Mack."

"He was just telling Melanie how much he loved that movie as a kid. Weren't you, Spencer?"

"I—"

"Great! It's settled! We'll see the two of you at Logan's house for movie night tomorrow. Say . . . six o'clock?" She was already pulling on her backpack and entwining her fingers with Logan's. They were so freaking adorable together it was almost nauseating. "See you then!"

And just like that the two of them strolled out of the ice-skating rink.

Leaving me alone with a hockey player who had just been shanghaied into a movie date with me that I didn't even want in the first place.

Because I was still stupidly hung up on someone else altogether.

I was *so* screwed.